NUTMEG

ISSUE 10

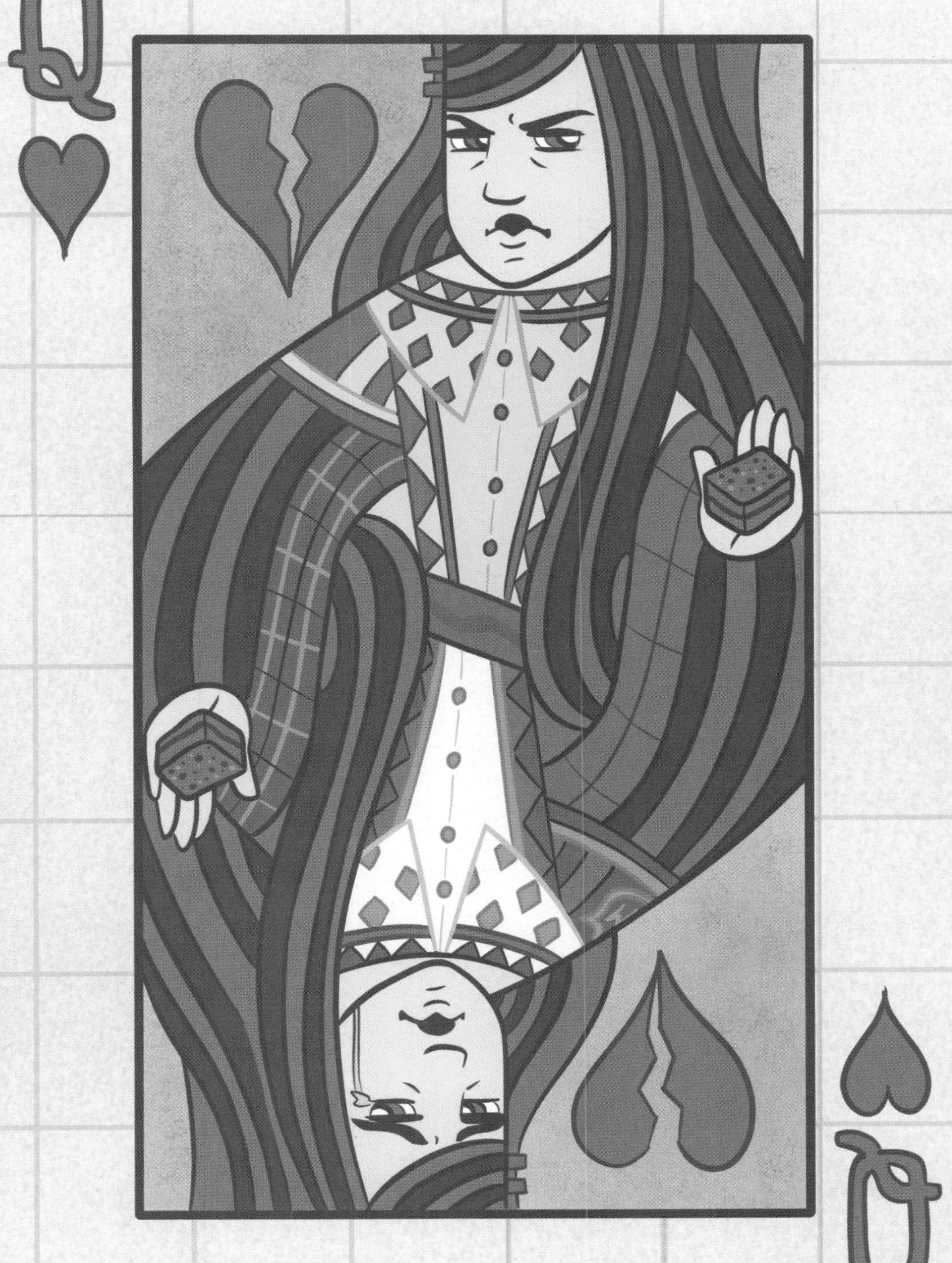

Bryan Seaton - Publisher • Kevin Freeman - President • Dave Dwonch - Creative Director • Shawn Gabborin - Editor In Chief
Jamal Igle - Co-Directors of Marketing • Chad Cicconi - ate all the brownies • Colleen Boyd - Associate Editor

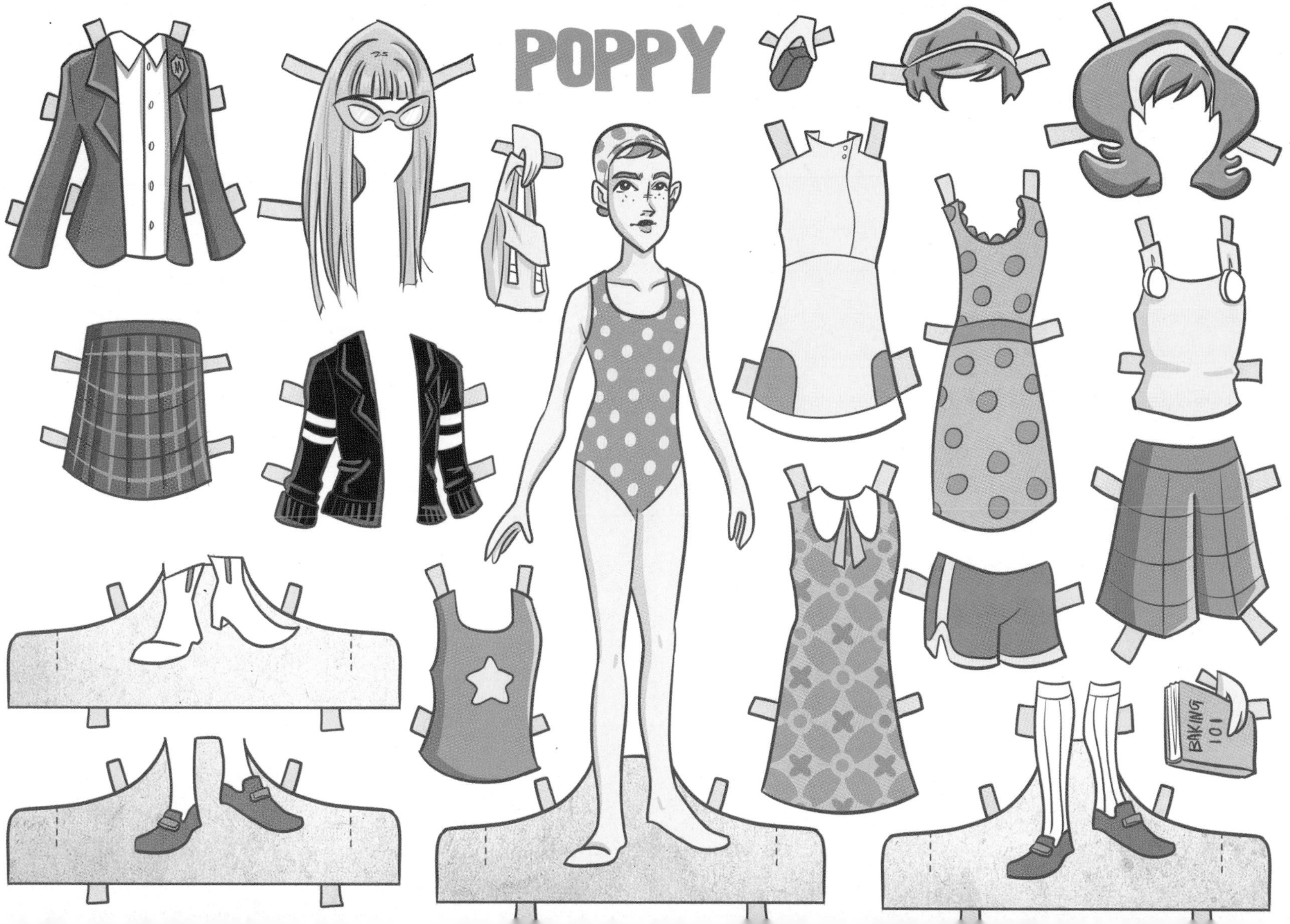
POPPY
BAKING 101

TEAM NUTMEG IN 2017

HEROES CON

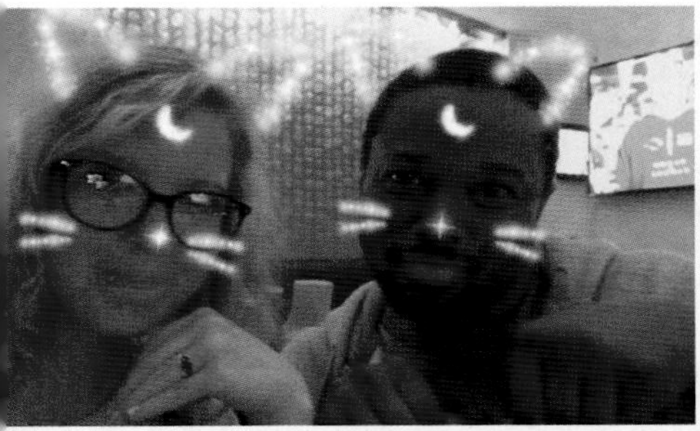

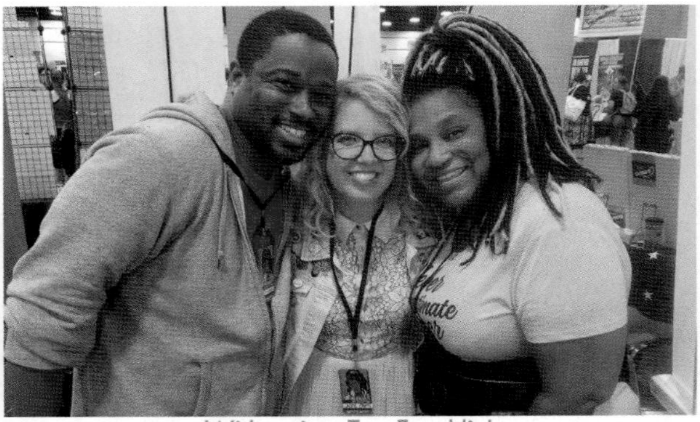

With writer Tee Franklin!

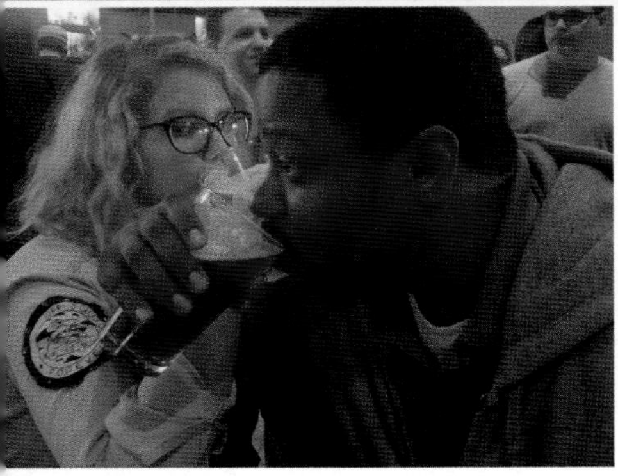

C2E2

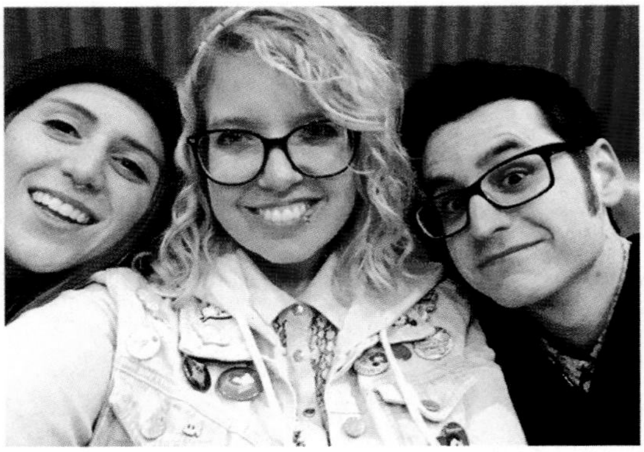

With artist/writers Nicole Goux & Dave Baker!

INDIANA COMIC CON

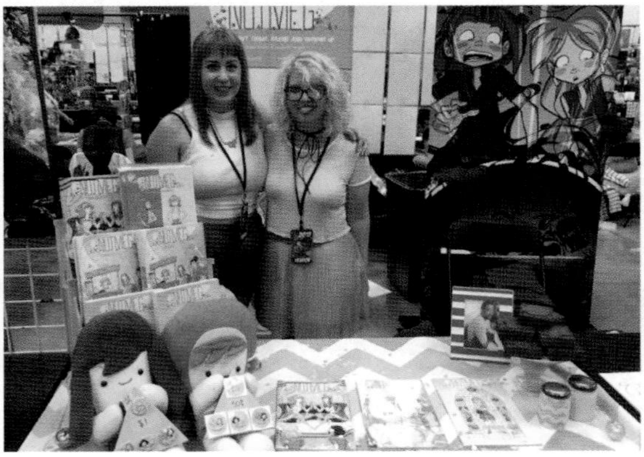

With best friend Becca!

VANCOUVER COMIC ARTS FESTIVAL

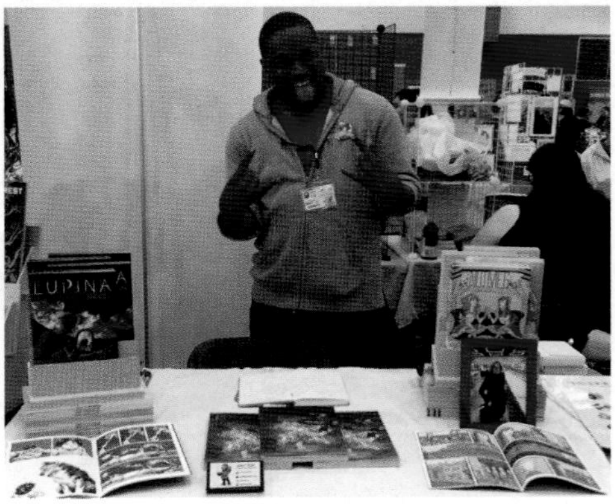
LUPINA

WONDERCON

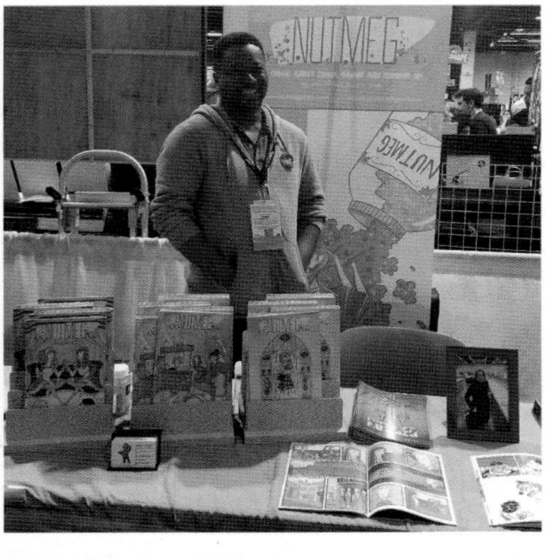
NUTMEG

ROSE CITY

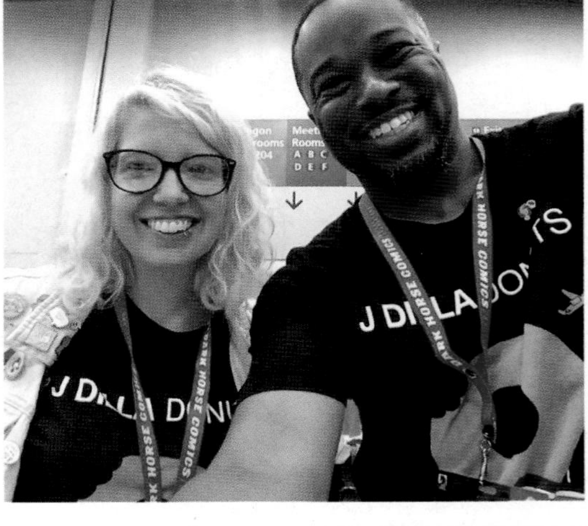

TEAM NUTMEG IN 2017

EMERALD CITY COMIC CON

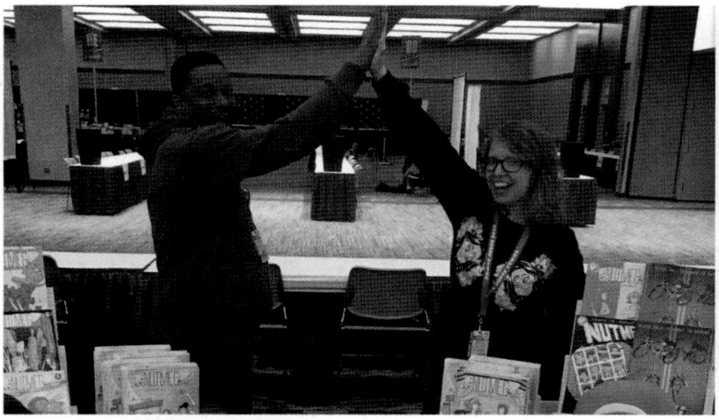

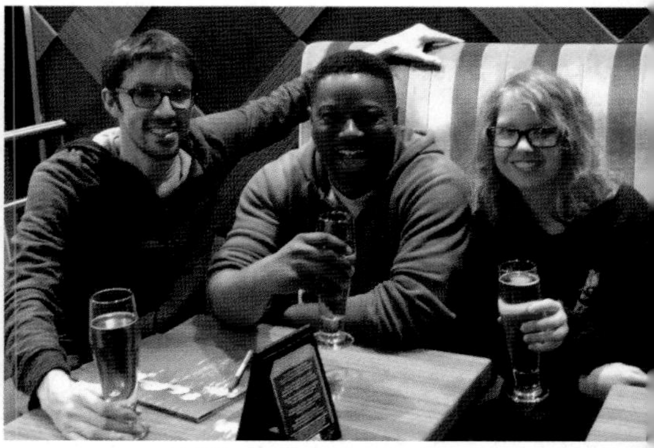

With our colorist, Josh Eckert!

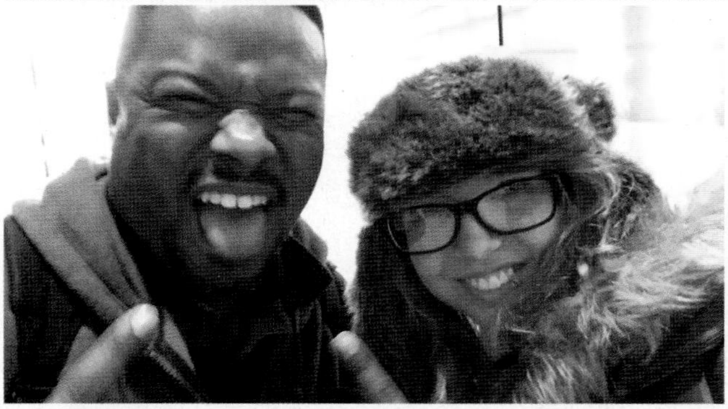

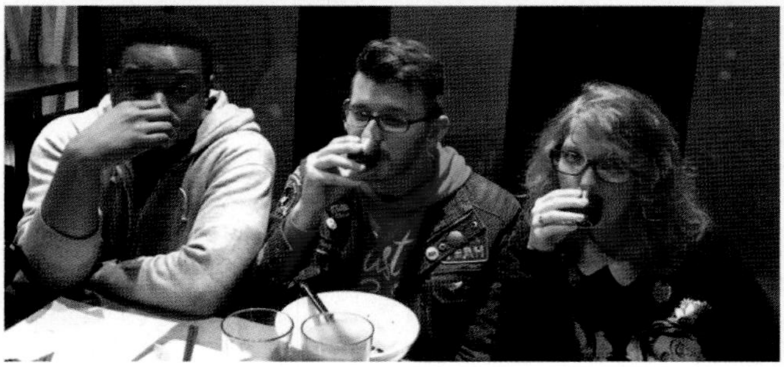

With artist Lee Cherolis!

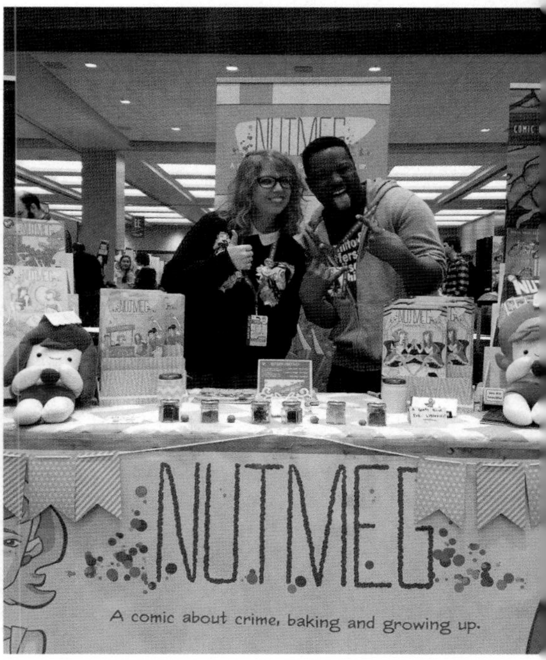
NUTMEG
A comic about crime, baking and growing up.

SAN DIEGO COMIC CON

With writer/artist Raina Telgemeier!

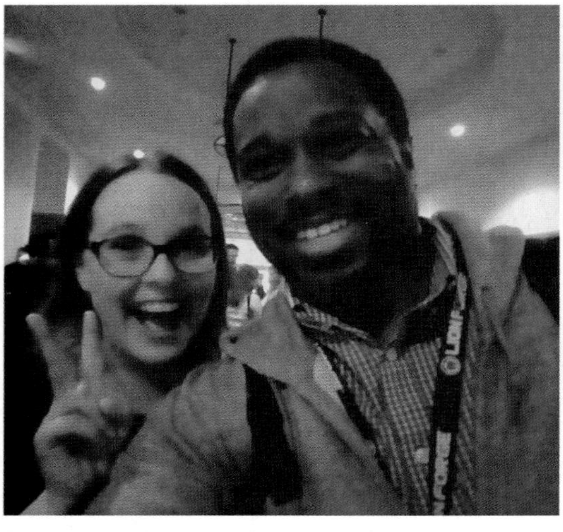

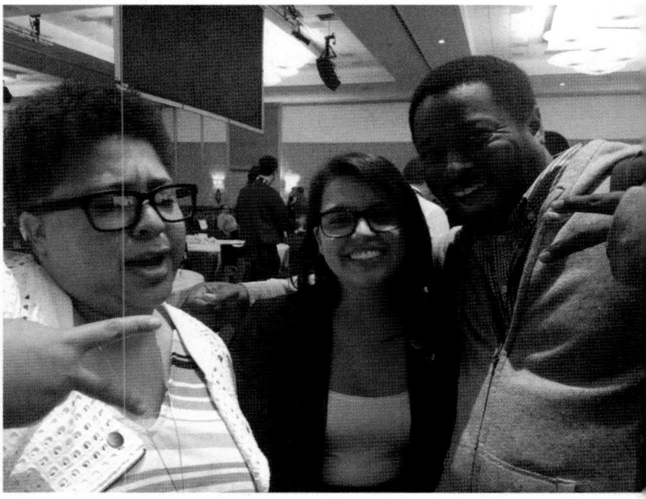

With editor Taneka Stotts and artist Sara DuVall!

TEAM NUTMEG IN 2016

TORONTO COMIC ARTS FESTIVAL

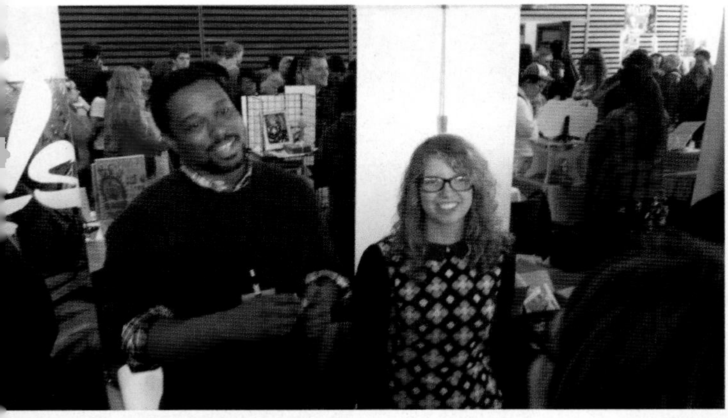

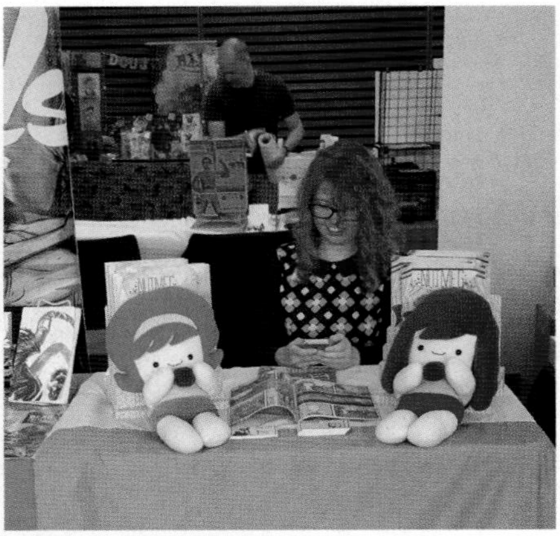

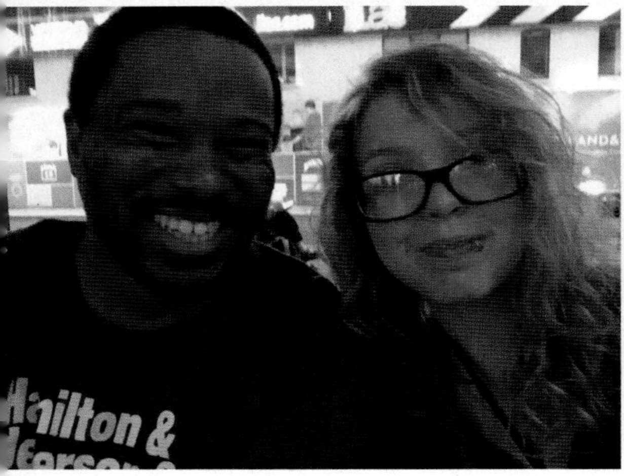

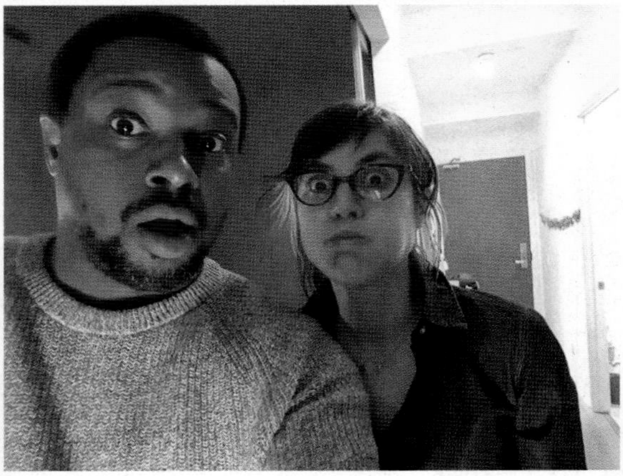

With our wonderful, hilarious host, Julie!

AN DIEGO COMIC CON

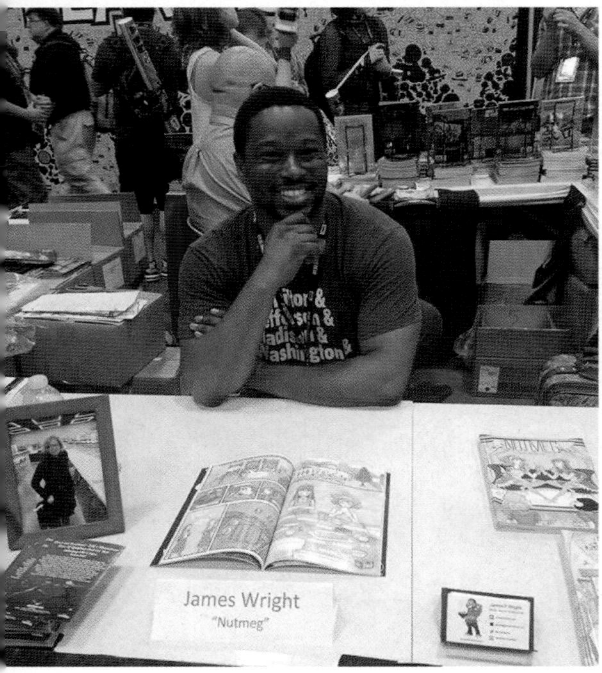
James Wright
"Nutmeg"

WONDERCON

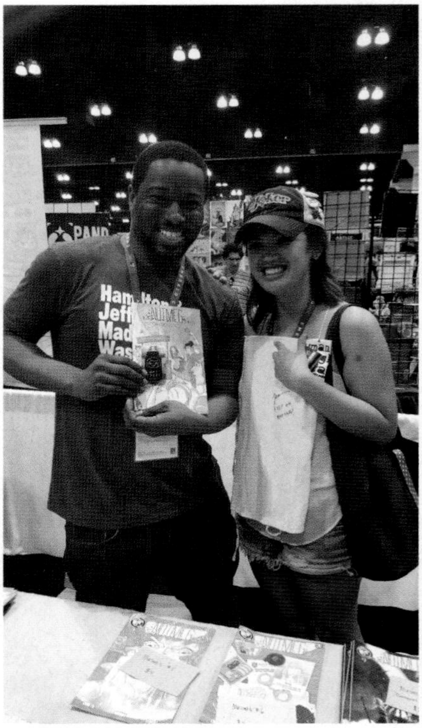

With Mai Bakes!

TEAM NUTMEG IN 2016

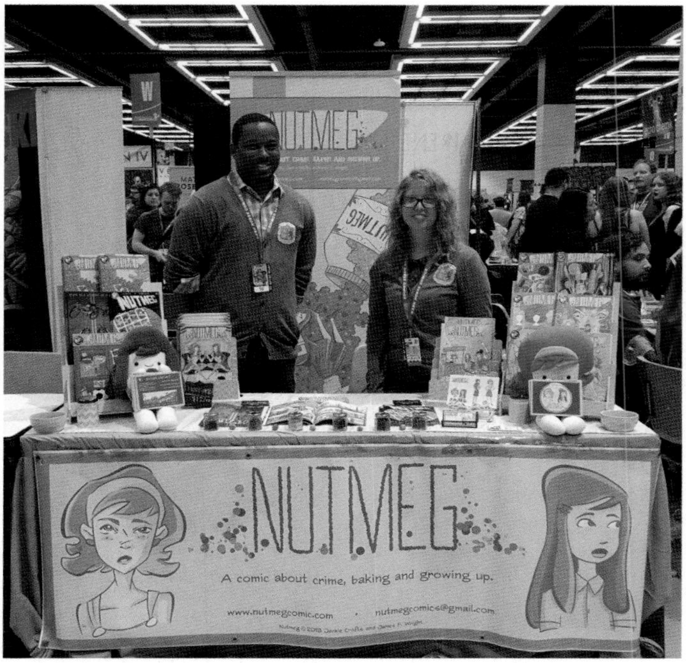
NUTMEG
A comic about crime, baking and growing up.
www.nutmegcomic.com
nutmegcomics@gmail.com

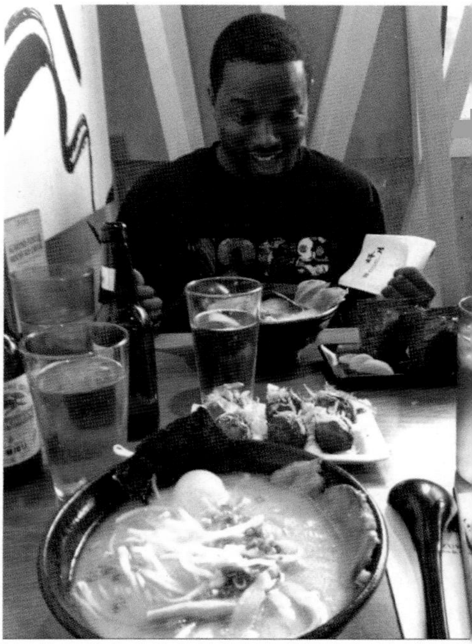

At Kizuki Ramen!

EMERALD CITY COMIC CON

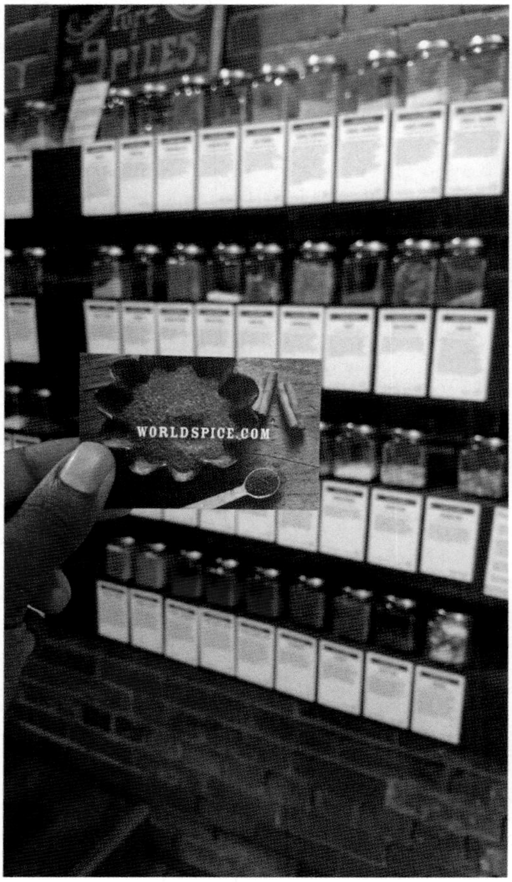
WORLDSPICE.COM

Spice shop!

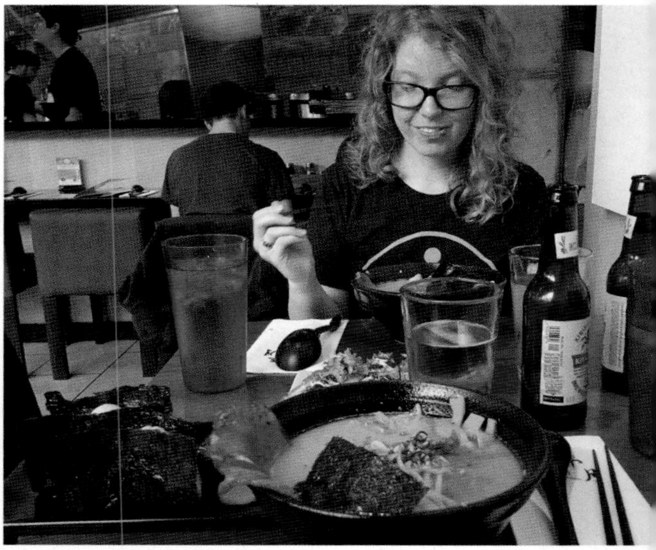

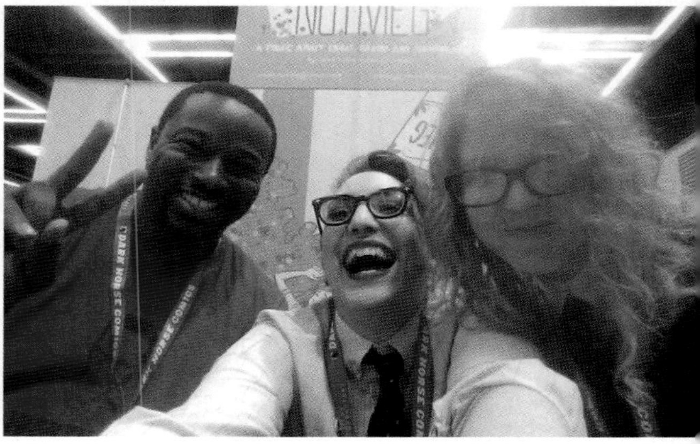

With colorist Marissa Louise!

Tony: *The recipes and tips I saw in the back of the issues. How are you guys coming up with these? Is it from years of experience? Are friends and family contributing?*

James: We're really big fans of the way a number of comics nowadays have a lot of fun with the backmatter content sections, and it feels like added value on their purchases. For us, our friends and family have been so incredibly supportive of this book and of us in its creation that we wanted a way to showcase them and the delicious foods they make. I do enjoy baking, though I don't do it as much as I'd like. Also, we want to give a huge thanks to our friend, Josh Eckert, who colored and lettered issues 5-10 of the series, and who also has been monumental in setting and laying out this backmatter section of our series. He's an absolute titan.

Tony: *Jackie, as a chef instructor, my students tell me that drawing creative plating ideas is really difficult. Do you find drawing food for Nutmeg more of a challenge or a fun thing to go wild with?*

Jackie: It's so fun! I always go back to memories of watching anime or reading manga where the food looked so amazing you just wish you could reach in and grab it. Spirited Away, Howl's Moving Castle, and Sailor Moon all come to mind. I want people to feel that way when they see the brownies and other sweets in the book!

Tony: *So what's next for Nutmeg?*

James: Jackie and I have discussed a follow-up to Nutmeg, a four-issue miniseries that takes place three years later in the summer between the girls' sophomore and junior year of high school. We're not sure if it will happen or not, but we've at least talked about it. And honestly, we think this book would be a hit in libraries, so if that proves to be the case we'll have a lot more leeway in our options moving forward.

Tony: *Do you have any non-Nutmeg ideas brewing?*

James: It's been a long, long journey to the end of Nutmeg, and I'm both happy and surprised that Jackie hasn't plotted my demise yet (or has she?) We've had a lot of fun working on this book--and some not fun things, as will happen with any creative endeavor-- and she's agreed to work with me again down the road. Once Nutmeg wraps, we're taking a crack at a Japanese-influenced short ghost story I pitched her a few months back. And we've talked a bit about our riff on the magical girls genre, which would be a miniseries if we can make that happen.

Jackie: I'm looking forward to doing some more stories with James and other creators too. I'd like to eventually write something myself as well, but we'll see when I have time for that!

Tony: *This is for both Jackie and James - if you could get 1 chef to do a crossover with the Lady Rangers - who would you choose?*

James: Michael Twitty. I admit I've only learned about him recently, but both his cooking and his background are things we don't really see much of (or enough of) in culinary circles. I can only imagine how great his brownies would be!

Jackie: James already knows how much I love Alton Brown (specifically Good Eats). I like the science behind food, and there's a lot of that when it comes to baking! We were lucky enough to meet him at San Diego Comic-Con one year and we talked to him about the book a little. Actually, he DOES have a brownie recipe: https://altonbrown.com/alton-brown-brownie-recipe/

Tony: *Lastly, for both Jackie and James - what is your least favorite thing to eat and does that play any sort of role in the series? Particularly, Saffron. Do you guys hate the spice and thus she's the antagonist?*

James: Haha! We have nothing against the spice saffron. With all of the girls in the series named after spices and herbs (Poppy, Cassia, Saffron, Marjoram, Anise, and Ginger), it just made sense for the rich girl to be named for one of the most expensive in the world. As it stands, my least favorite thing to eat is umeboshi, the salted, pickled plum that shows up in Japanese food. I've tried numerous times, and every time my brain just goes, "Nah, son."

Jackie: Seconding James here, I have no problems with Saffron! My brain is turning over trying to think of a food I don't like. I'm not a picky eater! I'd have to say maybe green pepper? I don't even fully dislike it, but I'll tell you that I don't prefer it on my pizza. No, sir.

* * *

The full interview is available here:
http://www.outrightgeekery.com/2017/11/06/
cooking-geeky-interview-nutmegs-co-creators-
james-f-wright-jackie-crofts

COOKING GEEKY

In November of 2017, Tony Dillard, a chef and contributor to the site Outright Geekery interviewed us for a series he does there called Cooking Geeky. We can't thank him enough for taking the time to speak to us about Nutmeg. He gave us permission to reprint a portion of that interview here, with minor edits for context and clarity.

Tony: *What was the inspiration for the series Nutmeg?*

James: There's a lot of answers to this question because so many elements led to the book's existence. But the simplest one is that one day, while the Girl Scouts were doing their cookie sales drive, we asked ourselves, "What if the Girl Scouts were a criminal organization?" Everything else seemed to flow from that one question. We'd seen decades of teen detective stories, from Nancy Drew to Scooby-Doo to Veronica Mars, even the movie Brick, but we hadn't seen very many stories focusing on the criminal side of that equation, particularly with girls as the chief operators. The way that kids of all genders interact at that age made sense as the perfect setting for a rise-and-fall kingpin story.

Jackie: I took inspiration from a lot of different places when I was designing the environments and characters for Nutmeg. I watched a lot of movies like Mean Girls, Clueless, and Grease to get into the mindset of remembering what it was like to be at school dealing with the weird social groups and bullying. I also looked at a lot of photo reference. I'd just try to find old photos of main streets, the girl scouts, old ads for stoves where they show the nice shiny kitchen with the happy family. When I designed Poppy and Cassia, James said "Have you seen Heavenly Creatures?!" I said no, and it turned out I'd designed the girls eerily similar and I had no idea that he'd taken influence from that movie for Nutmeg. I watched it the next day and it's one of my favorites now.

Tony: *Jackie, I see that you make learning games by day and in some of Nutmeg, the characters do RPG games. Are those games inspired by your work in the field? Could there ever be a Nutmeg game?*

Jackie: When the girls play Wyverns & Wastelands (essentially their version of D&D), I'm drawing from my own experiences playing games with my friends! During the winter, it can get pretty harsh in Indiana. Not many people want to go out of the house so it's easy to slump into a seasonal sadness kind of deal, especially once all the holidays pass. We try to do a campaign during the winter where we meet once a week for two or three months to play so we all see each other regularly still. You get to know people in a different way through playing games with them, especially table top RPGs where it's relying on your imagination and chemistry with the other players. At my job, I'm making learning games to train employees that work for companies, so I'm not sure much inspiration is coming from there, but maybe there is and I just don't realize it! I'd love to see Nutmeg as a top-down isometric point-and-click mystery adventure game.

Tony: *James, you go looking for the best ramen in LA. What's the best one you've found so far?*

James: This is surprisingly difficult because one place will have excellent broth, another the best noodles, and still another a good price range or location. Right now my two favorites are Kashira in Koreatown near the Wiltern, and Ramen Hood at the Grand Central Market downtown. Kashira has a wonderful broth, strong but not overpowering (which is my only real issue with Silver Lake Ramen in Silver Lake), and the golden wavy noodles I love. Ramen Hood surprised me out of the gate by being 100% vegan (the broth is a sesame seed base) and it's really grown on me since I first had it [in 2016]. The great thing about L.A., though, is that there's hundreds of places I haven't been to yet.

Tony: *James, as a male writing a series about young girls striving to become chefs, what are the challenges trying to make the story relatable for readers of both sexes? Are there advantages?*

James: At first I was worried about portraying an experience unfamiliar to me, and that never really went away, but I spoke with Jackie and a number of other friends about their junior high years, drawing on the highs and lows they went through. I read what I could- Rosalind Wiseman's Queen Bees & Wannabees, itself the inspiration for Mean Girls, proved invaluable- and watched films and TV series related to our subject matter. And even though my own experience was different from the girls' in our story, I knew there were still some aspects to growing up that I had gone through myself. All of which is to say that I didn't set out specifically to make a story relatable to readers of all gender identities, but rather to attempt to make the specific universal, even within the sort of heightened reality criminal element on display.

INSTRUCTIONS

1. Preheat the oven to 400°F. Grease 2 baking sheets.

2. In a saucepan, combine the milk, butter & salt and bring to a simmer, stirring constantly. Add in the flour and mix it in thoroughly so that a dough forms. Keep stirring it over low heat for a minute or two – until the dough dries a bit & pulls away from the pan.

3. Move the dough into a bowl and let it cool for a minute. Then one by one, beat the eggs into the dough until thoroughly mixed. Mix in the cheese and the spices.

4. If you have a pastry bag, then pipe tablespoon-sized balls onto the baking sheets, leaving a good bit of room between each one. If you don't have a pastry bag, then just use a spoon to scoop the dough into mounds. ← (IF YOU HAVE EXTRA CHEESE, SPRINKLE SOME ON TOP!)

5. Bake for 22 minutes or until they're golden brown. Serve them hot! (Or you can freeze them for later — in which case you should pop them back in the oven to get them toasty again!)

6. DEVOUR THEM!!!

(ADAPTED FROM ALAIN DUCASSE'S RECIPE)

It's French!
You pronounce it roughly like "goo-jair".

(Think of a cheesy version of cream puffs! They're super easy to make and utterly delicious.)

INGREDIENTS

1 cup MILK
1 stick BUTTER, cut into pieces
1 teaspoon SALT
1 cup FLOUR
4 EGGS
1 cup GRUYÈRE CHEESE ← COMTÉ ALSO WORKS
A pinch of PEPPER
A pinch of NUTMEG

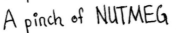

ALMOND BUTTER BANANA SHAKE

2 ripe bananas
1 ½-2 cups almond milk (or any nut milk)
A big spoonful of almond butter (or peanut butter if that's what you got)

Throw all of the ingredients in a blender and liquidize them. Liquidize them good. If your shake is too thick, add more milk. If it's too thin, add more banana and almond butter and blend again. Pour into a huge glass and drink it!

CHOCOLATE CINNAMON CHIA MOUSSE

1 can coconut milk
½ cup almond milk
2 tablespoons maple syrup, honey, or agave nectar
¼ cup raw cocoa powder (non-raw is perfectly fine)
1 tsp vanilla extract
½ tsp cinnamon
A dash of nutmeg
¼ cup chia seeds.

Put all the ingredients except for the chia seeds in a blender. Blend on high until everything is smooth and well mixed. Pour into a bowl or tupperware and add the chia seeds. Mix together until all the chia seeds have been coated with the mixture. Cover and set in fridge for 15 minutes. Take the mousse out of the fridge and stir. Put it back in the fridge for another 45 minutes or overnight so that it gets super think and you have to basically carve it out with a spoon! My favorite garnishes to add are banana, chopped almonds, and dried coconut flakes. Strawberries and dates also kick this desert up a notch.

Leila del Duca is the artist of SLEEPLESS, SHUTTER and the writer of AFAR, all published by Image Comics. She lives in Portland, Oregon and cooks every day. You can contact her through email at leiladelduca@gmail.com, on Twitter at @leiladelduca, or on Instagram at @leiladelduck.

TWO RECIPES FROM LEILA DEL DUCA

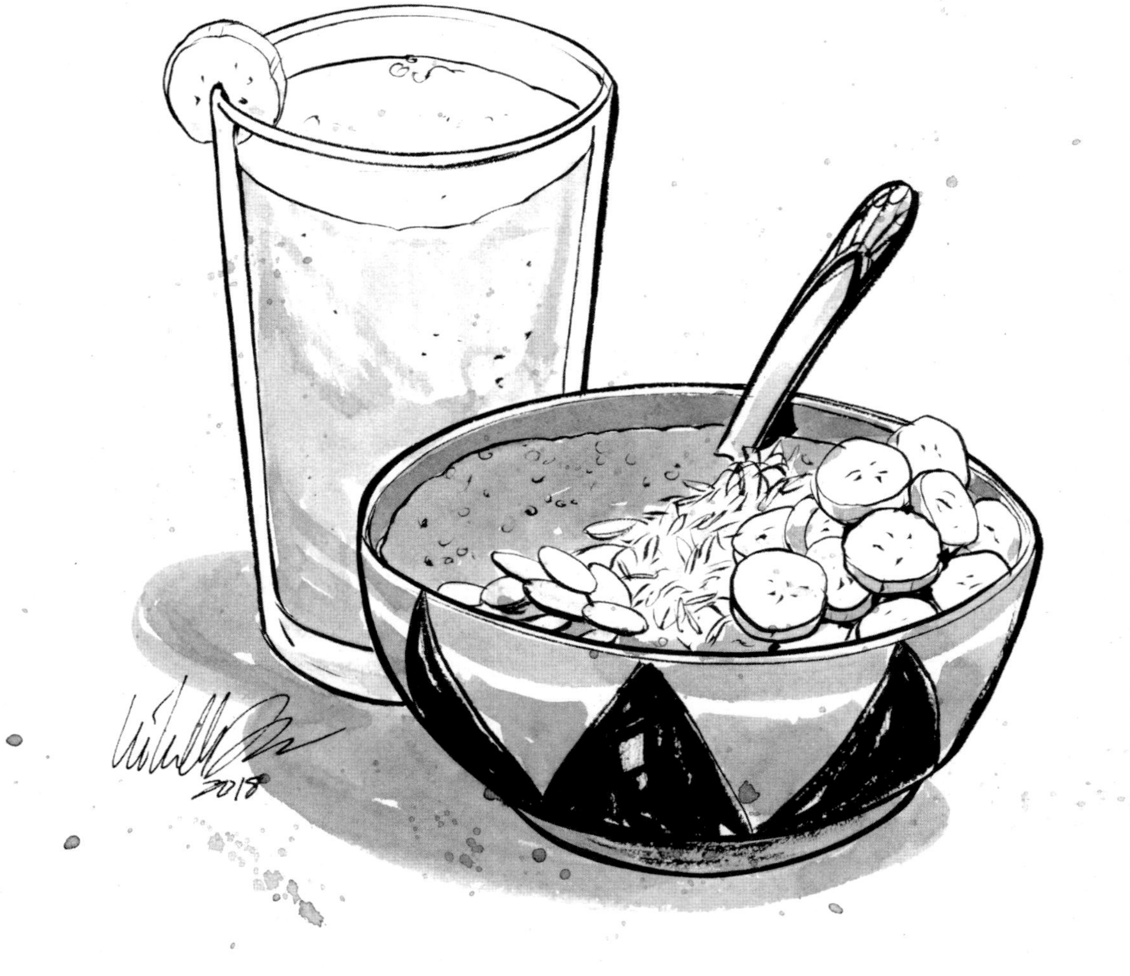

A couple years ago I was living in a second story apartment in Portland, Oregon during a super-hot, air-condition-less summer. Around that time I was trying really hard to stay away from sweets, but I had such a big sweet tooth I was failing miserably! In an attempt to satiate my sugar addiction and not contribute to the heat in my apartment, I started searching for "sugarless, no-cook deserts" on the internet and eventually found a boundless rabbit hole of raw food snacks. The ingredient lists and the delicious-looking pictures were enticing, and once I tried it I was pleasantly surprised! They didn't taste quite the same or deliver that sugar high good old fashioned sweets have, but I didn't crash hard after eating them, and I felt good knowing I was putting more nutrients in my body instead of fats and sugars that are bad for me. Chocolate chip cookie dough, brownie balls, and banana ice cream all entered my diet on a regular basis. Seriously, raw deserts rock! Since then, I've come up with some recipes of my own and here are two of my favorites, both sweet and perfect for hot summer days.

COOKIE DIRECTIONS

1. Line two cookie sheets with parchment paper.

2. Sift together the dry ingredients in a medium bowl. Whisk in any larger bits that are leftover in the sieve.

3. In a large mixing bowl or the bowl of your stand mixer, cream the butter on medium-high until it lightens in colour, about 1-2 minutes.

4. Add the sugars to the butter, and beat on medium-high until light and fluffy, about 2-3 minutes. Scrape down the sides of the bowl with a spatula.

5. Add the molasses to the butter mixture and beat on medium-high until just incorporated, about another 1-2 minutes.

6. Add the egg and beat on medium-high until incorporated, about 1-2 minutes. Scrape down the sides of the bowl again.

7. Add the flour mixture and mix on low until just combined.

8. Measure out roughly Tablespoon-sized scoops of dough and roll into little balls (roughly 1 inch in diameter).

9. Using the flat bottom of a glass, gently press down on each dough ball until they are roughly between ⅜ and ½ inches tall. They are now dough discs!

10. If using the **Crunchy Cardamom** or **Cinnamon Sugar** finishing option, combine the two ingredients in a small or medium bowl and whisk to incorporate.

11. One-by-one, place each dough disc in the finishing option bowl of your choice and liberally coat with the sugar/spice combo. Transfer each dough disc onto the prepared cookie sheet. For baking, they will need to be spread about 2 inches apart.

12. Put prepared dough in the fridge to chill for about one hour.

13. Preheat the oven to 350°F.

14. Bake cookies in the centre rack of the oven for 10-13 minutes (mine came about the best just before 12 minutes). They should be slightly darker brown around the edges.

15. Allow cookies to cool on the cookie sheet for about 5 minutes, then transfer to cooling rack to cool completely.

16. If using, prepare the **Molasses Glaze**: combine sugar, molasses, and milk in a small to medium bowl and whisk to combine. I used the glaze on the plain cookies, but feel free to mix it up!

17. If using, allow the Molasses Glaze up to an hour to set.

18. Eat the cookies and fill yourself up with fall coziness.

AMADON'S
FALL SPICE COOKIES
THEBOTTOMLESSBAKER.COM

These are fairly flat cookies (think ginger snaps) with slightly crisp edge
and a soft middle — a fine balance! A general note before you ba
I enjoy bold flavours — if you prefer a simpler cookie, adjust the spi
to suit your taste preferences but please give it a try as-is first!

Yield: about 36 cookies

Notes: Be sure to leave enough time for the dough to chill (at least an hour) before baking. I tried this recipe both with chilled and room temperature dough. Chilling it will prevent it from spreading out too much and will slow down the baking, providing a softer cookie. If you don't have time to chill the dough, err on a shorter baking time.

Below are a few options for finishing the cookies. I encourage you to try more than one and see which you prefer, or come up with your own combinations!

1. Keep them plain!
2. Crunchy Cardamom (see below)
3. Cinnamon Sugar (see below)
4. Molasses Glaze (see below)

COOKIE INGREDIENTS

Dry

2 cups all-purpose flour
¾ tsp baking soda
¼ tsp baking powder
1 tsp ground cardamom
¾ tsp ground cinnamon
¾ tsp ground ginger
¾ tsp ground black pepper
¾ tsp salt
½ tsp allspice
¼ tsp ground cloves
¼ tsp Chinese 5 spice

Wet

1 cup unsalted butter, room temperature
¾ cup granulated sugar
½ cup brown sugar
2 Tbsp molasses
1 large egg

COOKIE FINISHING INGREDIENTS

Crunchy Cardamom:

3 Tbsp raw (turbinado) sugar
½ tsp ground cardamom

Cinnamon Sugar:

3 Tbsp granulated sugar
1 tsp ground cinnamon

Molasses Glaze:

½ cup confectioners' (icing) sugar
1 Tbsp molasses
1 ½ Tbsp milk

AYLA'S BASIC BISCUITS

"HONESTLY this is the best biscuit recipe I've found but I recommend adding 1.5-3tsp of sweet paprika and garlic powder for a fun addition. It also isn't clear enough in the recipe, but basically mix all the ingredients together very loosely, until they just hold together, then roll it out and cut and bake. Do not work the dough at ALL otherwise it makes the FLATTEST biscuits I've ever seen also GRATE THE BUTTER! It is the single best thing I've done for my baking. I hope that's helpful - they're super simple and quick to make, and seriously delicious!"

INGREDIENTS

2 cups all-purpose flour

1 tablespoon baking powder

½ teaspoon salt

½ cup shortening

¾ cup milk

DIRECTIONS

1. Preheat oven to 450 degrees F (230 degrees C).

2. In a large mixing bowl sift together flour, baking powder and salt. Cut in shortening with fork or pastry blender until mixture resembles coarse crumbs.

3. Pour milk into flour mixture while stirring with a fork. Mix in milk until dough is soft, moist and pulls away from the side of the bowl.

4. Turn dough out onto a lightly floured surface and toss with flour until no longer sticky. Roll dough out into a 1/2 inch thick sheet and cut with a floured biscuit or cookie cutter. Press together unused dough and repeat rolling and cutting procedure.

5. Place biscuits on ungreased baking sheets and bake in preheated oven until golden brown, about 10 minutes.

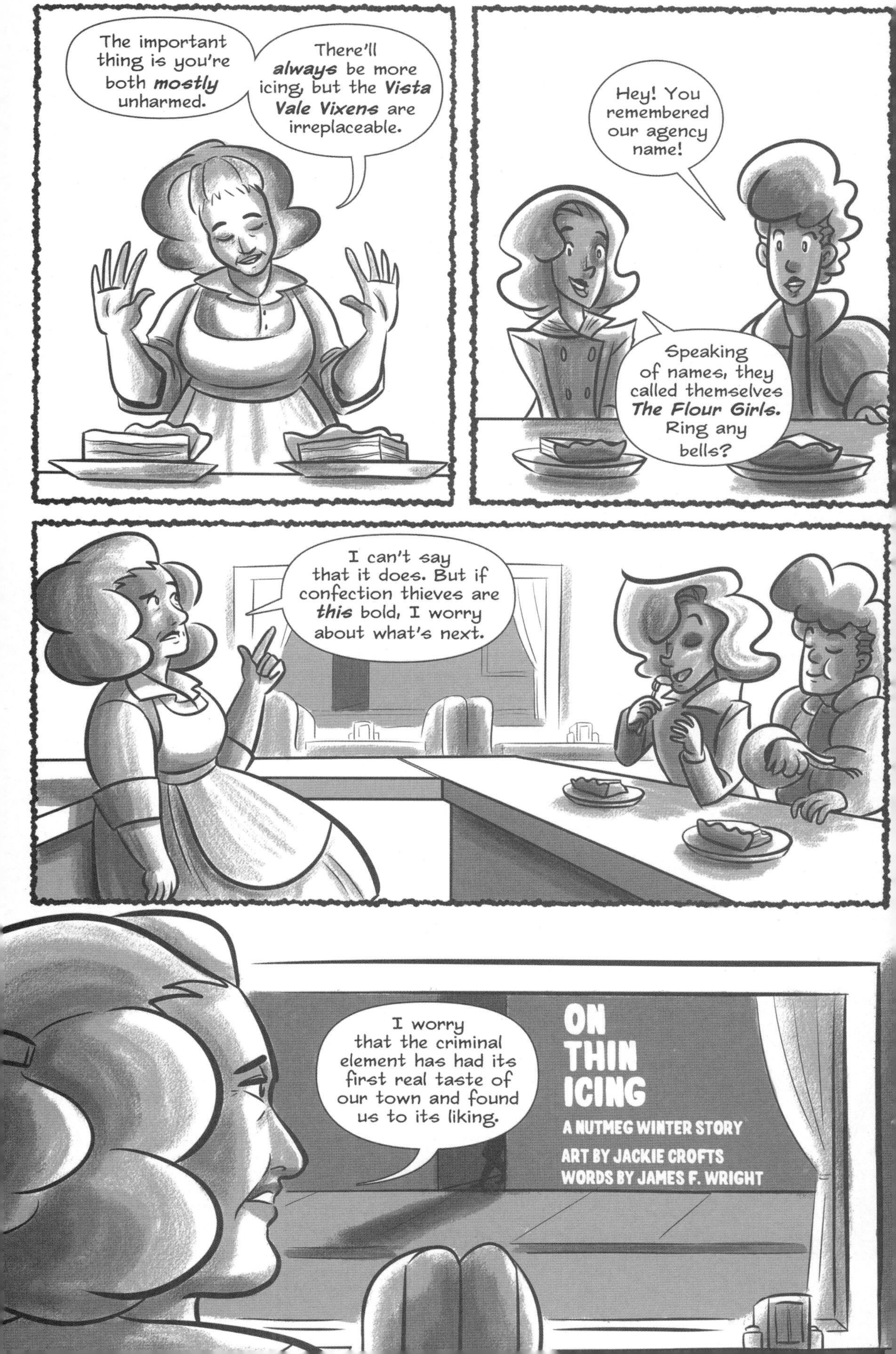

The important thing is you're both mostly unharmed.
There'll always be more icing, but the Vista Vale Vixens are irreplaceable.
Hey! You remembered our agency name!
Speaking of names, they called themselves The Flour Girls. Ring any bells?
I can't say that it does. But if confection thieves are this bold, I worry about what's next.
I worry that the criminal element has had its first real taste of our town and found us to its liking.
ON THIN ICING
A NUTMEG WINTER STORY
ART BY JACKIE CROFTS
WORDS BY JAMES F. WRIGHT

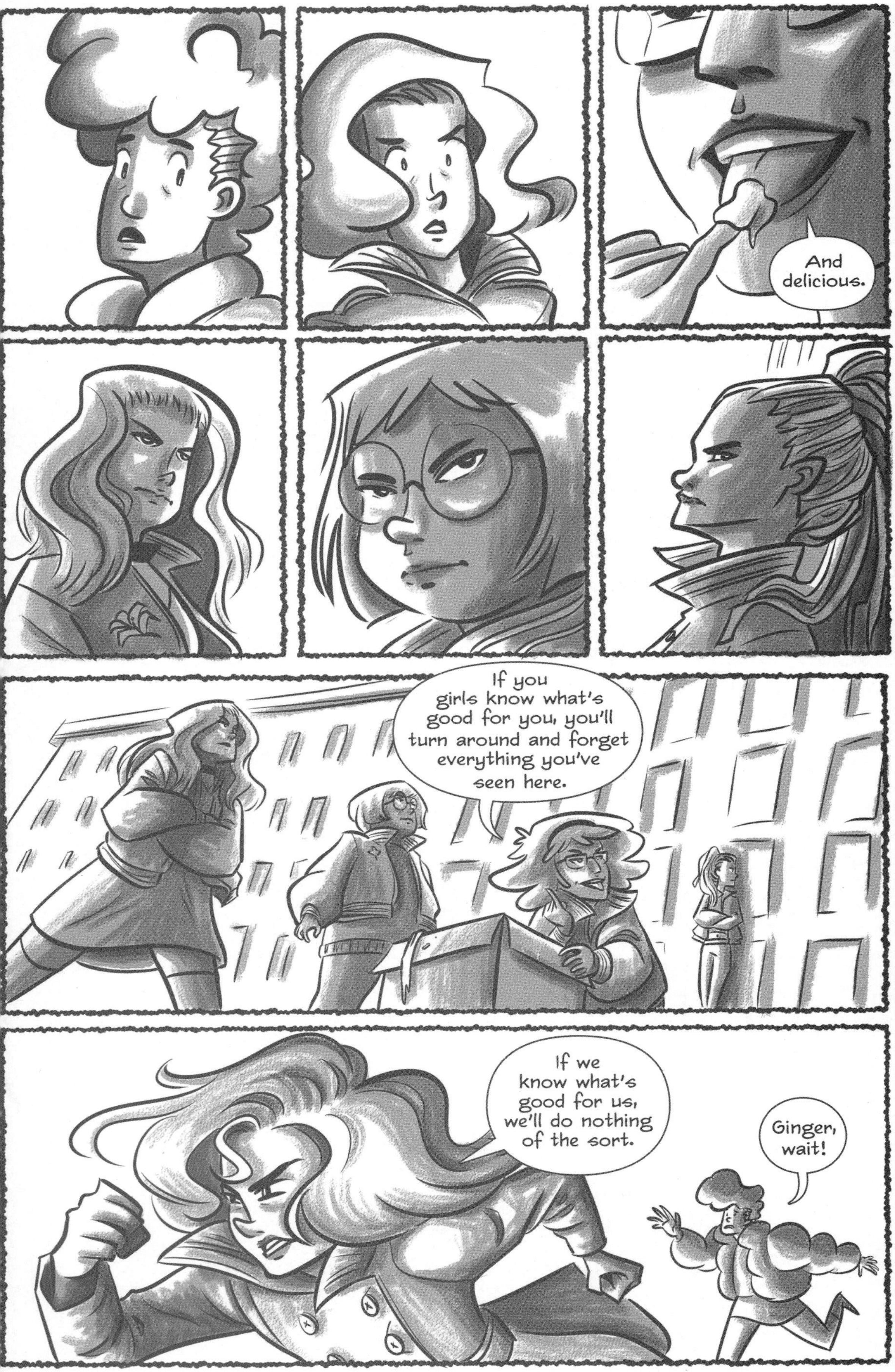
And delicious.
If you girls know what's good for you, you'll turn around and forget everything you've seen here.
If we know what's good for us, we'll do nothing of the sort.
Ginger, wait!

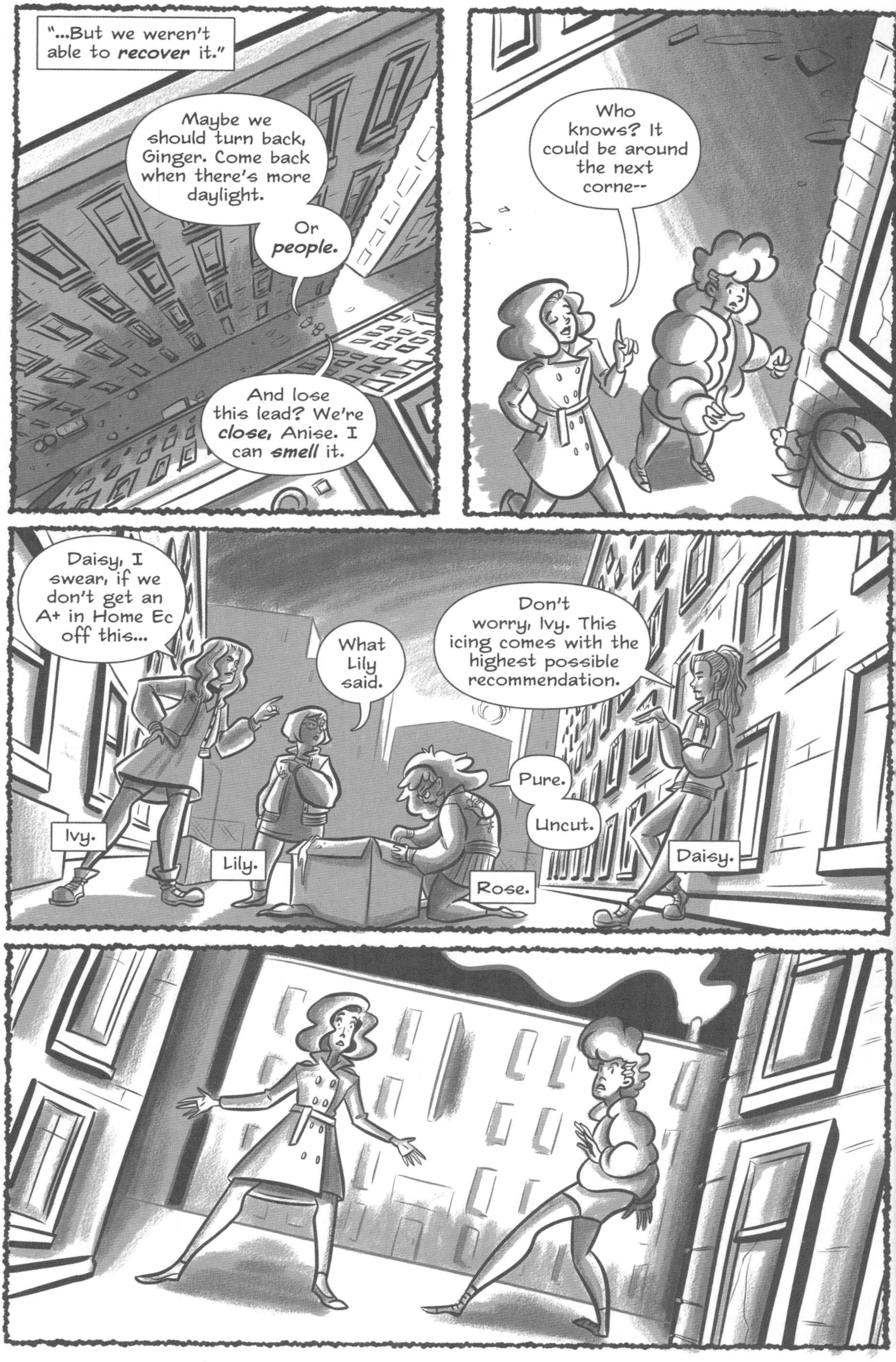
"...But we weren't able to *recover* it."
Maybe we should turn back, Ginger. Come back when there's more daylight.
Or *people.*
And lose this lead? We're *close,* Anise. I can *smell* it.
Who knows? It could be around the next corne--
Daisy, I swear, if we don't get an A+ in Home Ec off this...
What Lily said.
Don't worry, Ivy. This icing comes with the highest possible recommendation.
Pure.
Uncut.
Ivy.
Lily.
Rose.
Daisy.

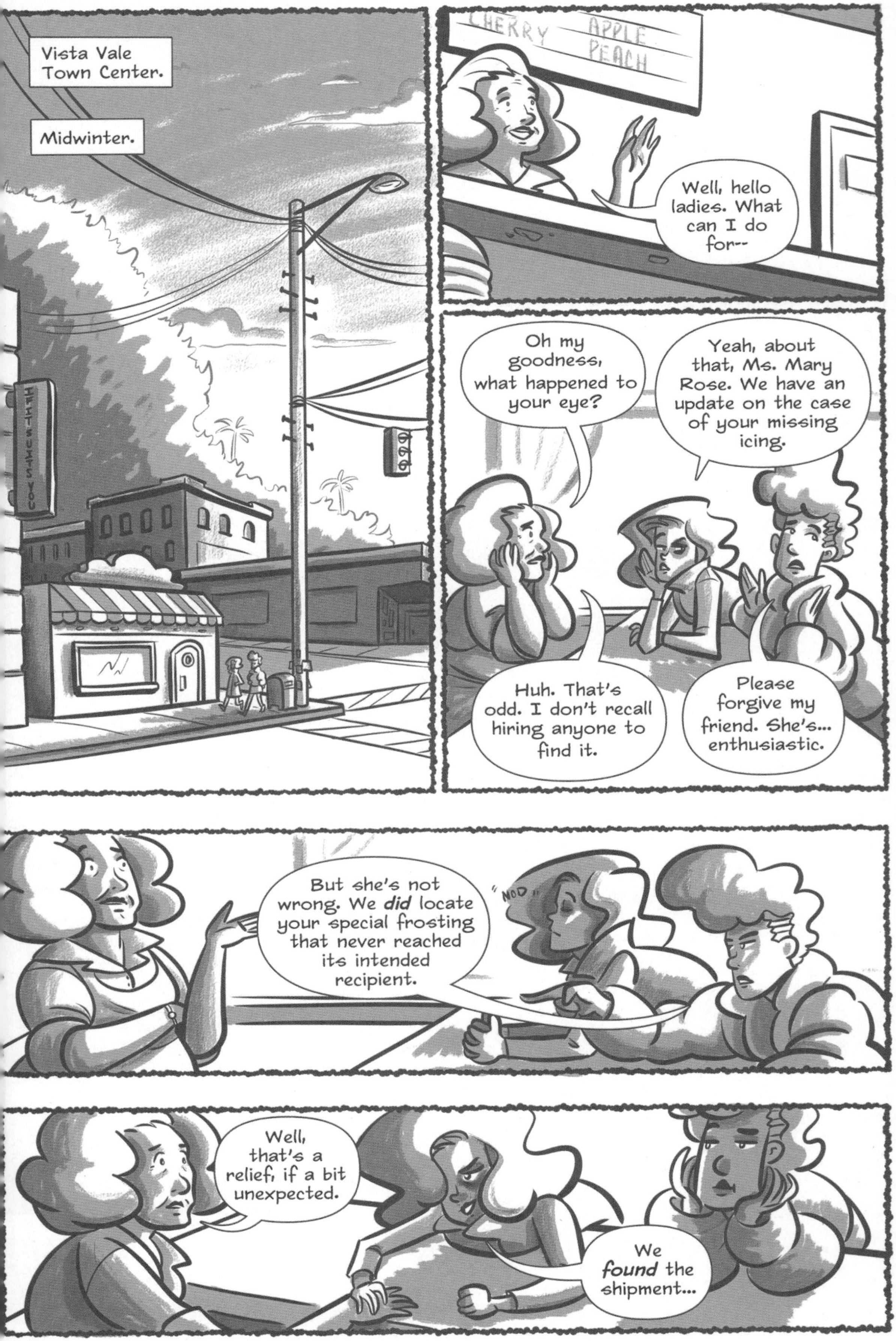
Vista Vale Town Center.
Midwinter.
IF IT SUITS YOU
CHERRY
APPLE
PEACH
Well, hello ladies. What can I do for--
Oh my goodness, what happened to your eye?
Yeah, about that, Ms. Mary Rose. We have an update on the case of your missing icing.
Huh. That's odd. I don't recall hiring anyone to find it.
Please forgive my friend. She's... enthusiastic.
But she's not wrong. We *did* locate your special frosting that never reached its intended recipient.
"NOD"
Well, that's a relief, if a bit unexpected.
We *found* the shipment...

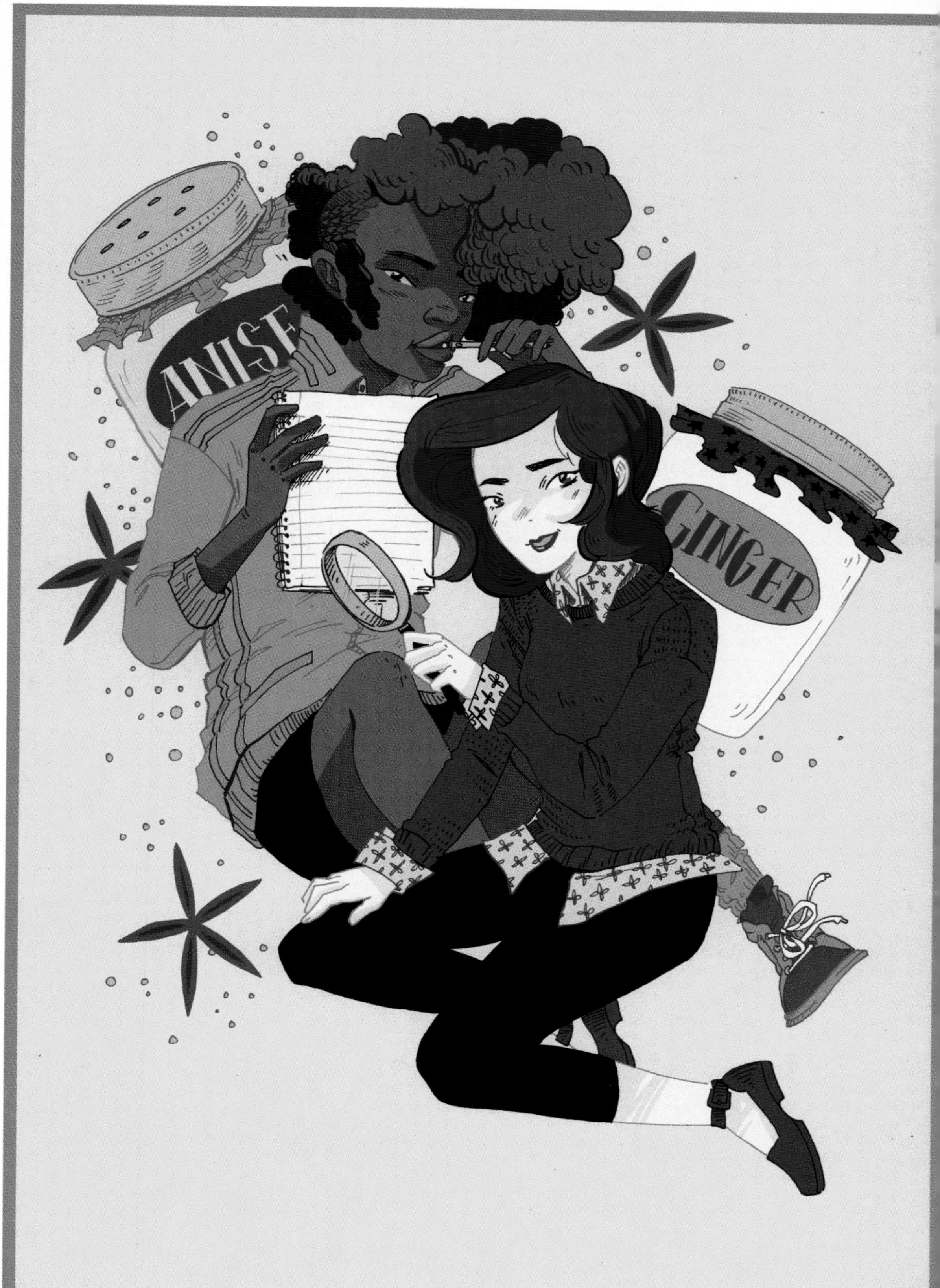
ANISE
GINGER

ART BY NICOLE GOUX

THE COOLING RACK

CONTACT: @NutmegComic NutmegComics@gmail.com

Avatars by Genue Revuelta

Yeah. We know things got a little darker for Poppy and Cassia, but don't worry because there's still some more story to tell. At the very least, we've got a couple of pick-me-ups right here. Our friend Lisa Uyemura has shared her Blondies recipe with us and they are delicious! And our friend and wonderfully talented artist, Nicole Goux, did a dope pinup featuring teen journalist and detective Anise Stark and Ginger Westlake!

LISA UYEMURA'S BLONDIES

INGREDIENTS

1 1/2 sticks (3/4 cup) unsalted butter, softened
1 1/2 cups firmly packed light brown sugar
2 large eggs
2 teaspoons vanilla
1/2 teaspoon salt
1 1/2 teaspoons double-acting baking powder
1 1/2 cups all purpose flour
1 1/2 cups white chocolate chips
2 cups sweetened flaked coconut, toasted and cooled

INSTRUCTIONS

* In a bowl with an electric mixer, cream together the butter and brown sugar, beating the mixture until it is light and fluffy

* Add the eggs, one at a time, beating well after each addition, and beat in the vanilla

* In a small bowl whisk together the salt, the baking powder and the flour.

* Add the flour to the butter mixture and beat the batter until it is just combined. Stir in the chocolate chips and the coconut.

* Spread the batter evenly in a buttered and floured 13x9 inch baking pan and bake it in the middle of a preheated 350* oven for 25 to 30 minutes, or until it begins to pull away from the sides of the pan and crumbs adhere to a tester.

* Let the mixture cool completely in the pan on a rack and cut it into squares.

HOW TO TOAST COCONUT: Pour coconut in a thin layer on a baking sheet. Bake at 300* for about 20 minutes or until toasted light brown, stirring frequently to prevent burning.

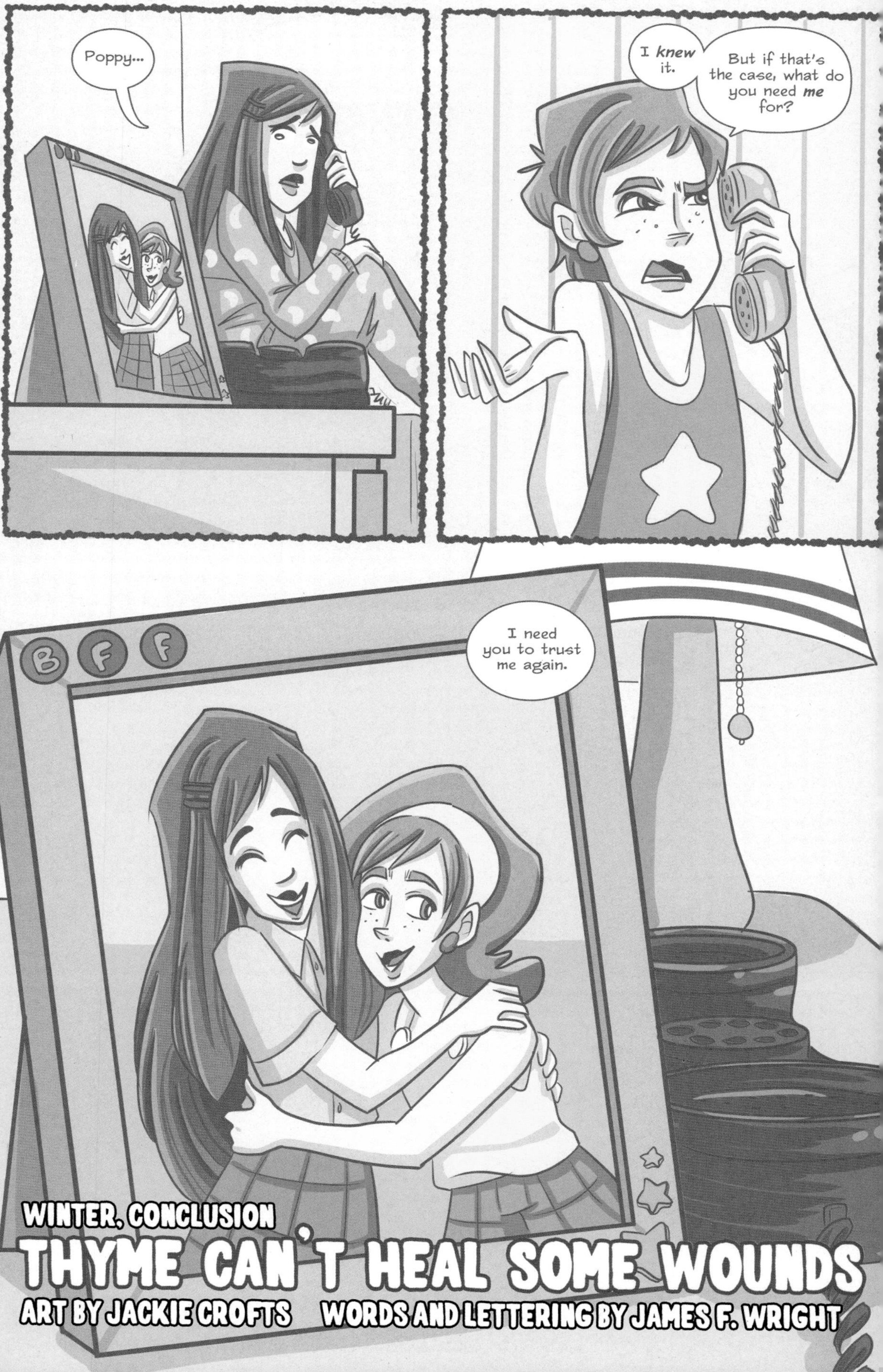

Poppy...
I *knew* it.
But if that's the case, what do you need *me* for?
I need you to trust me again.
B F F
WINTER, CONCLUSION
THYME CAN'T HEAL SOME WOUNDS
ART BY JACKIE CROFTS
WORDS AND LETTERING BY JAMES F. WRIGHT

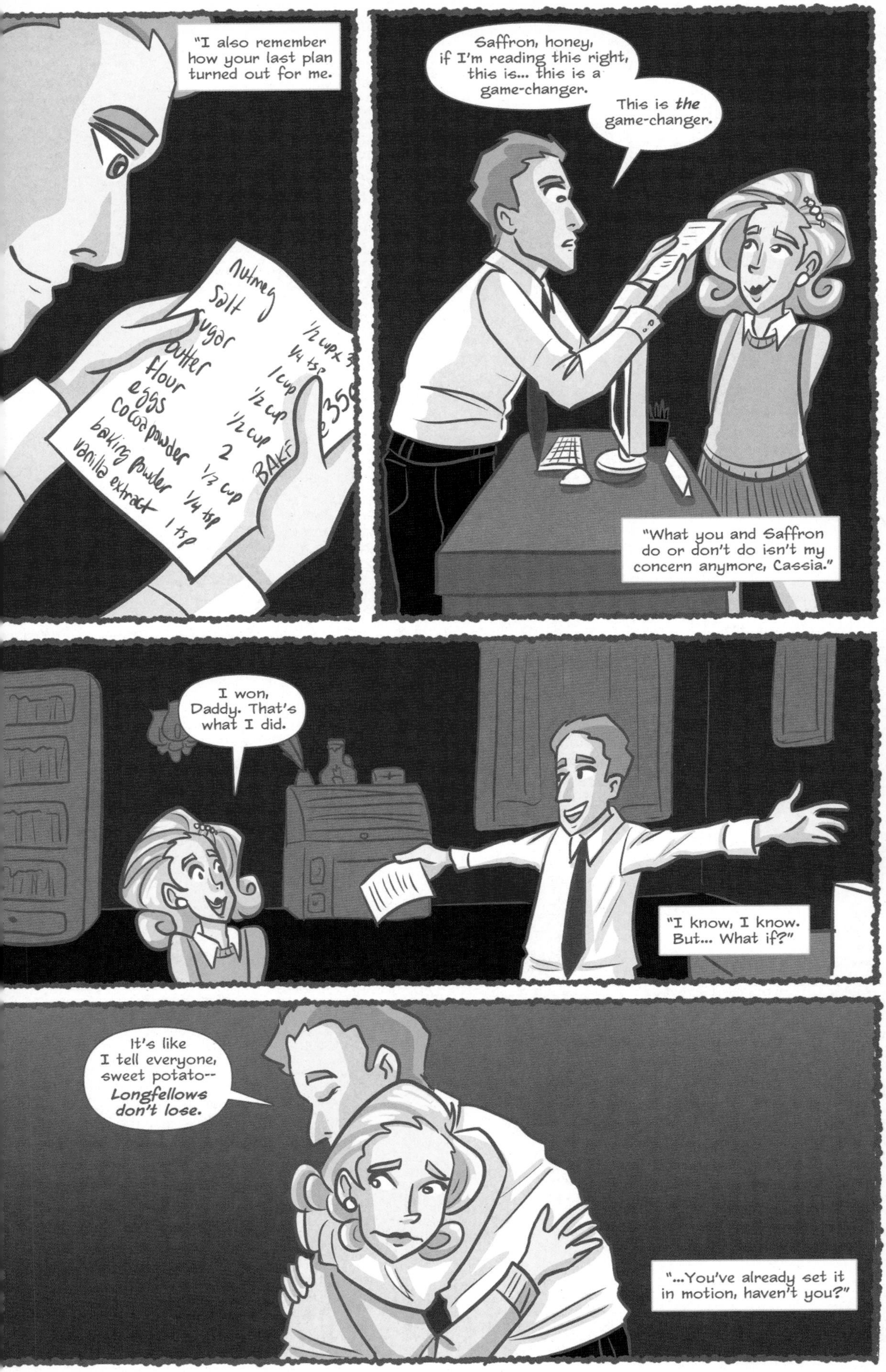

"I also remember how your last plan turned out for me.
nutmeg
salt
sugar
butter
flour
eggs
cocoa powder
baking powder
vanilla extract
1/2 cup
1/4 tsp
1 cup
1/2 cup
1/2 cup
2
1/3 cup
1/4 tsp
1 tsp
Saffron, honey, if I'm reading this right, this is... this is a game-changer.
This is *the* game-changer.
"What you and Saffron do or don't do isn't my concern anymore, Cassia."
I won, Daddy. That's what I did.
"I know, I know. But... What if?"
It's like I tell everyone, sweet potato-- ***Longfellows don't lose.***
"...You've already set it in motion, haven't you?"

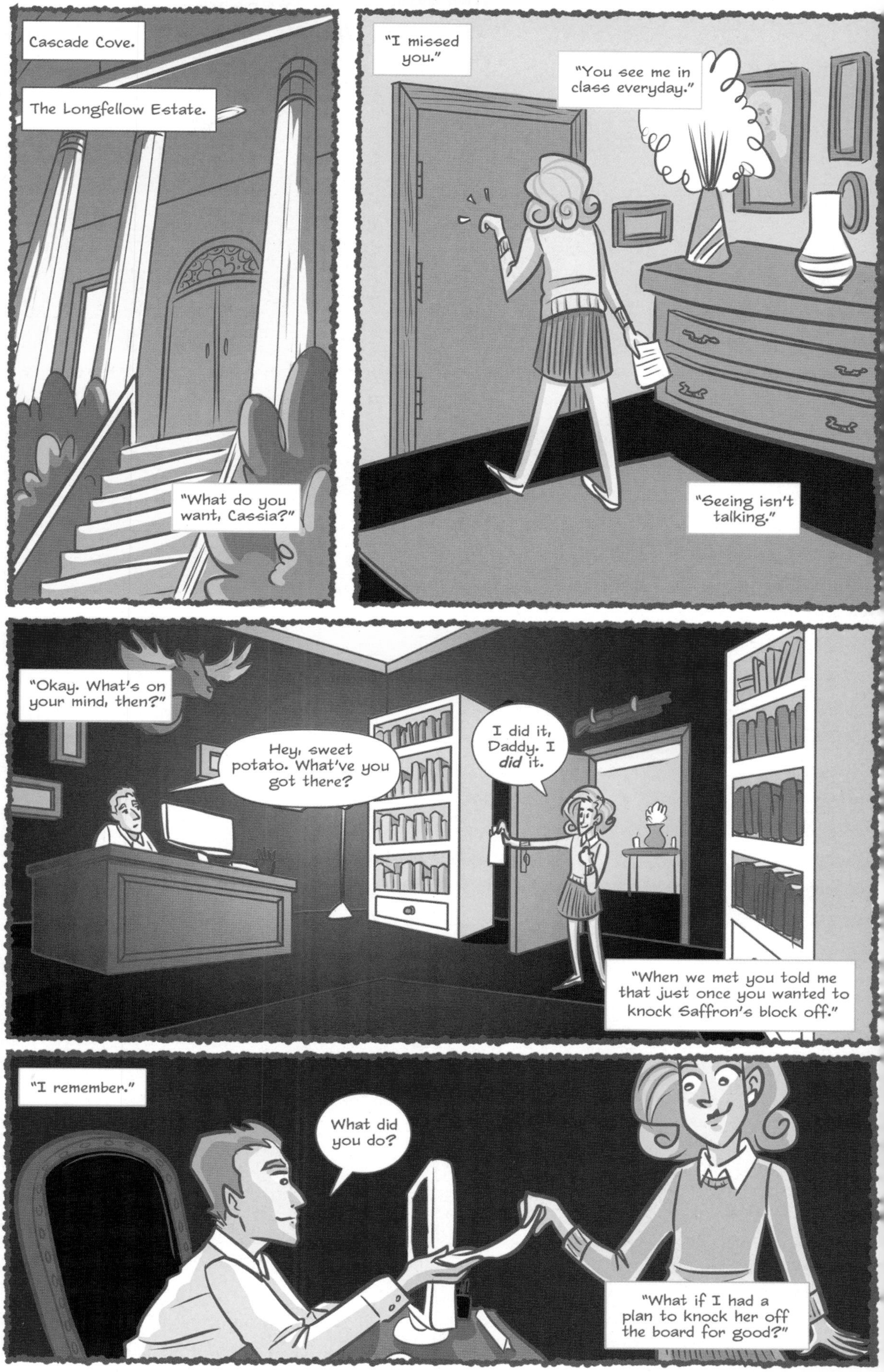
Cascade Cove.
The Longfellow Estate.
"What do you want, Cassia?"
"I missed you."
"You see me in class everyday."
"Seeing isn't talking."
"Okay. What's on your mind, then?"
Hey, sweet potato. What've you got there?
I did it, Daddy. I *did* it.
"When we met you told me that just once you wanted to knock Saffron's block off."
"I remember."
What did you do?
"What if I had a plan to knock her off the board for good?"

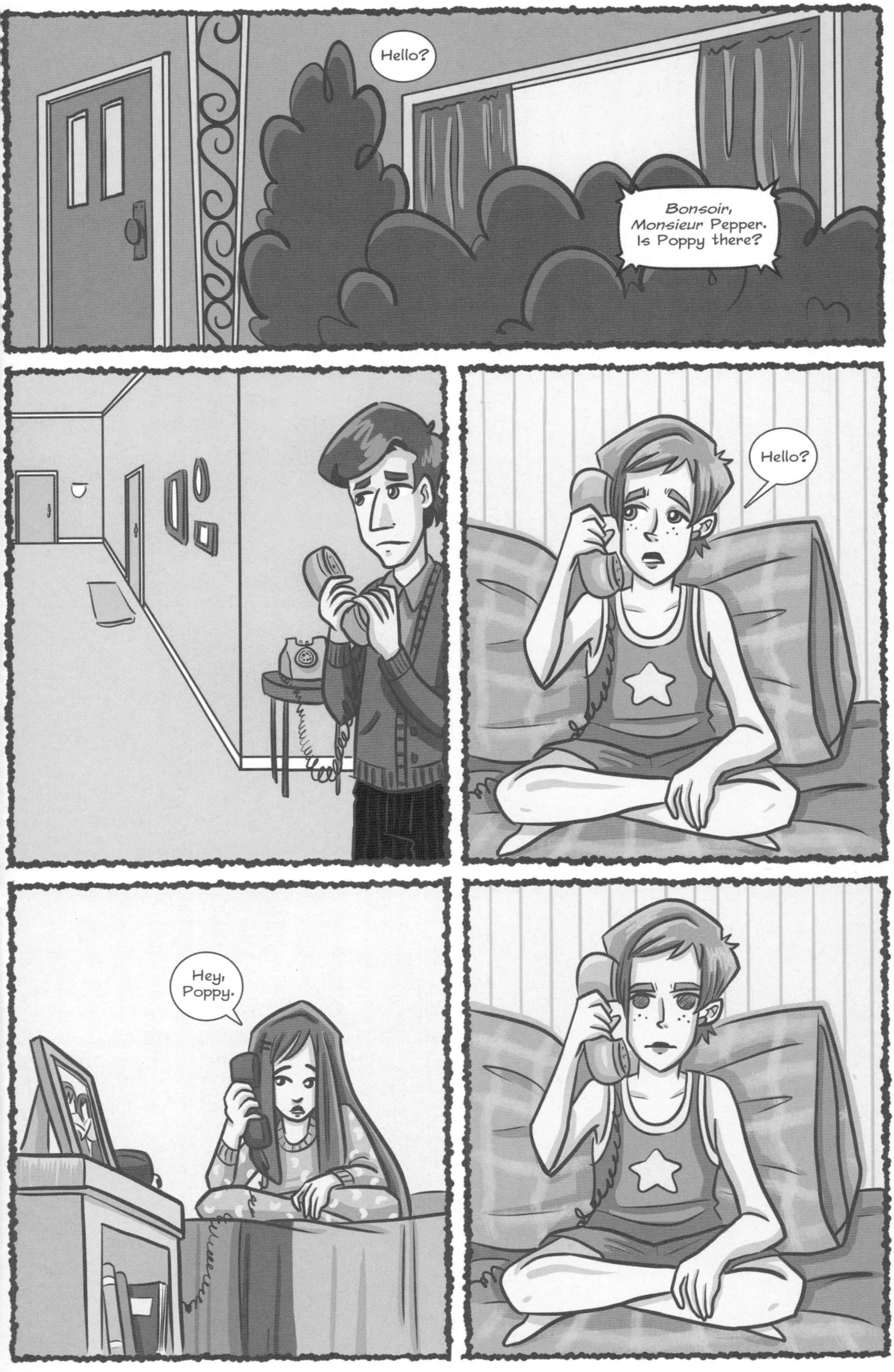
Hello?
Bonsoir, Monsieur Pepper. Is Poppy there?
Hello?
Hey, Poppy.

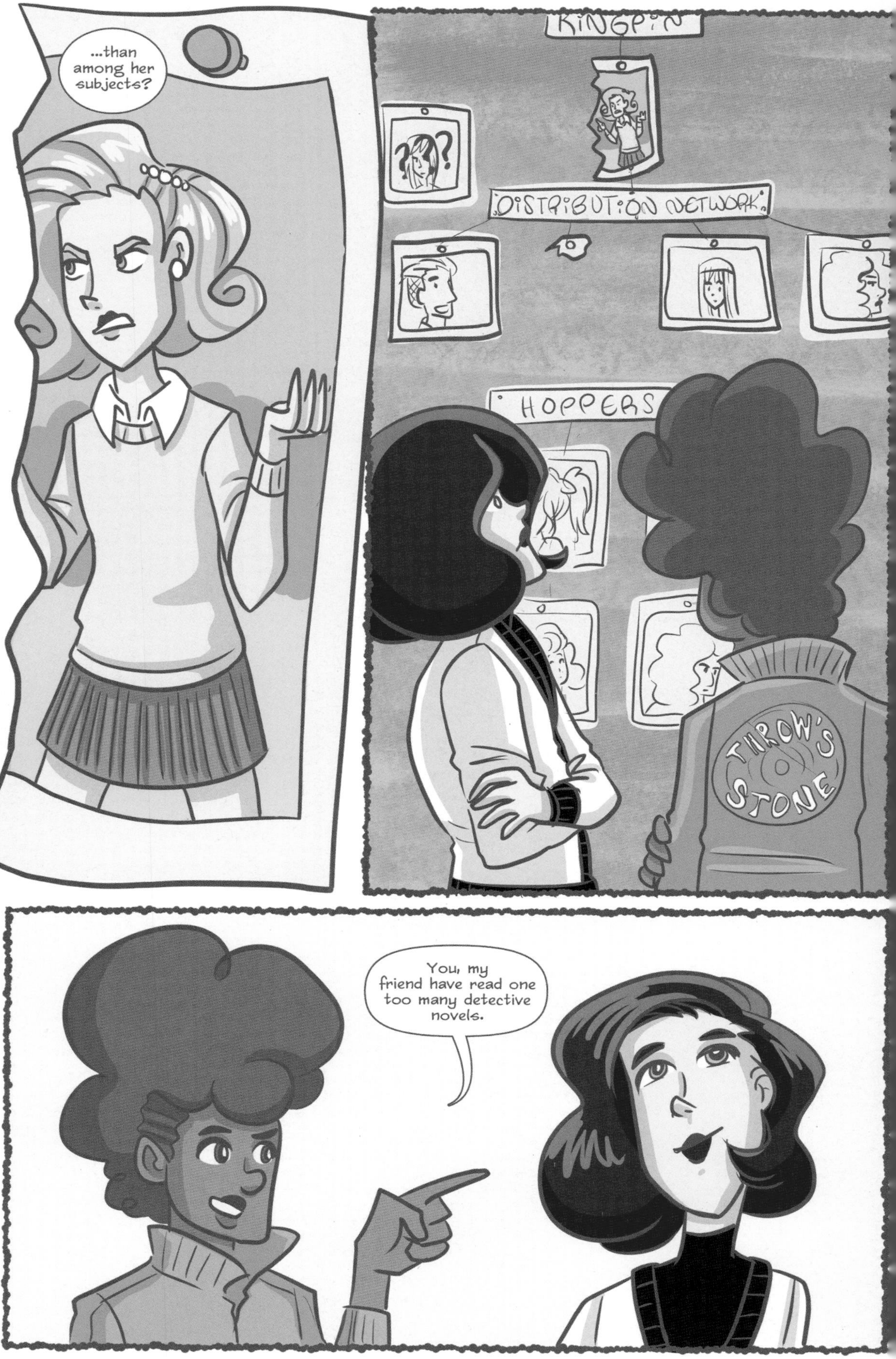
...than among her subjects?
KINGPIN
DISTRIBUTION NETWORK
HOPPERS
THROW'S STONE
You, my friend have read one too many detective novels.

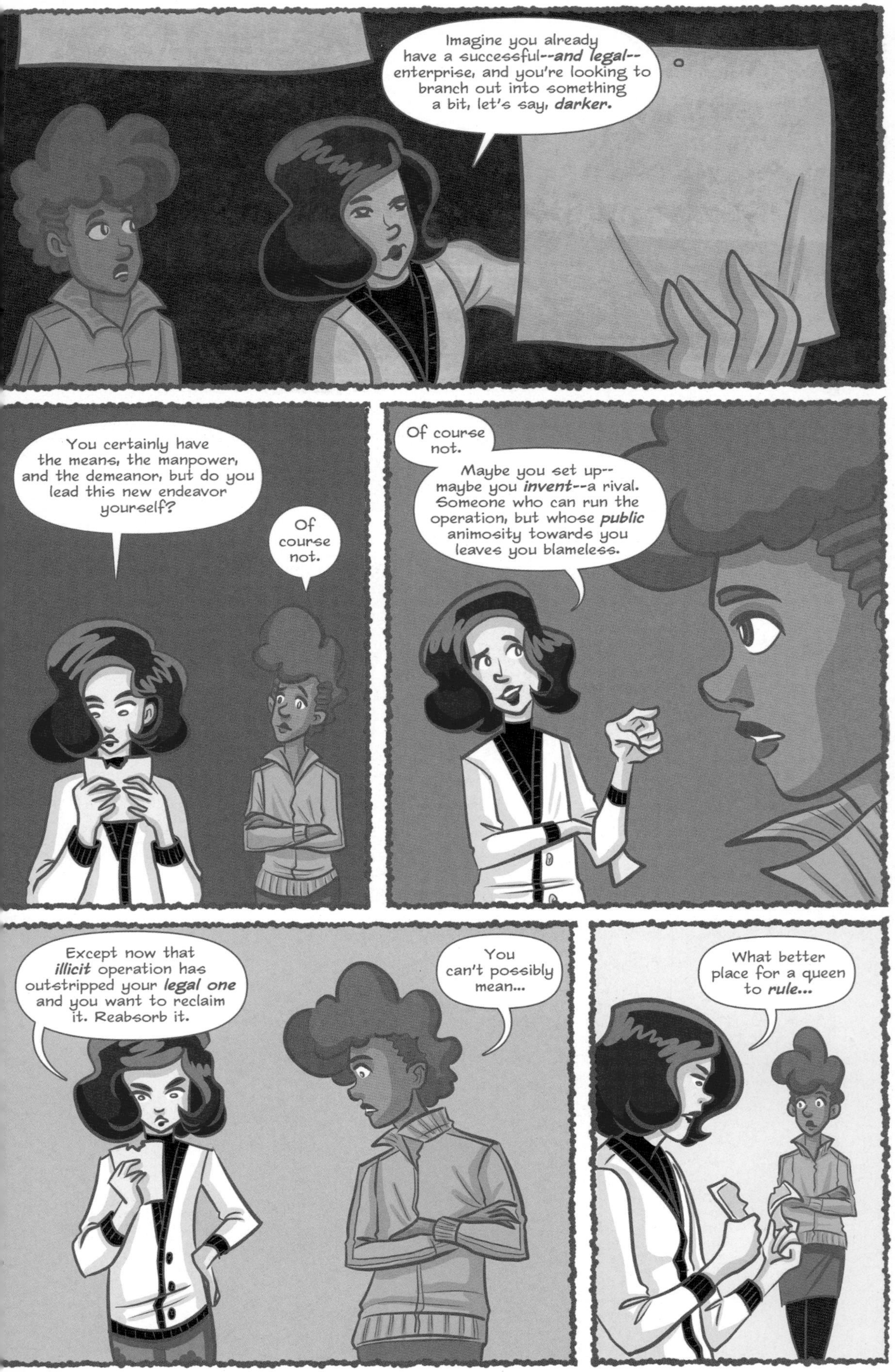

Imagine you already have a successful--*and legal*--enterprise, and you're looking to branch out into something a bit, let's say, *darker.*
You certainly have the means, the manpower, and the demeanor, but do you lead this new endeavor yourself?
Of course not.
Of course not.
Maybe you set up--maybe you *invent*--a rival. Someone who can run the operation, but whose *public* animosity towards you leaves you blameless.
Except now that *illicit* operation has outstripped your *legal one* and you want to reclaim it. Reabsorb it.
You can't possibly mean...
What better place for a queen to *rule...*

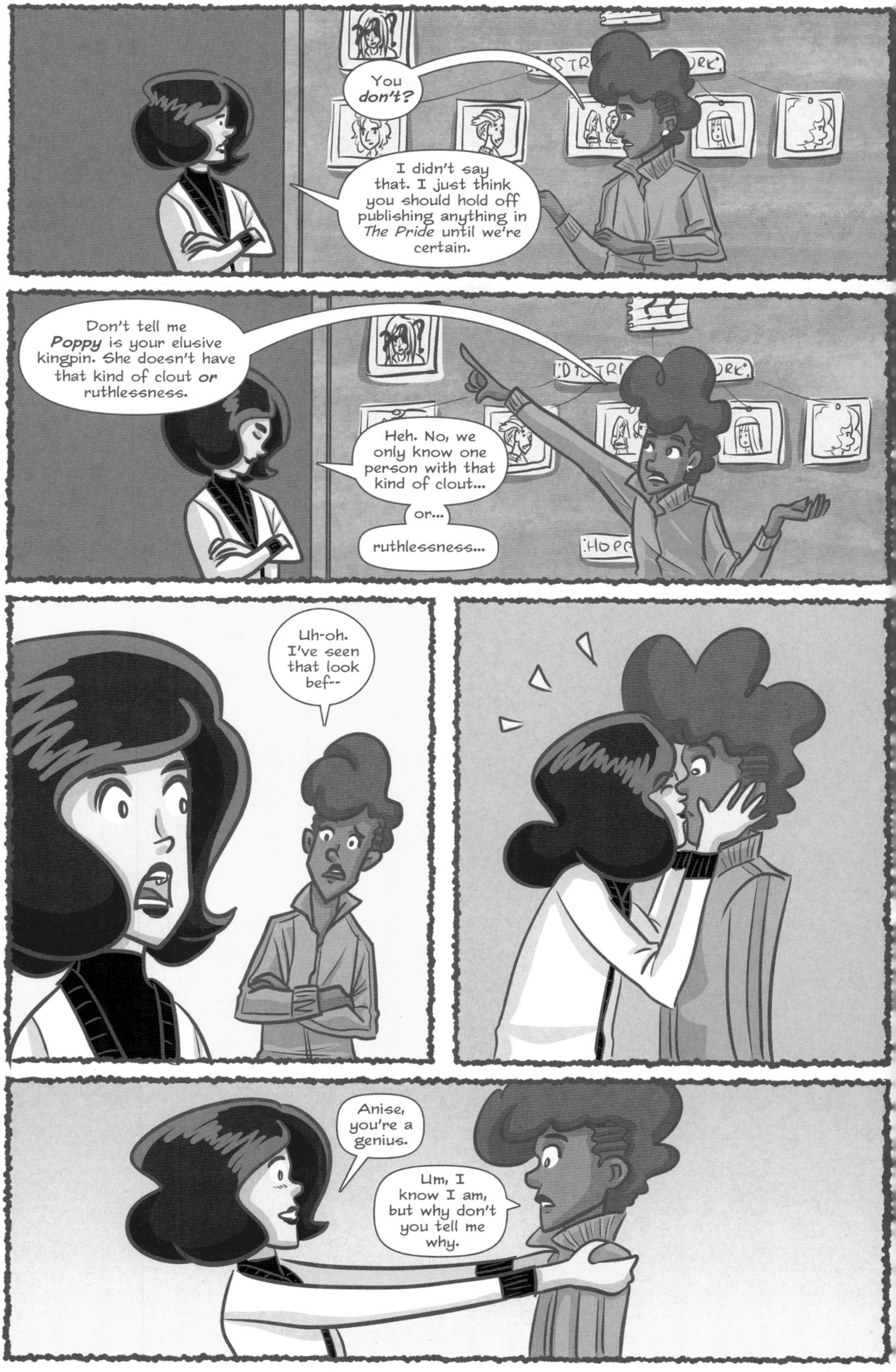
You *don't?*
I didn't say that. I just think you should hold off publishing anything in *The Pride* until we're certain.
Don't tell me **Poppy** is your elusive kingpin. She doesn't have that kind of clout **or** ruthlessness.
Heh. No, we only know one person with that kind of clout...
or...
ruthlessness...
HOPP
Uh-oh. I've seen that look bef--
Anise, you're a genius.
Um, I know I am, but why don't you tell me why.

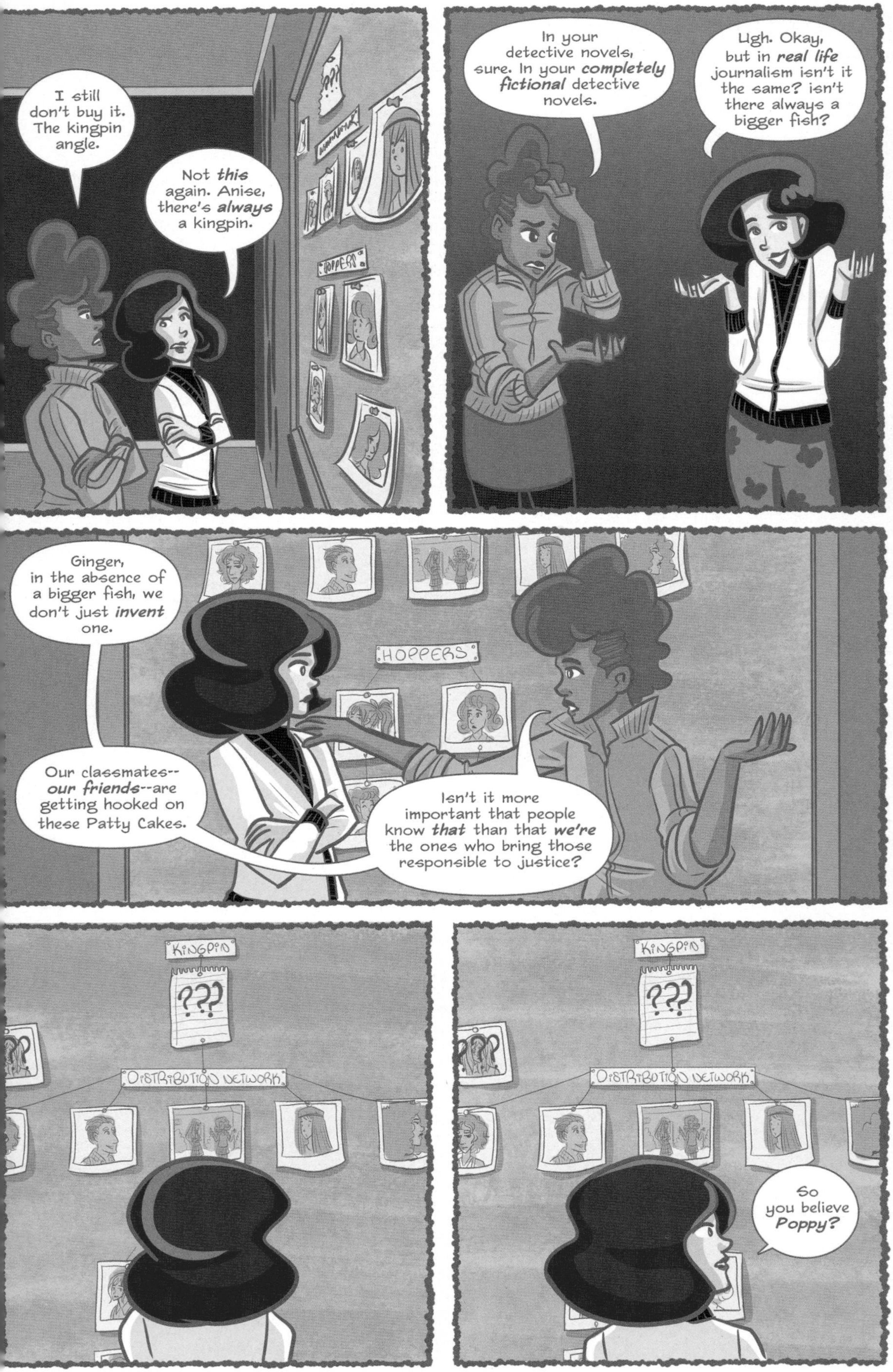
I still don't buy it. The kingpin angle.
Not *this* again. Anise, there's *always* a kingpin.
HOPPERS
In your detective novels, sure. In your *completely fictional* detective novels.
Ugh. Okay, but in *real life* journalism isn't it the same? isn't there always a bigger fish?
Ginger, in the absence of a bigger fish, we don't just *invent* one.
HOPPERS
Our classmates-- *our friends*--are getting hooked on these Patty Cakes.
Isn't it more important that people know *that* than that *we're* the ones who bring those responsible to justice?
KINGPIN
???
DISTRIBUTION NETWORK
KINGPIN
???
DISTRIBUTION NETWORK
So you believe *Poppy?*

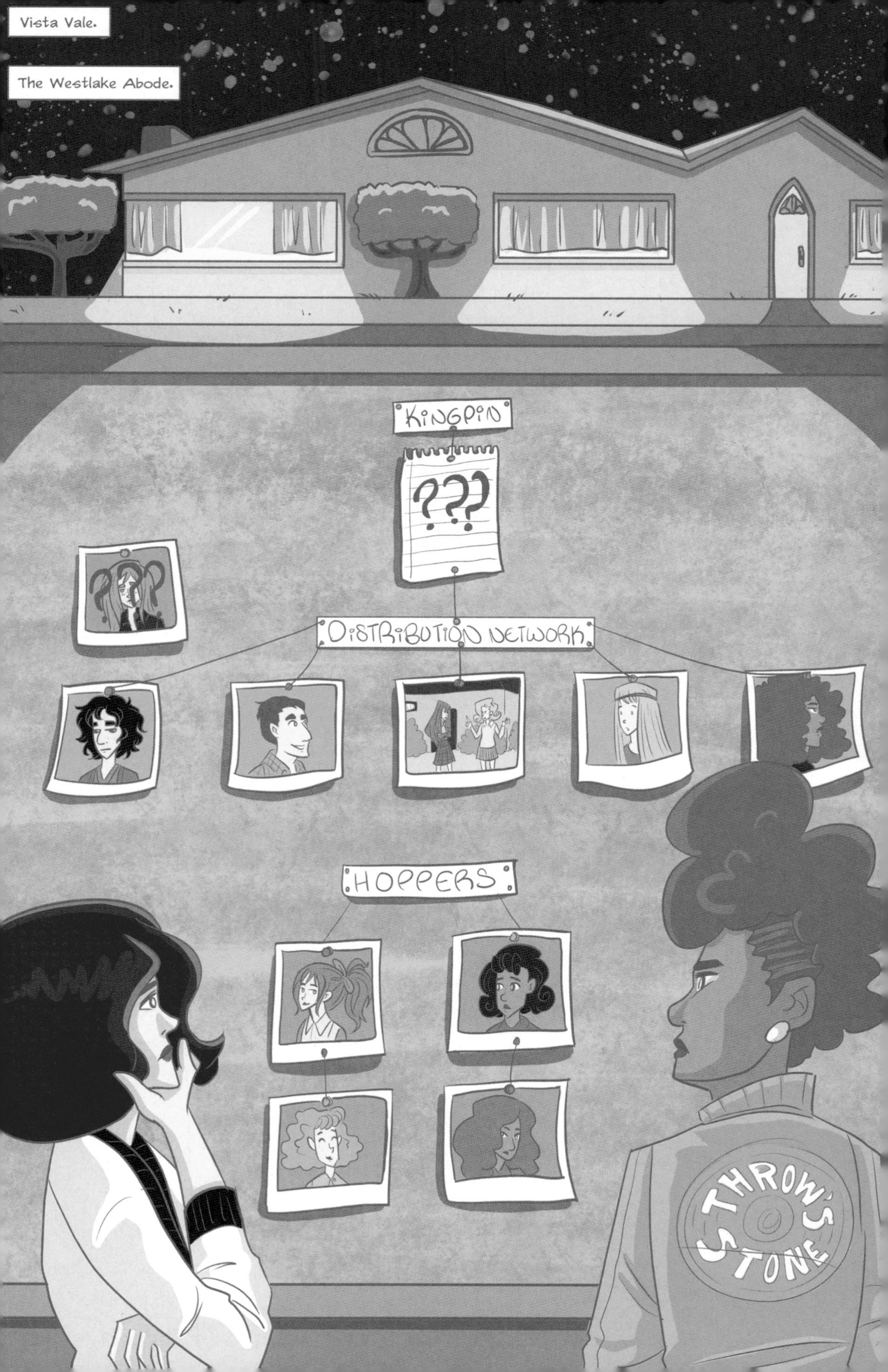
Vista Vale.
The Westlake Abode.
KINGPIN
???
DISTRIBUTION NETWORK
HOPPERS
THROW'S STONE

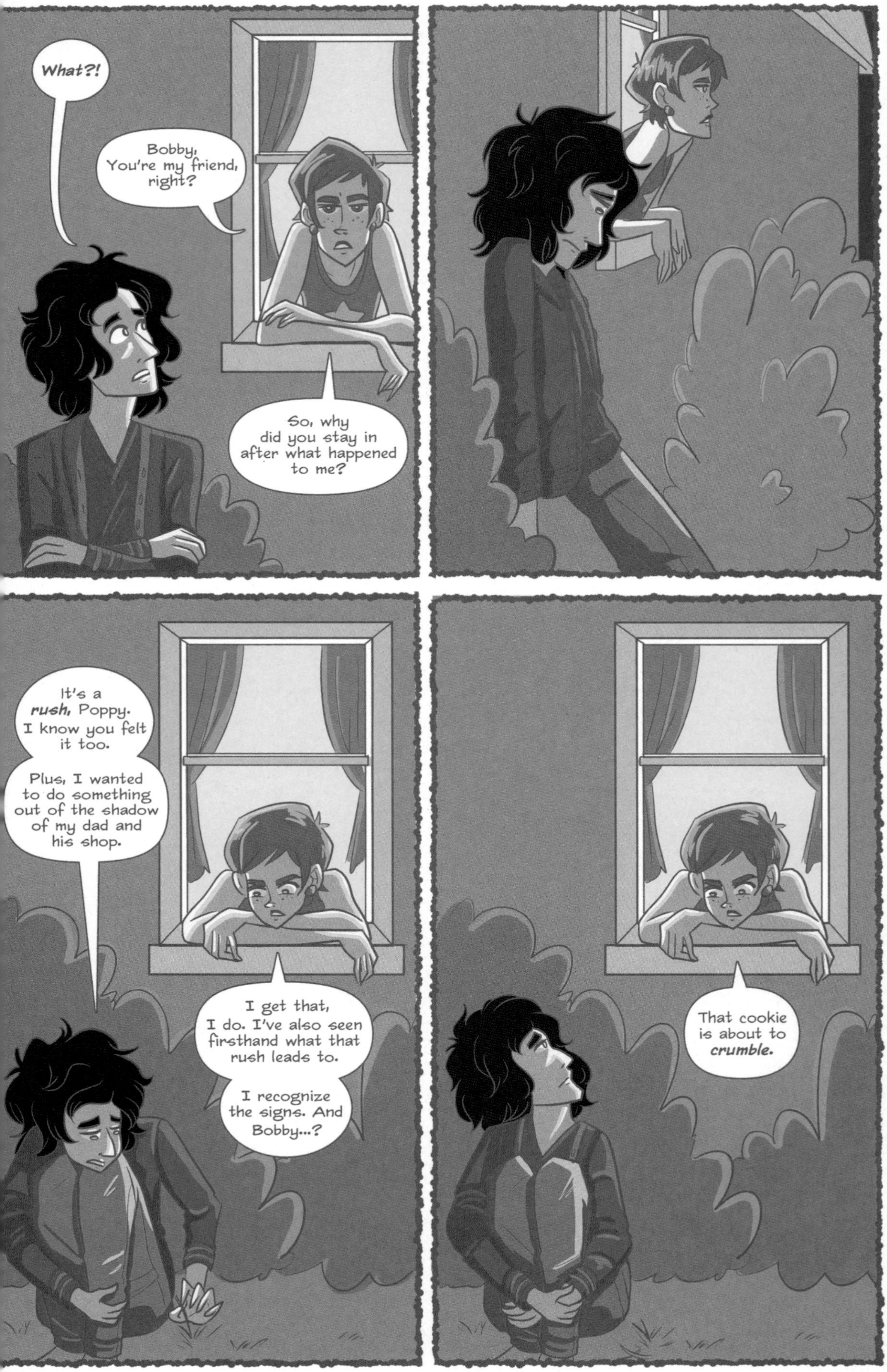
What?!
Bobby, You're my friend, right?
So, why did you stay in after what happened to me?
It's a **rush,** Poppy. I know you felt it too.
Plus, I wanted to do something out of the shadow of my dad and his shop.
I get that, I do. I've also seen firsthand what that rush leads to.
I recognize the signs. And Bobby...?
That cookie is about to ***crumble.***

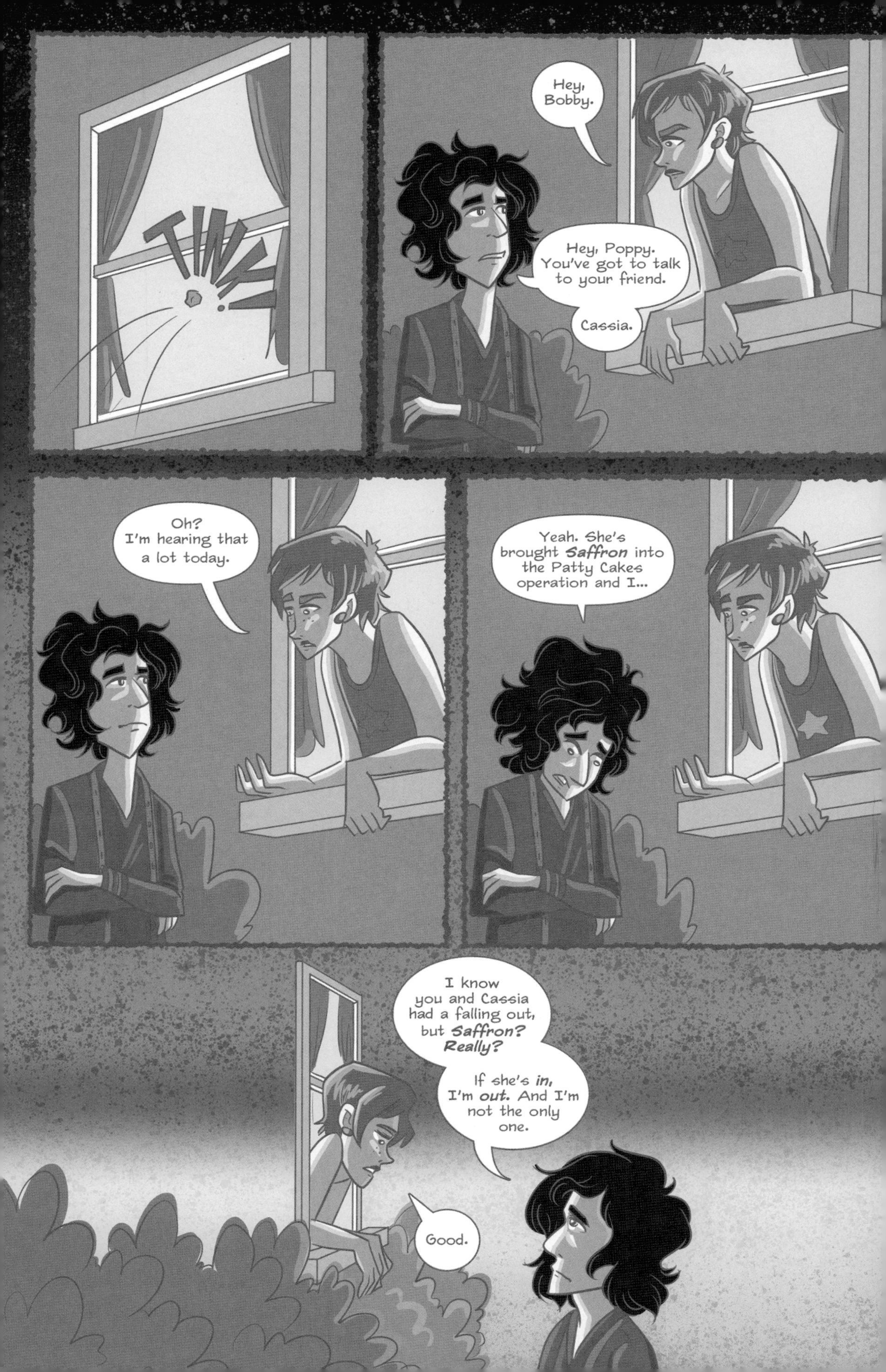
TINK
Hey, Bobby.
Hey, Poppy. You've got to talk to your friend.
Cassia.
Oh? I'm hearing that a lot today.
Yeah. She's brought Saffron into the Patty Cakes operation and I...
I know you and Cassia had a falling out, but Saffron? Really?
If she's in, I'm out. And I'm not the only one.
Good.

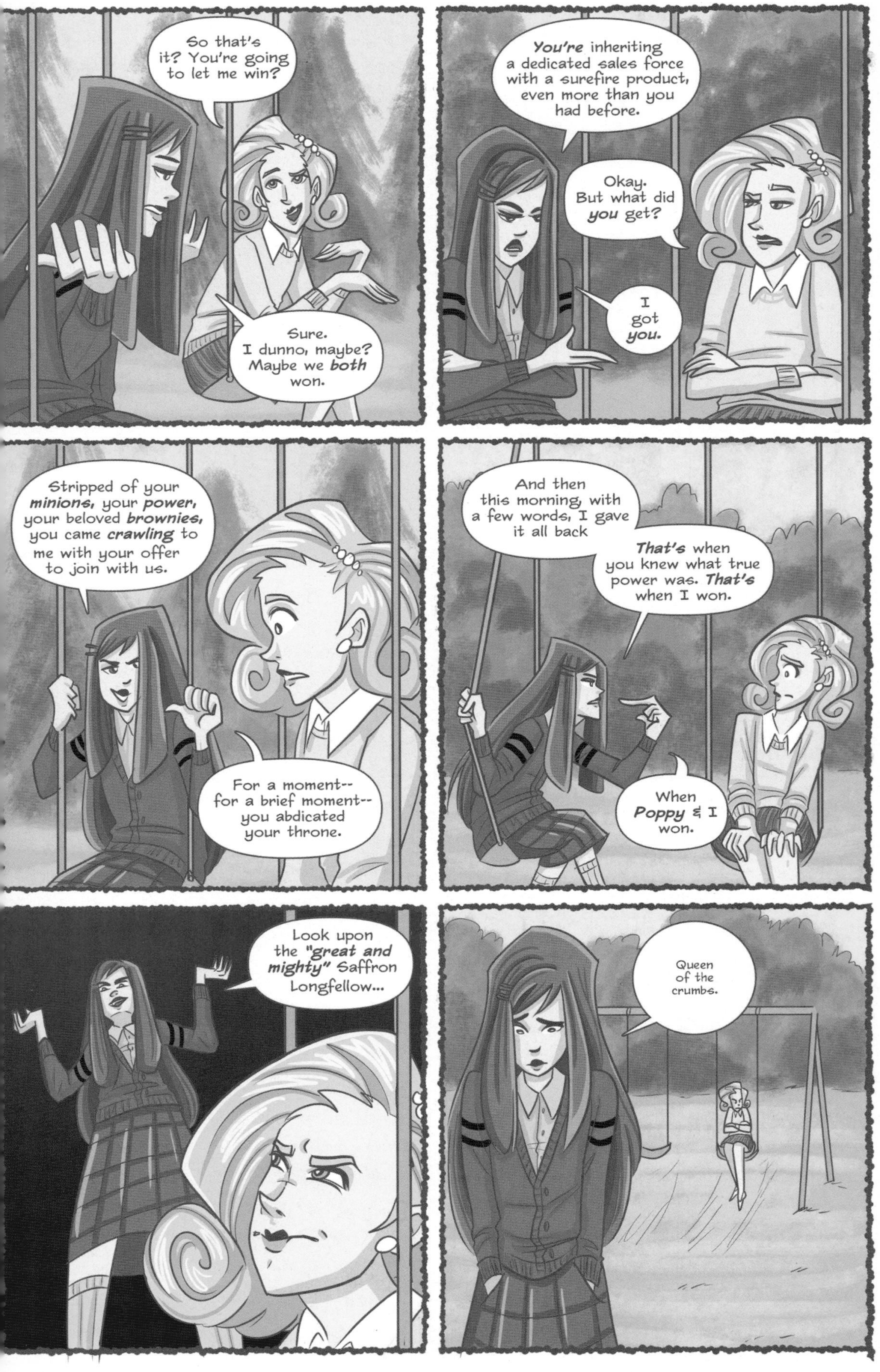
So that's it? You're going to let me win?
Sure. I dunno, maybe? Maybe we *both* won.
You're inheriting a dedicated sales force with a surefire product, even more than you had before.
Okay. But what did ***you*** get?
I got ***you.***
Stripped of your ***minions,*** your ***power,*** your beloved ***brownies,*** you came ***crawling*** to me with your offer to join with us.
For a moment-- for a brief moment-- you abdicated your throne.
And then this morning, with a few words, I gave it all back
That's when you knew what true power was. ***That's*** when I won.
When ***Poppy*** & I won.
Look upon the ***"great and mighty"*** Saffron Longfellow...
Queen of the crumbs.

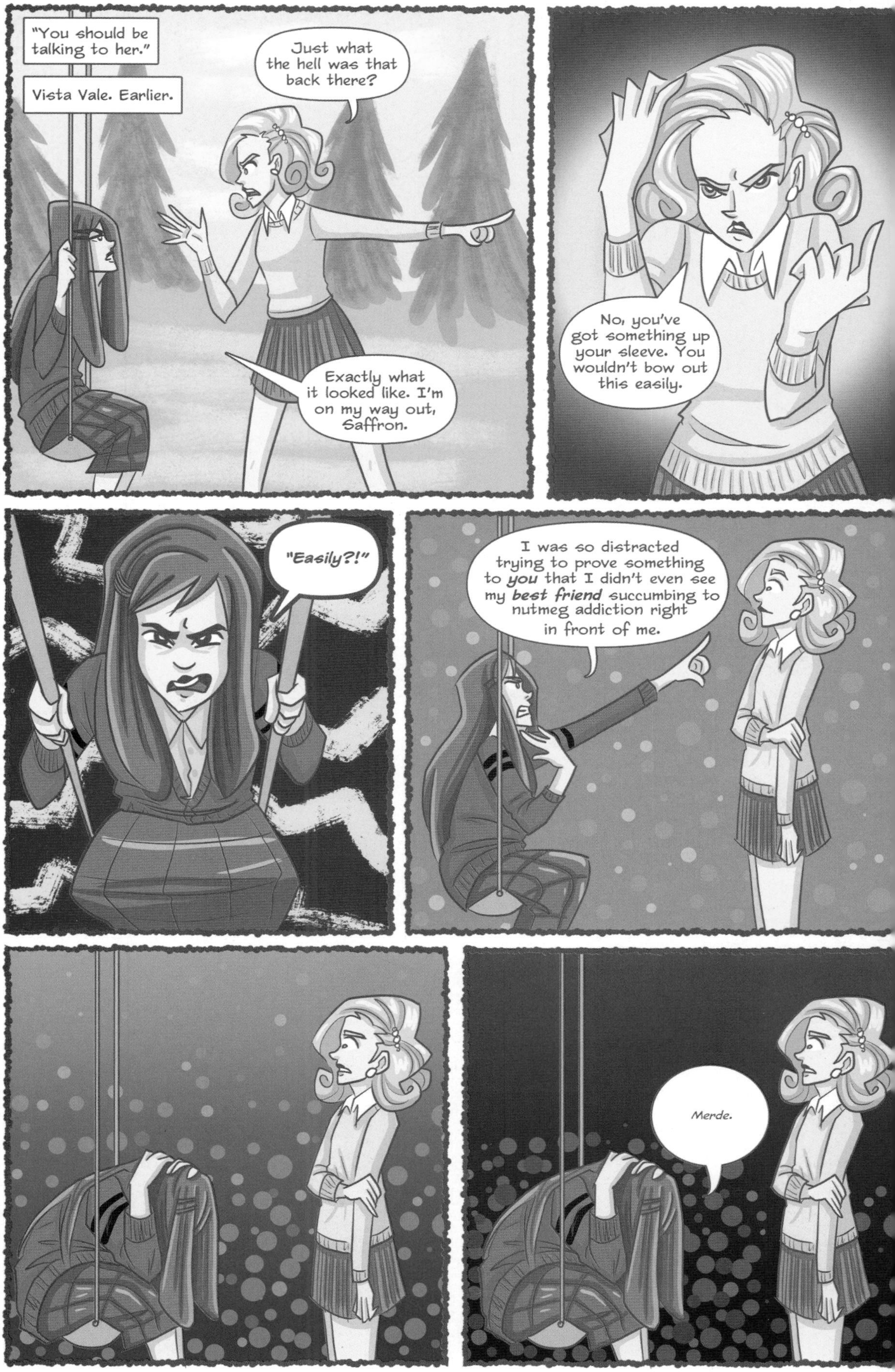
"You should be talking to her."
Vista Vale. Earlier.
Just what the hell was that back there?
Exactly what it looked like. I'm on my way out, Saffron.
No, you've got something up your sleeve. You wouldn't bow out this easily.
"Easily?!"
I was so distracted trying to prove something to you that I didn't even see my best friend succumbing to nutmeg addiction right in front of me.
Merde.

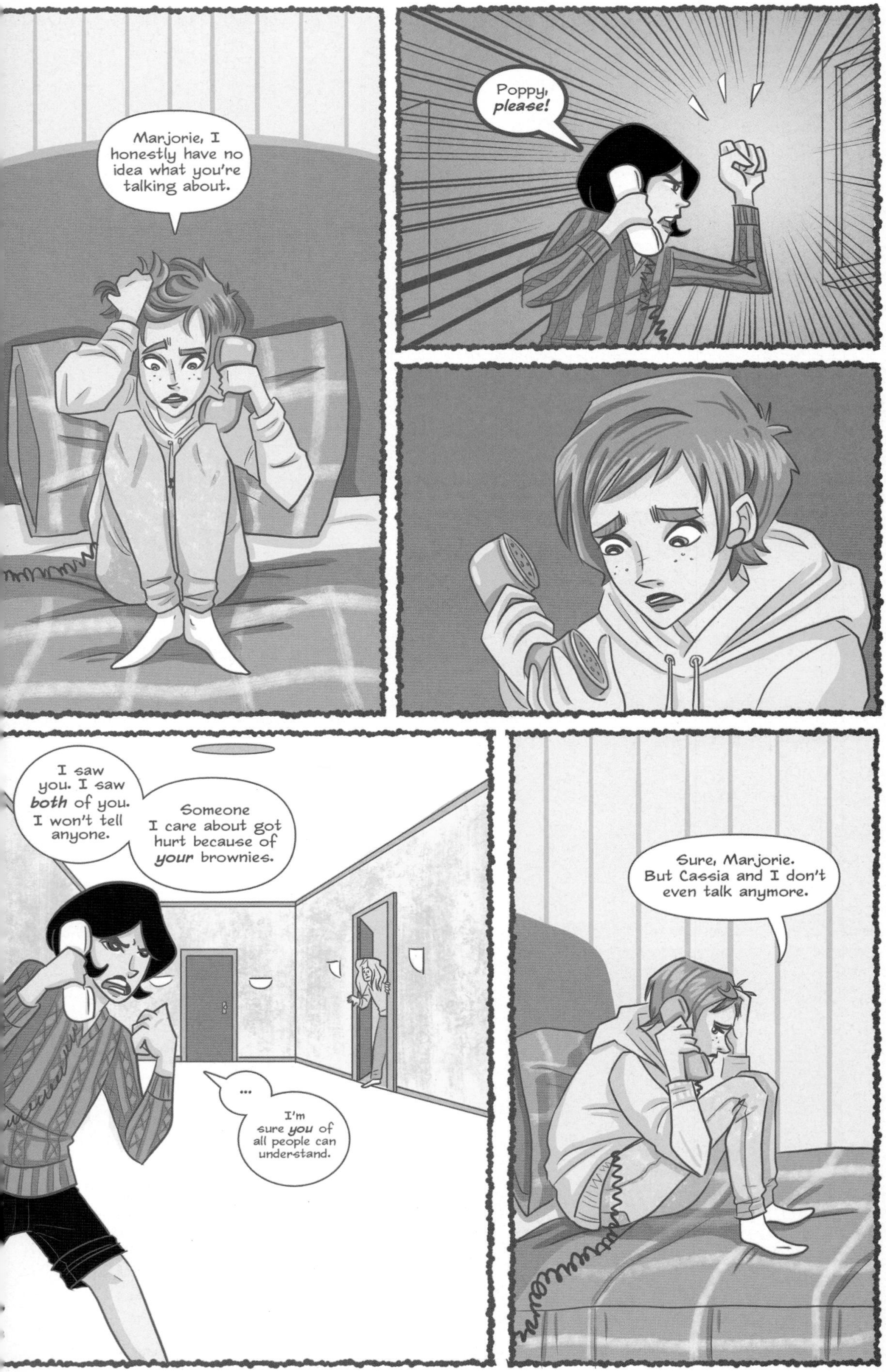
Marjorie, I honestly have no idea what you're talking about.
Poppy, *please!*
I saw you. I saw *both* of you. I won't tell anyone.
Someone I care about got hurt because of *your* brownies.
...
I'm sure *you* of all people can understand.
Sure, Marjorie. But Cassia and I don't even talk anymore.

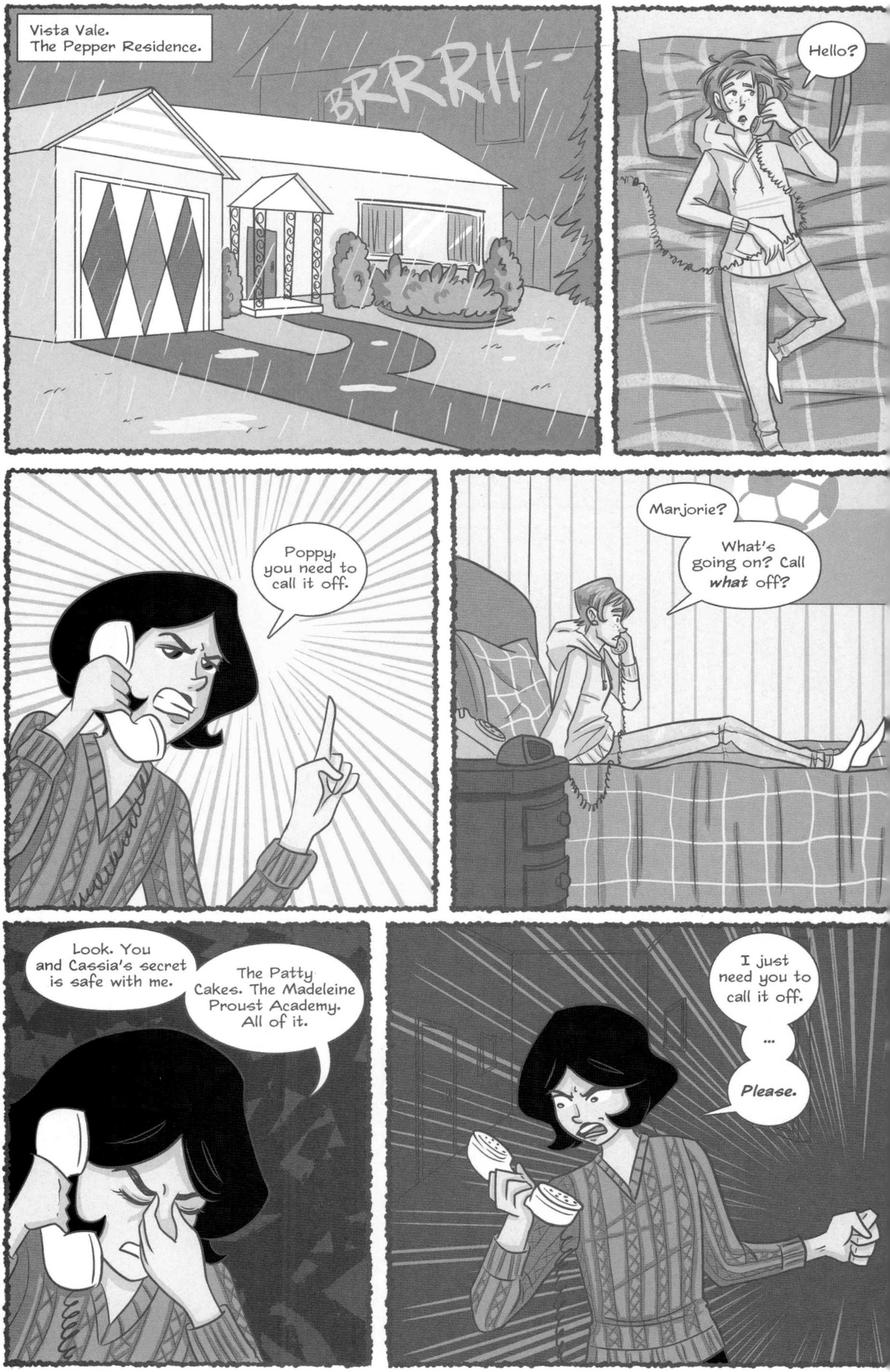
Vista Vale.
The Pepper Residence.
BRRRII--
Hello?
Poppy, you need to call it off.
Marjorie?
What's going on? Call *what* off?
Look. You and Cassia's secret is safe with me.
The Patty Cakes. The Madeleine Proust Academy. All of it.
I just need you to call it off.
...
Please.

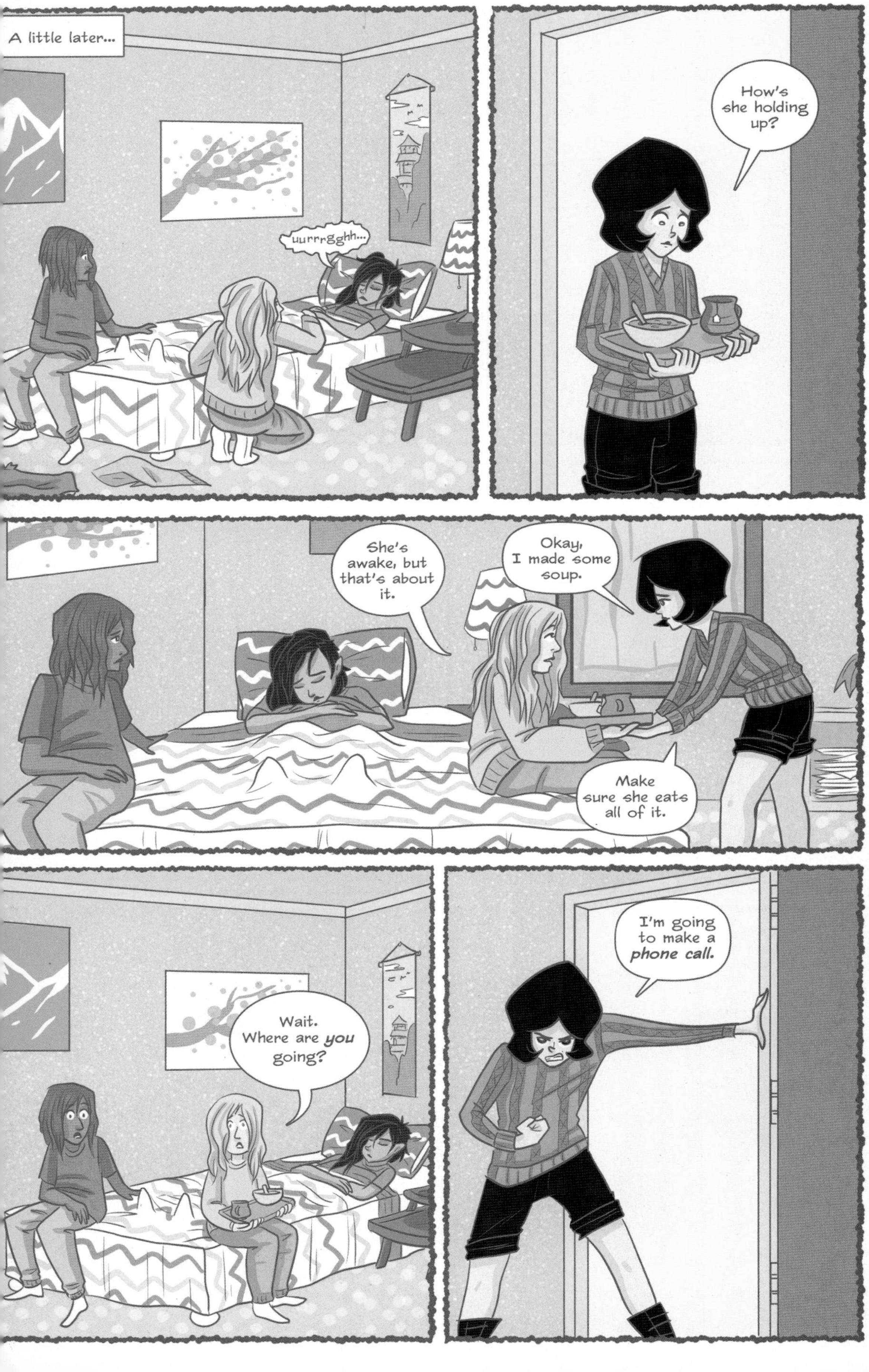
A little later...
uurrrgghh...
How's she holding up?
She's awake, but that's about it.
Okay, I made some soup.
Make sure she eats all of it.
Wait. Where are *you* going?
I'm going to make a ***phone call.***

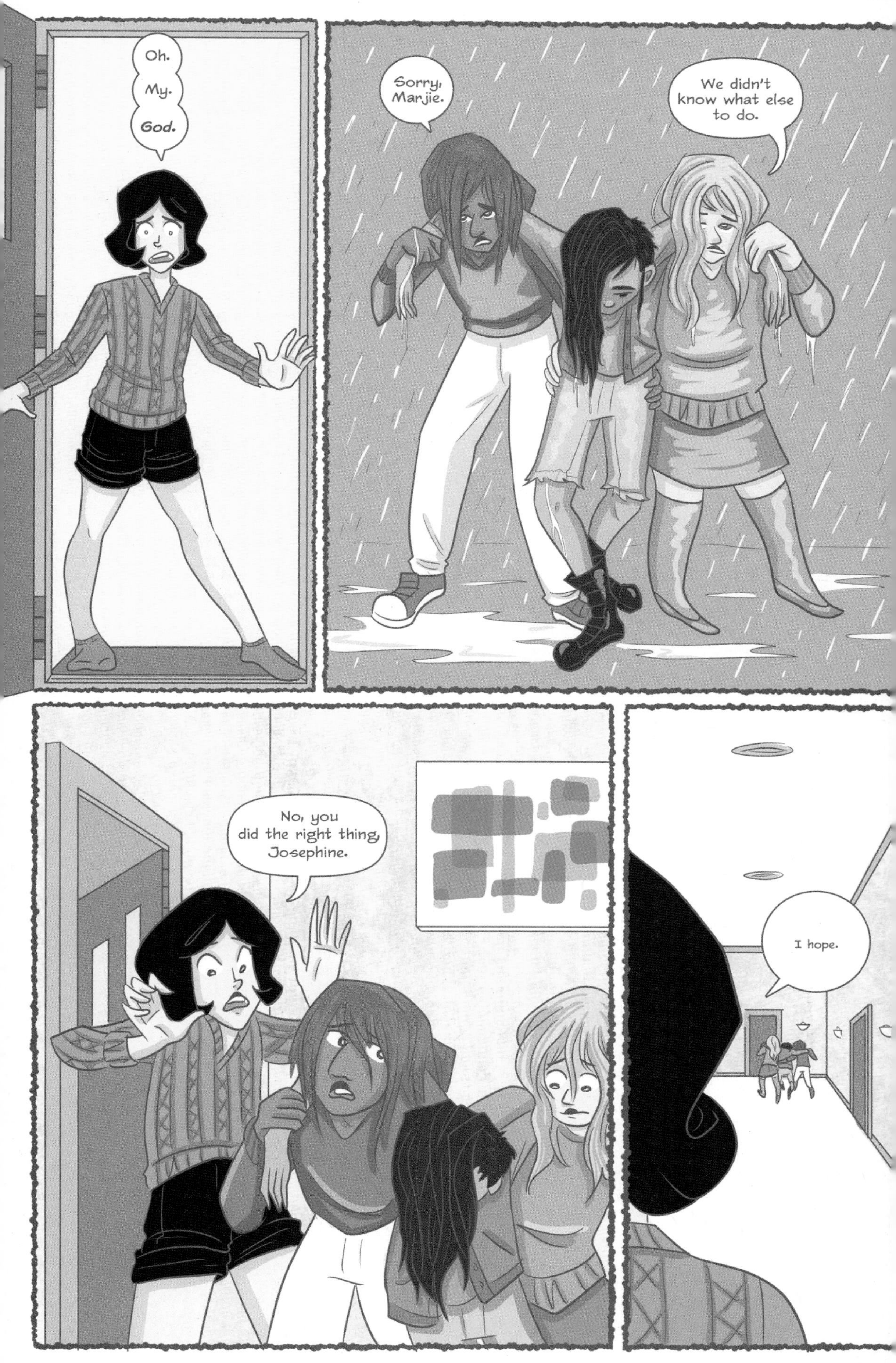
Oh.
My.
God.
Sorry, Marjie.
We didn't know what else to do.
No, you did the right thing, Josephine.
I hope.

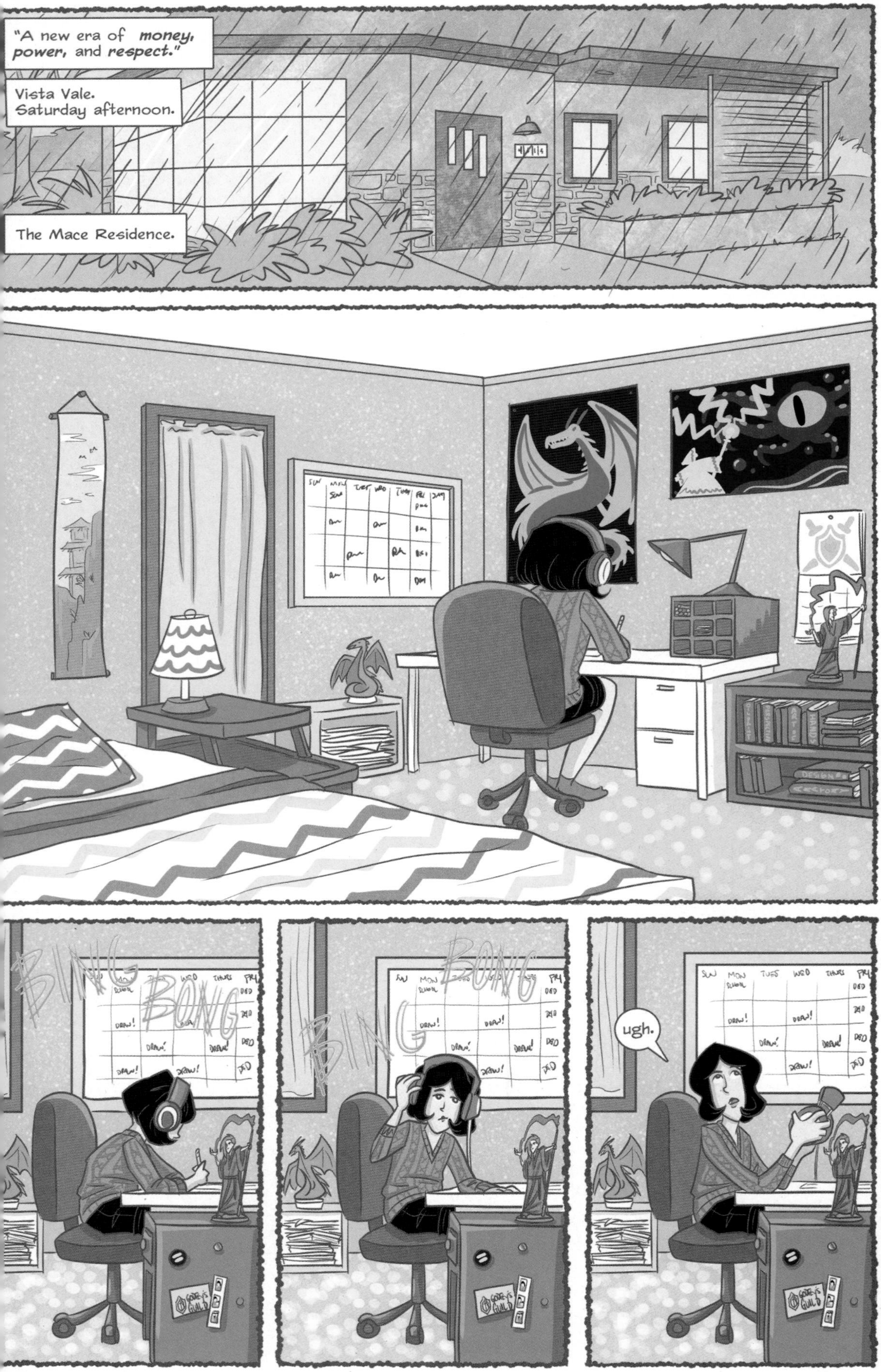
"A new era of *money, power,* and *respect.*"
Vista Vale.
Saturday afternoon.
The Mace Residence.
BING
BONG
BING
BONG
ugh.

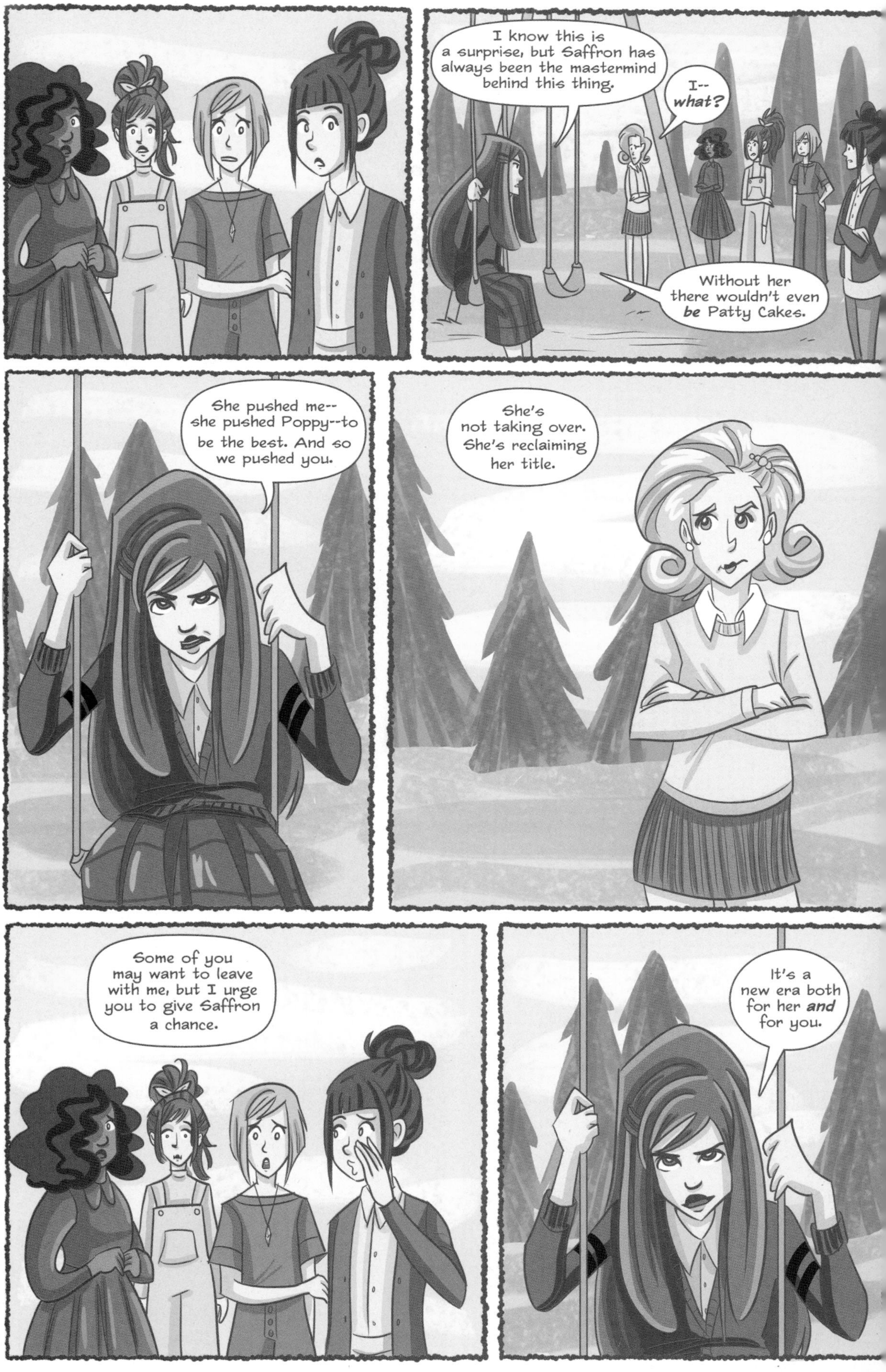
I know this is a surprise, but Saffron has always been the mastermind behind this thing.
I-- *what?*
Without her there wouldn't even *be* Patty Cakes.
She pushed me-- she pushed Poppy--to be the best. And so we pushed you.
She's not taking over. She's reclaiming her title.
Some of you may want to leave with me, but I urge you to give Saffron a chance.
It's a new era both for her *and* for you.

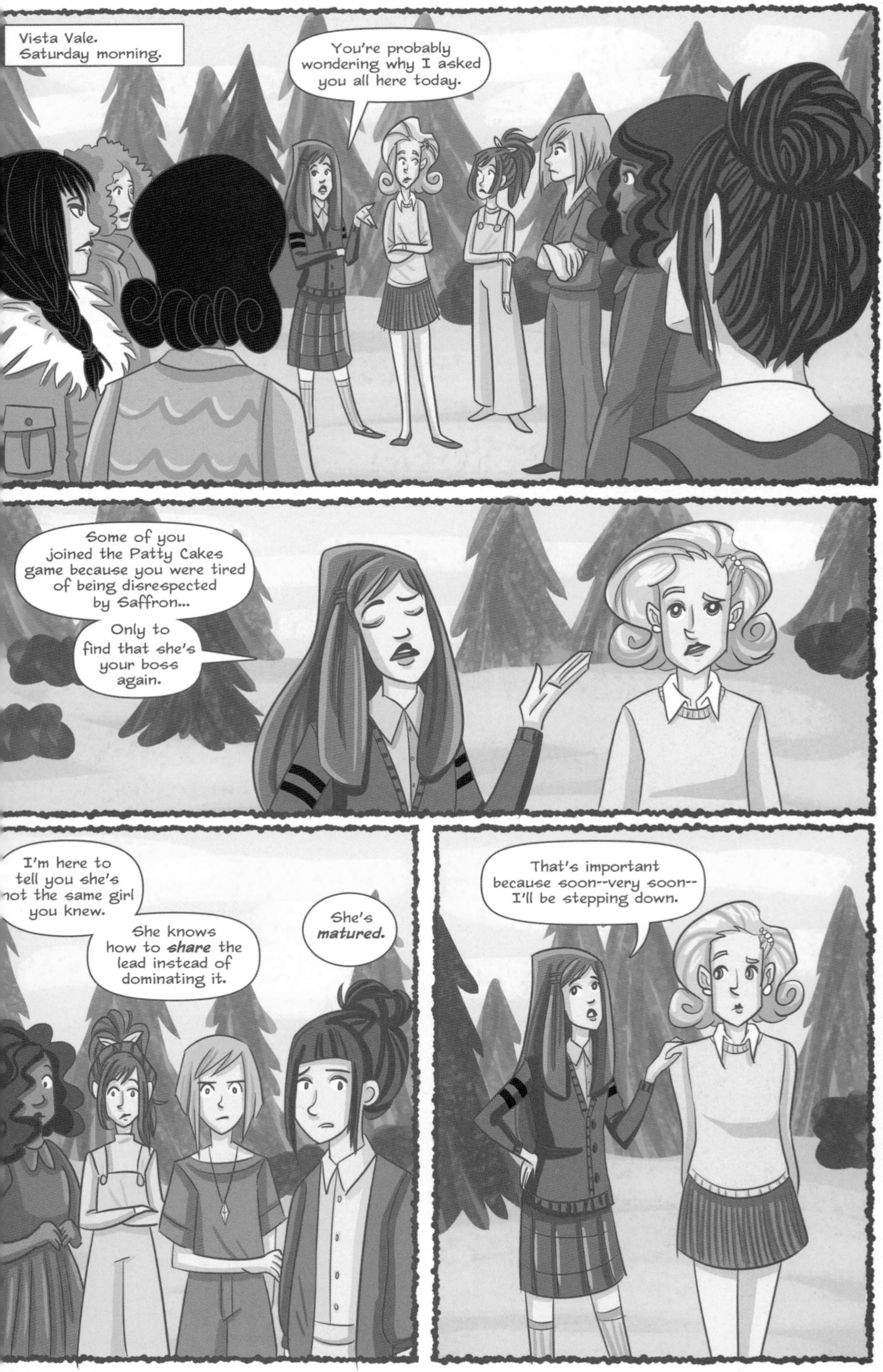
Vista Vale.
Saturday morning.
You're probably wondering why I asked you all here today.
Some of you joined the Patty Cakes game because you were tired of being disrespected by Saffron...
Only to find that she's your boss again.
I'm here to tell you she's not the same girl you knew.
She knows how to *share* the lead instead of dominating it.
She's ***matured.***
That's important because soon--very soon--I'll be stepping down.

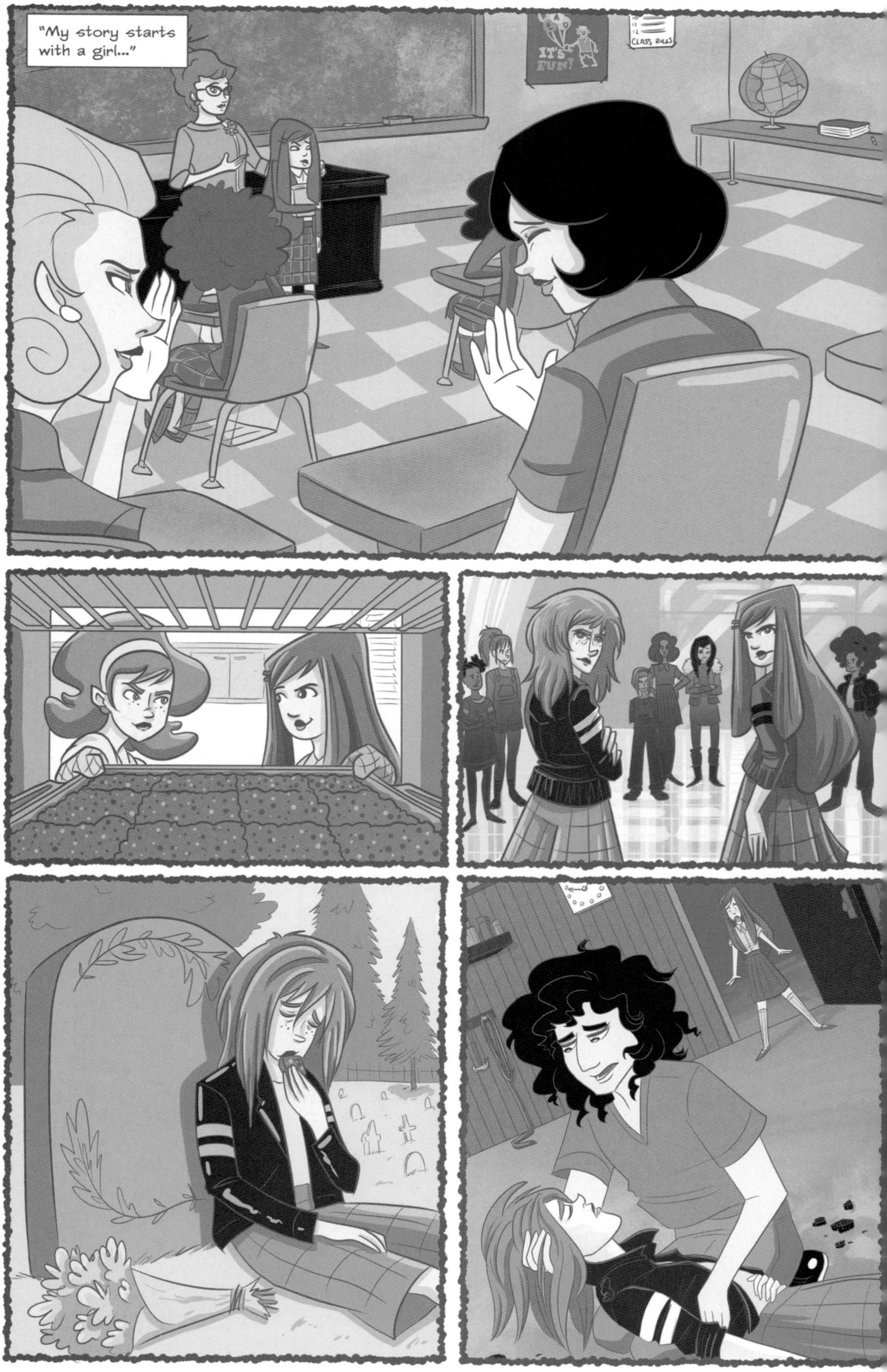
"My story starts with a girl..."
IT'S FUN!
CLASS RULES

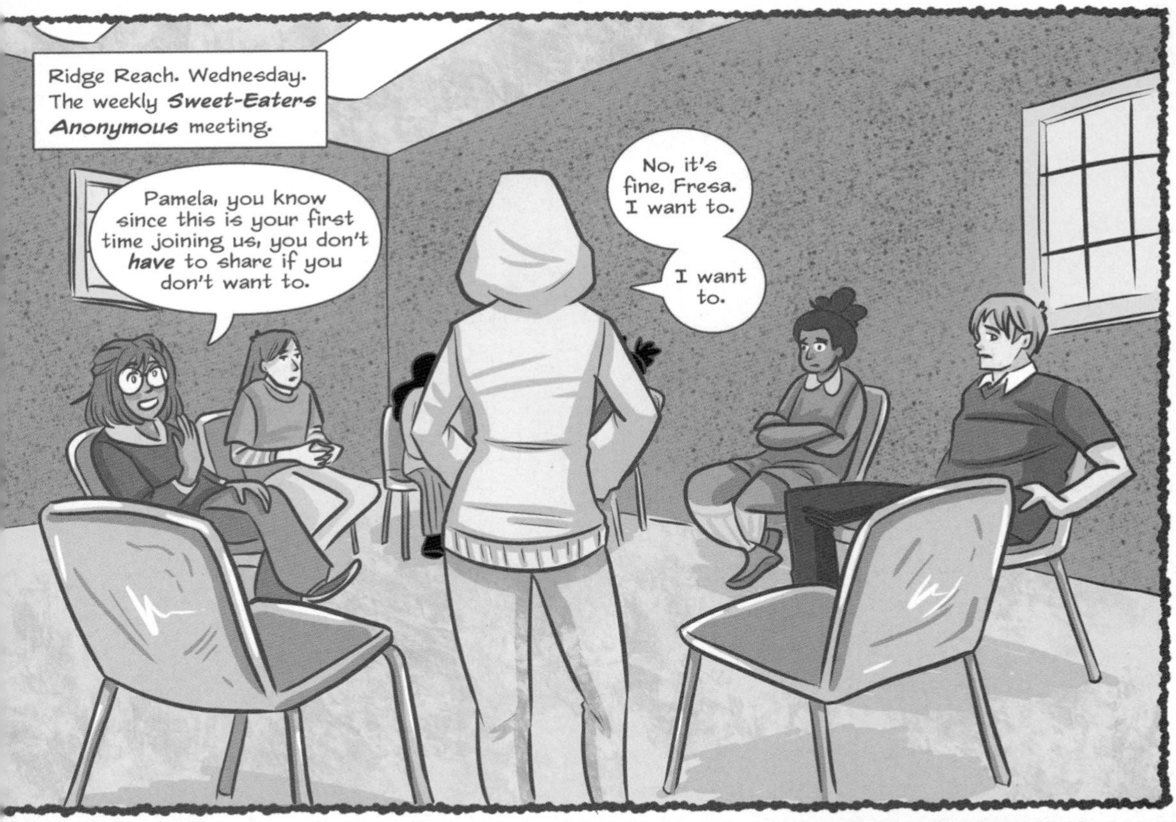
Ridge Reach. Wednesday. The weekly Sweet-Eaters Anonymous meeting.
Pamela, you know since this is your first time joining us, you don't have to share if you don't want to.
No, it's fine, Fresa. I want to.
I want to.

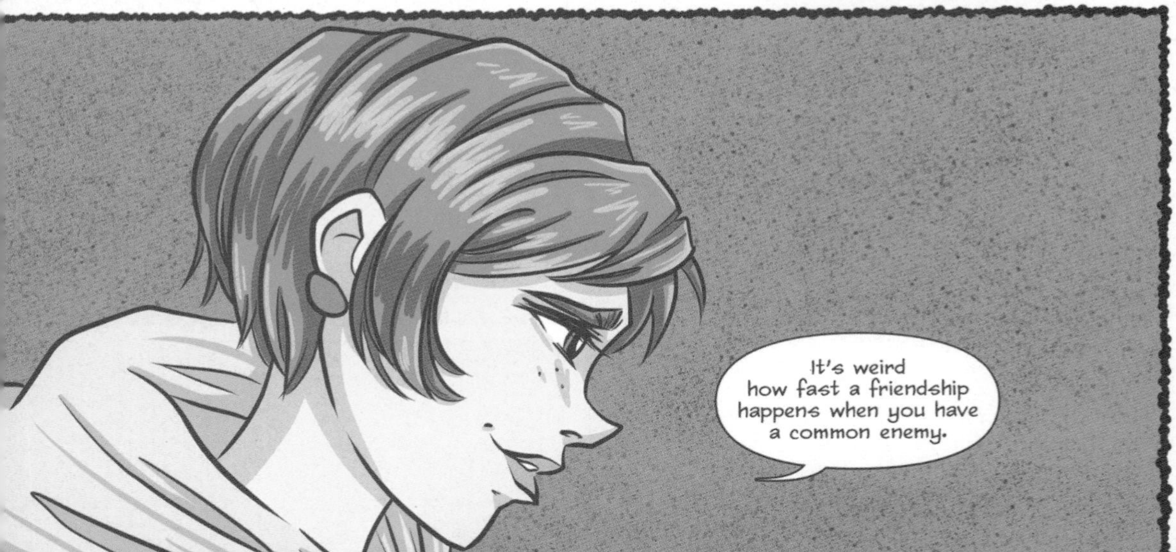
It's weird how fast a friendship happens when you have a common enemy.

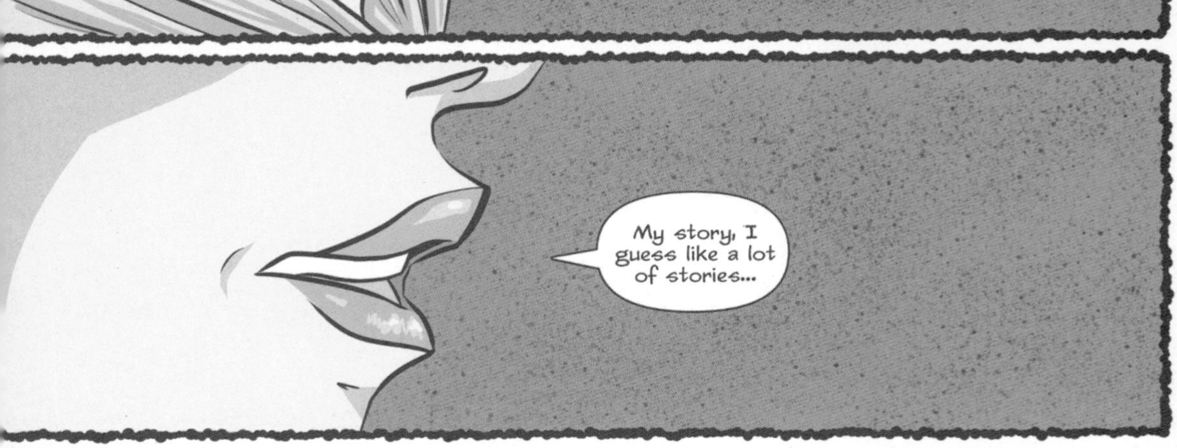
My story, I guess like a lot of stories...

Bryan Seaton - Publisher • Kevin Freeman - President • Dave Dwonch - Creative Director • Shawn Gabborin - Editor In Chief
Jamal Igle - Co-Directors of Marketing • Chad Cicconi - ate all the brownies • Colleen Boyd - Associate Editor

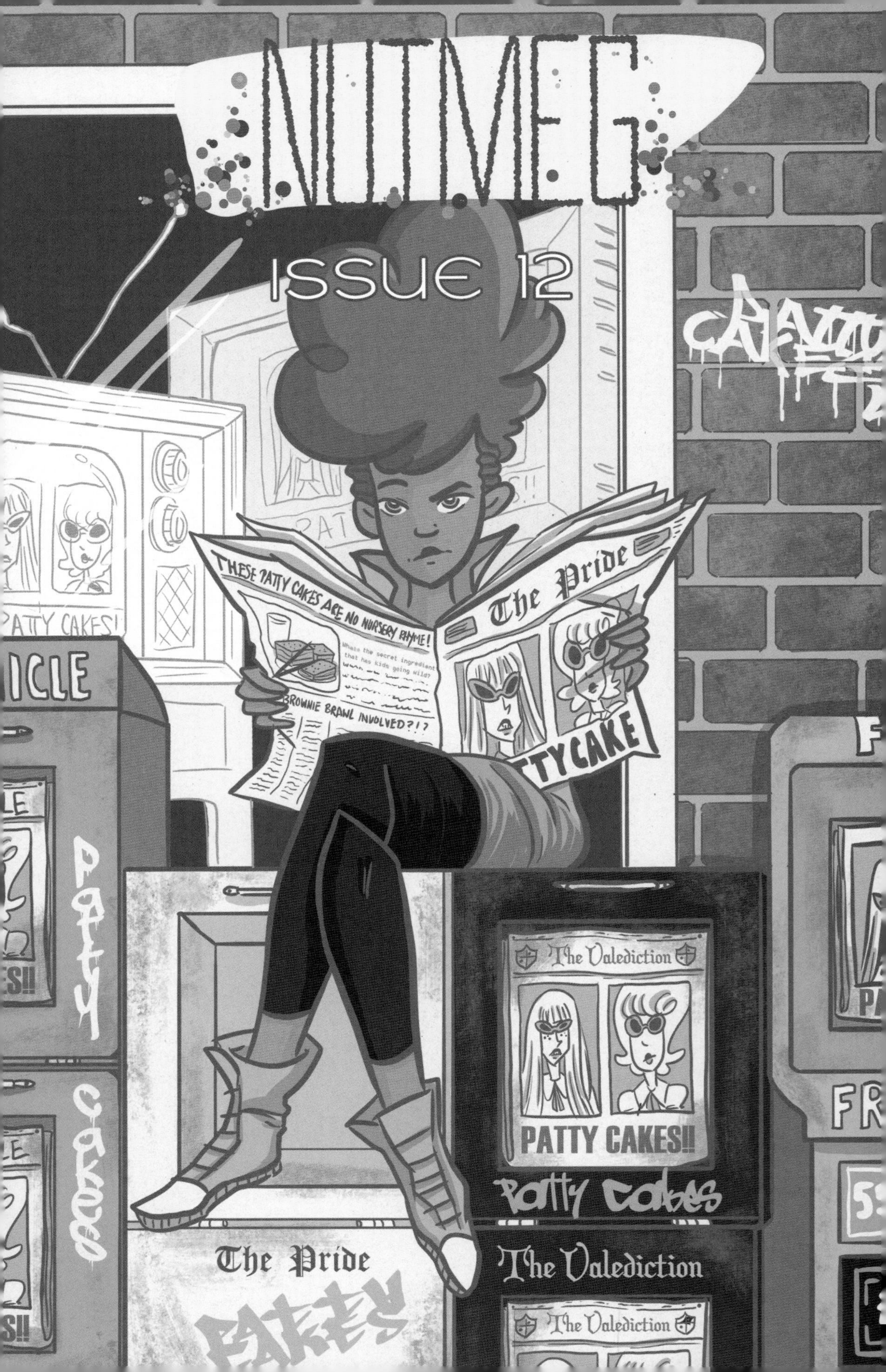
NUTMEG
ISSUE 12
THESE PATTY CAKES ARE NO NURSERY RHYME!
The Pride
BROWNIE BRAWL INVOLVED?!?
TTYCAKE
PATTY CAKES!
The Valediction
PATTY CAKES!!
Patty Cakes
The Pride
The Valediction

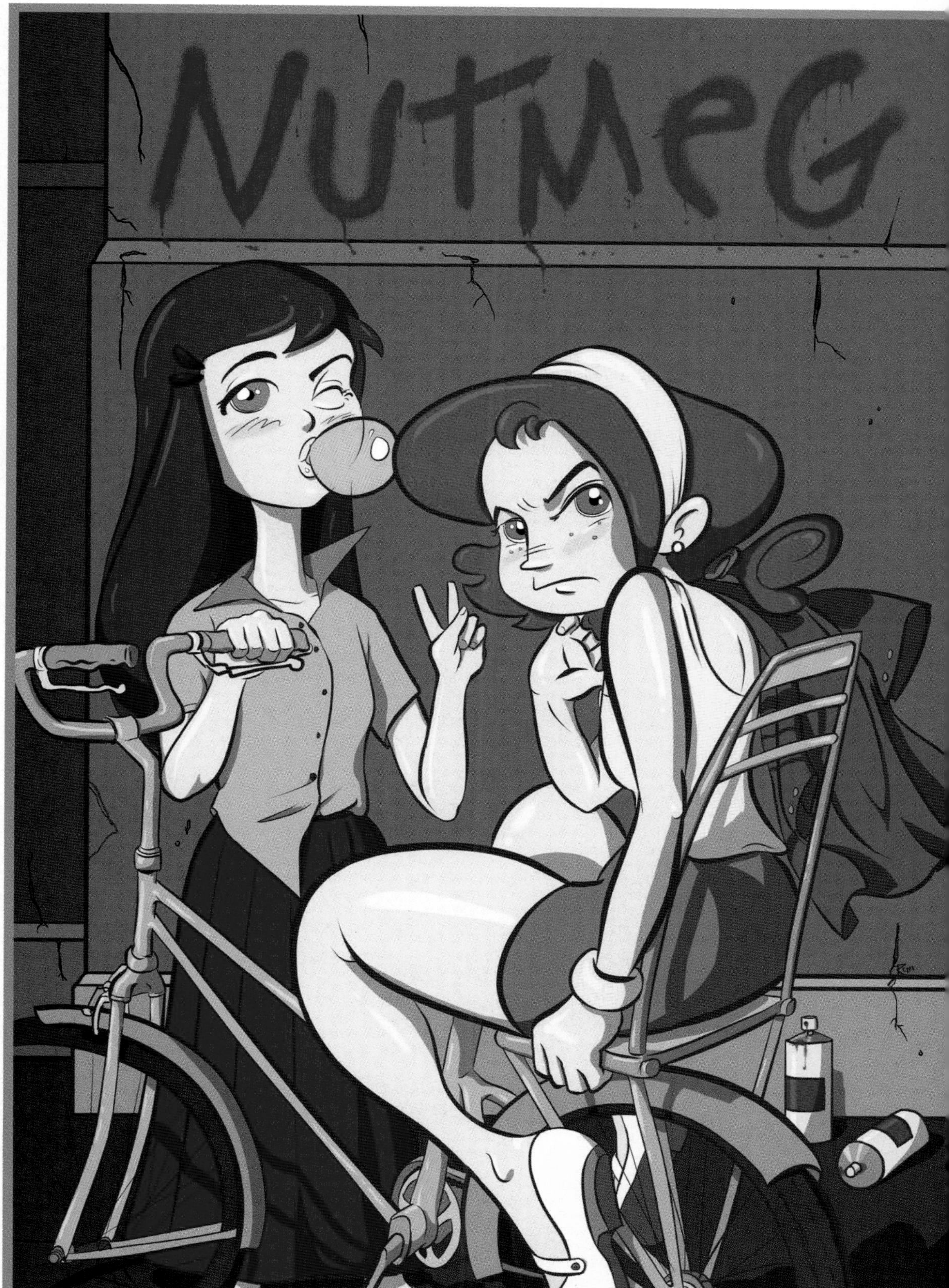
NUTMEG

ART BY BRIAN REYES

THE COOLING RACK

CONTACT: @NutmegComic   NutmegComics@gmail.com

Avatars by Genue Revuelta

Thank goodness for Anise and Sweet-Eaters Anonymous, because Poppy can get the help she needs. Hopefully it will be enough. In the meantime, we've got some sweet sweets for you this go-round. Our buddy Kei Taniguchi has shared with us his Mug Cake recipes. And our friend Brian Reyes did a really cool pinup of Poppy and Cassia.

KEI TANIGUCHI'S MUG CAKES

1. BLUEBERRY MUFFIN MUG CAKES

INGREDIENTS

2 Tbsp butter
1 medium egg
1 Tbsp milk
1 tsp vanilla extract
4 Tbsp self-raising flour
1/4 tsp ground cinnamon
pinch of salt
3 Tbsp fresh blueberries
1/2 tsp brown sugar.

INSTRUCTIONS

* Pop the butter in a large mug and microwave until melted

* Add the egg, milk and vanilla, then whisk with a fork until combined.

* Mix in the sugar, flour, cinnamon and beat until smooth.

* Mix in 2 tbsp of the blueberries, top with the other 1 tbsp.

* Sprinkle over the brown sugar, then microwave for 2 minutes at 800W.

2. CHOCOLATE PEAR GINGER MUG CAKES

INGREDIENTS

1 Tbsp butter
1 oz dark chocolate, finely chopped*
1/2 medium egg, beaten
1 Tbsp milk
2 Tbsp caster sugar
2 Tbsp self raising flour.
1/4 tsp ground ginger
pinch of salt
1 Tbsp preserved stem ginger, finely chopped
1 ripe pear, peeled

*If you like, you can substitute white chocolate for dark, and add a dash of vanilla.

INSTRUCTIONS

* Melt the butter and chocolate together in a large mug (10-20 sec in microwave)

* Add milk and egg, beat until smooth.

* Add the sugar, flour, ground ginger and salt and beat to a smooth batter.

* Fold through the chopped ginger

* Slice the base off the pear so it will stand upright and gently press into the mixture.

* Microwave for 1:50 at 800W

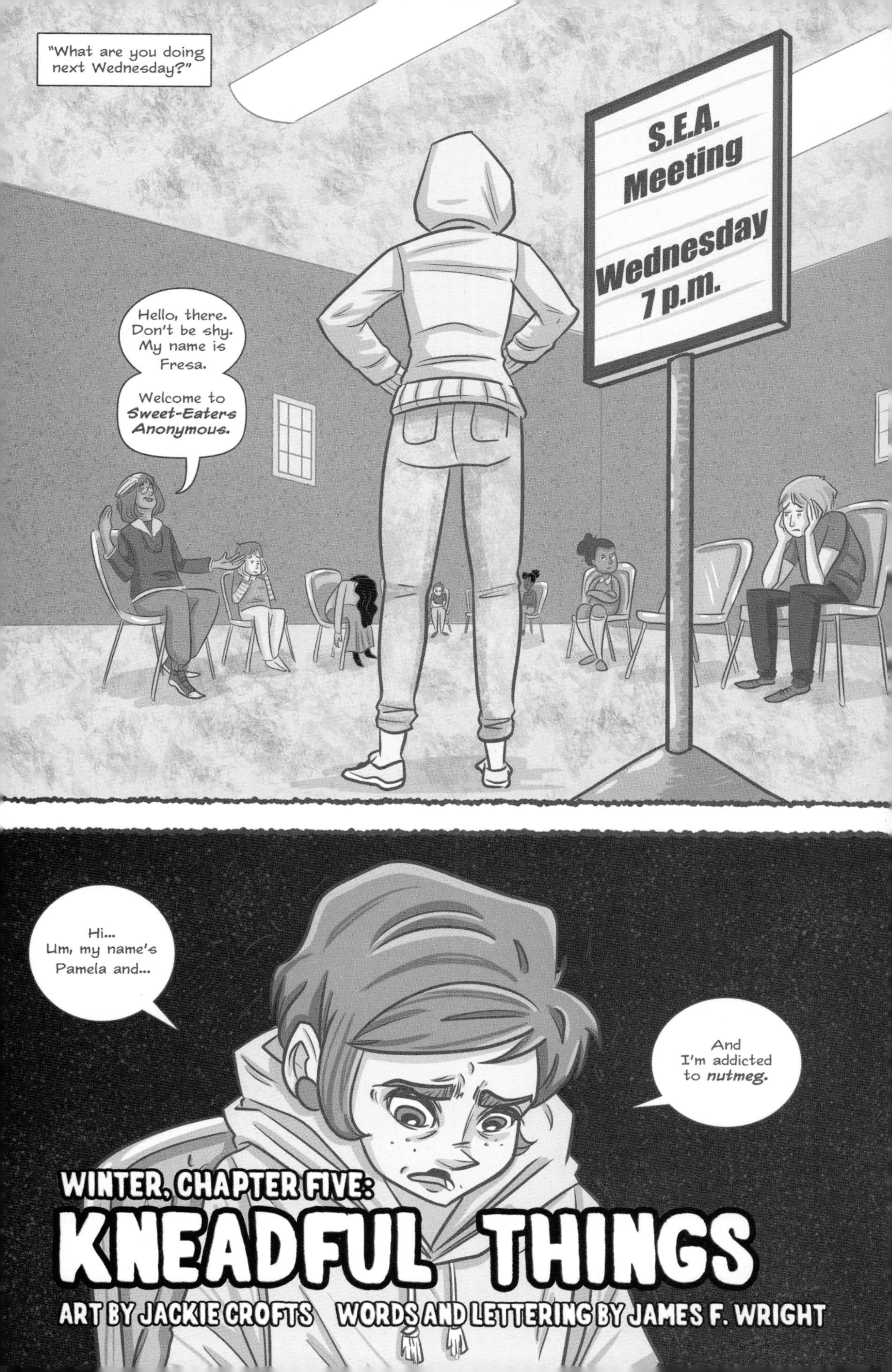
"What are you doing next Wednesday?"
S.E.A. Meeting Wednesday 7 p.m.
Hello, there. Don't be shy. My name is Fresa.
Welcome to Sweet-Eaters Anonymous.
Hi... Um, my name's Pamela and...
And I'm addicted to nutmeg.
WINTER, CHAPTER FIVE:
KNEADFUL THINGS
ART BY JACKIE CROFTS WORDS AND LETTERING BY JAMES F. WRIGHT

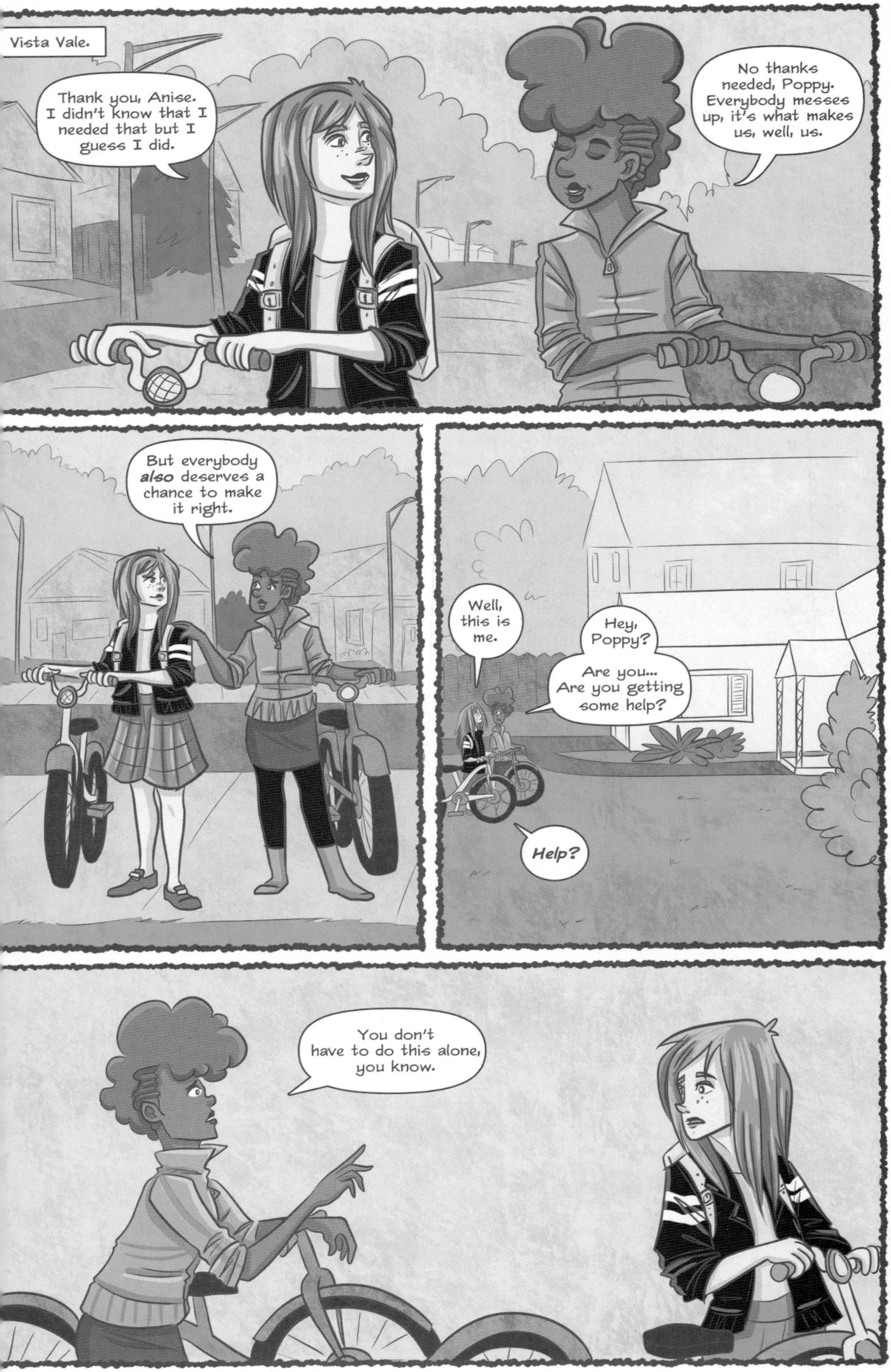
Vista Vale.
Thank you, Anise. I didn't know that I needed that but I guess I did.
No thanks needed, Poppy. Everybody messes up, it's what makes us, well, us.
But everybody *also* deserves a chance to make it right.
Well, this is me.
Hey, Poppy?
Are you... Are you getting some help?
Help?
You don't have to do this alone, you know.

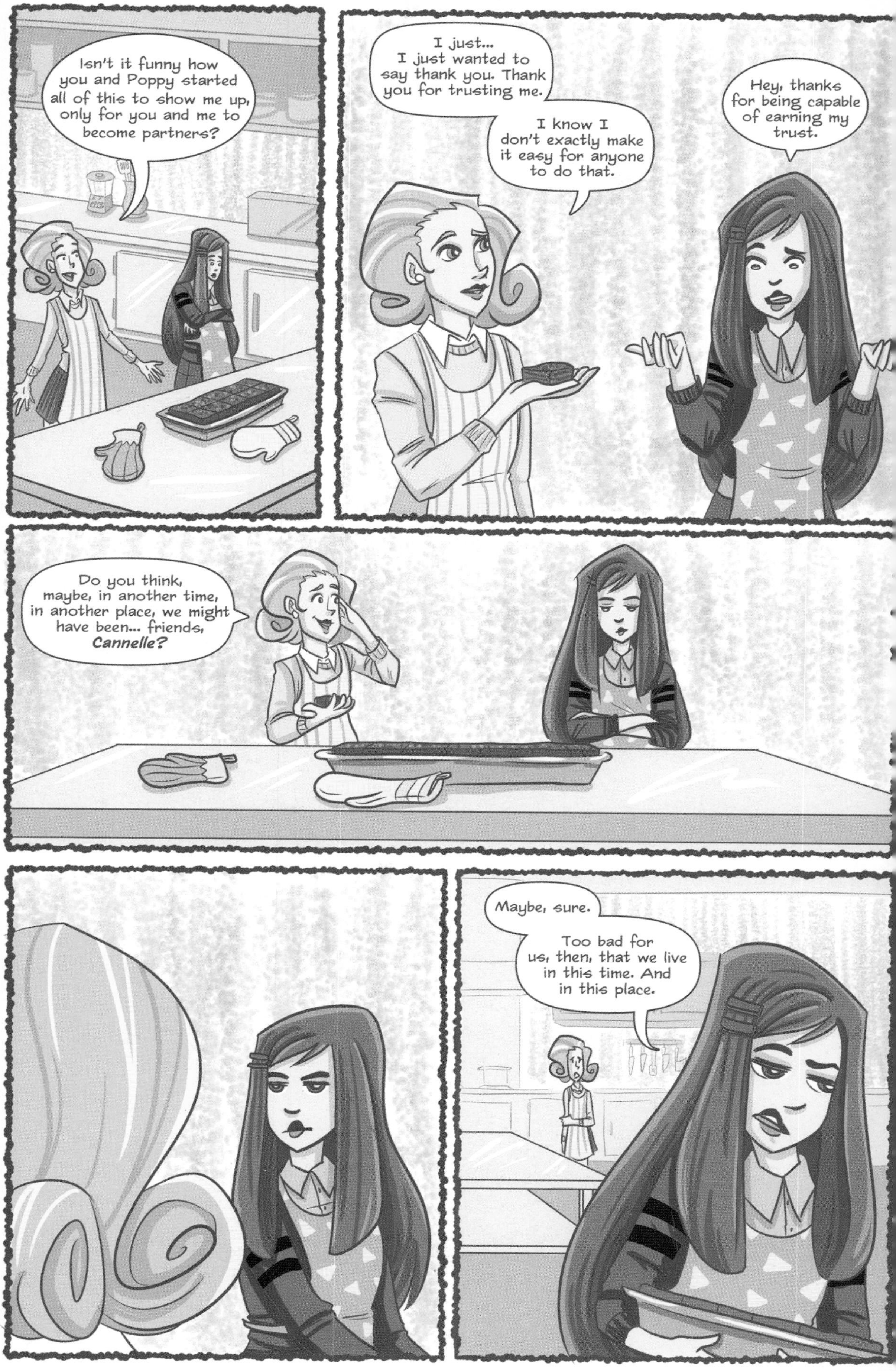
Isn't it funny how you and Poppy started all of this to show me up, only for you and me to become partners?
I just... I just wanted to say thank you. Thank you for trusting me.
I know I don't exactly make it easy for anyone to do that.
Hey, thanks for being capable of earning my trust.
Do you think, maybe, in another time, in another place, we might have been... friends, *Cannelle?*
Maybe, sure.
Too bad for us, then, that we live in this time. And in this place.

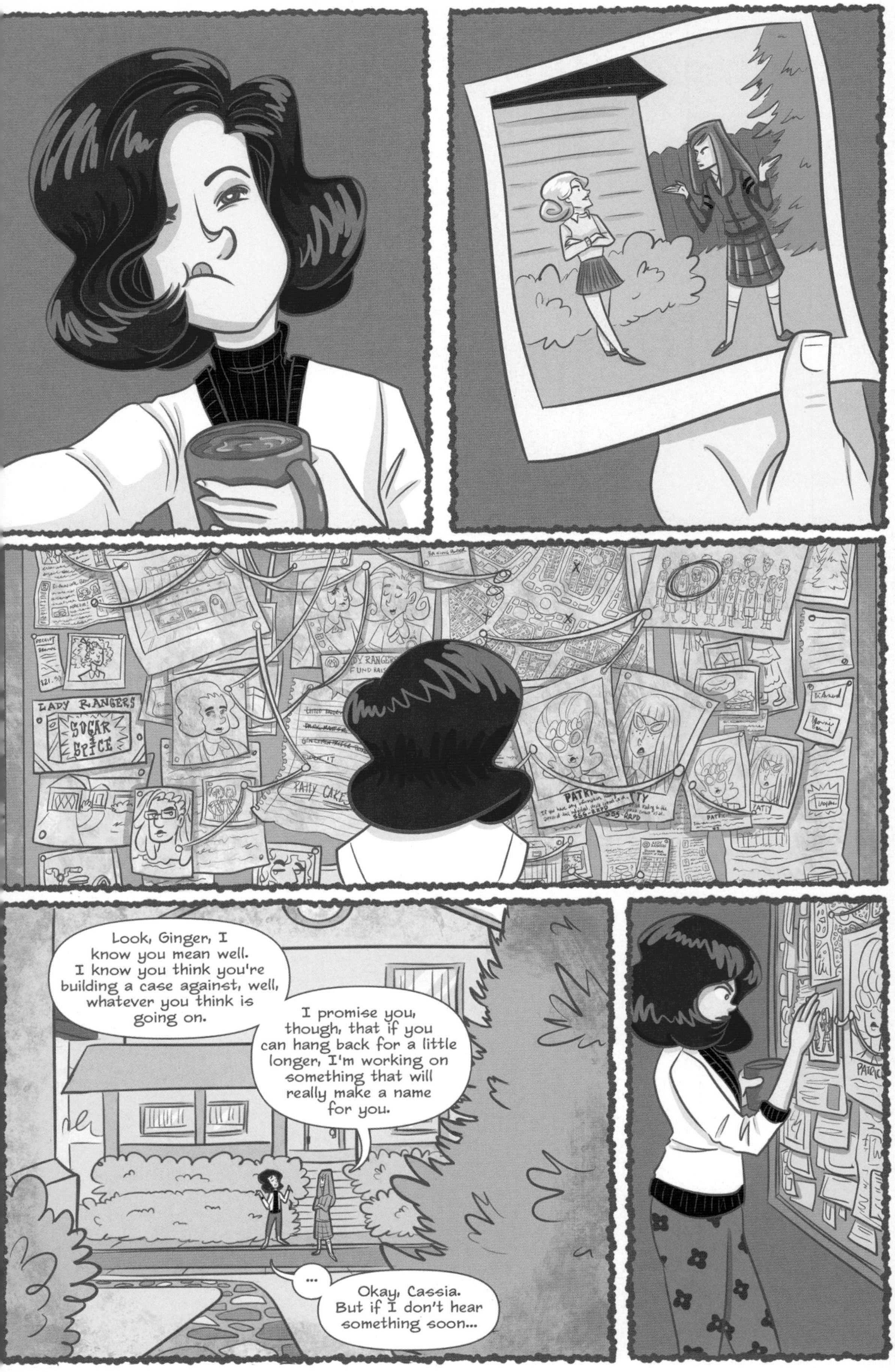
LADY RANGERS
Look, Ginger, I know you mean well. I know you think you're building a case against, well, whatever you think is going on.
I promise you, though, that if you can hang back for a little longer, I'm working on something that will really make a name for you.
...
Okay, Cassia. But if I don't hear something soon...

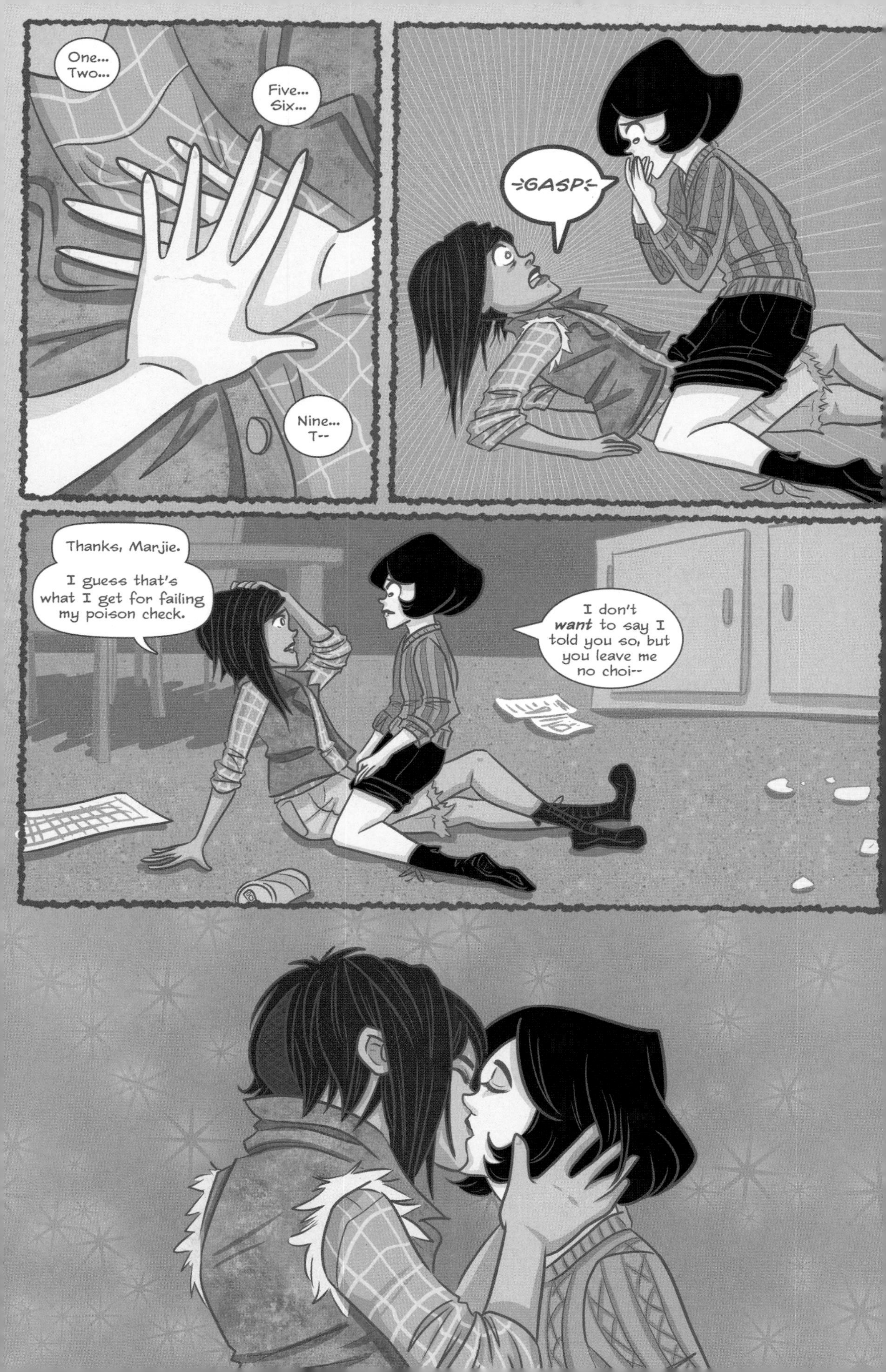

One... Two...
Five... Six...
Nine... T--
-=GASP=-
Thanks, Marjie.
I guess that's what I get for failing my poison check.
I don't *want* to say I told you so, but you leave me no choi--

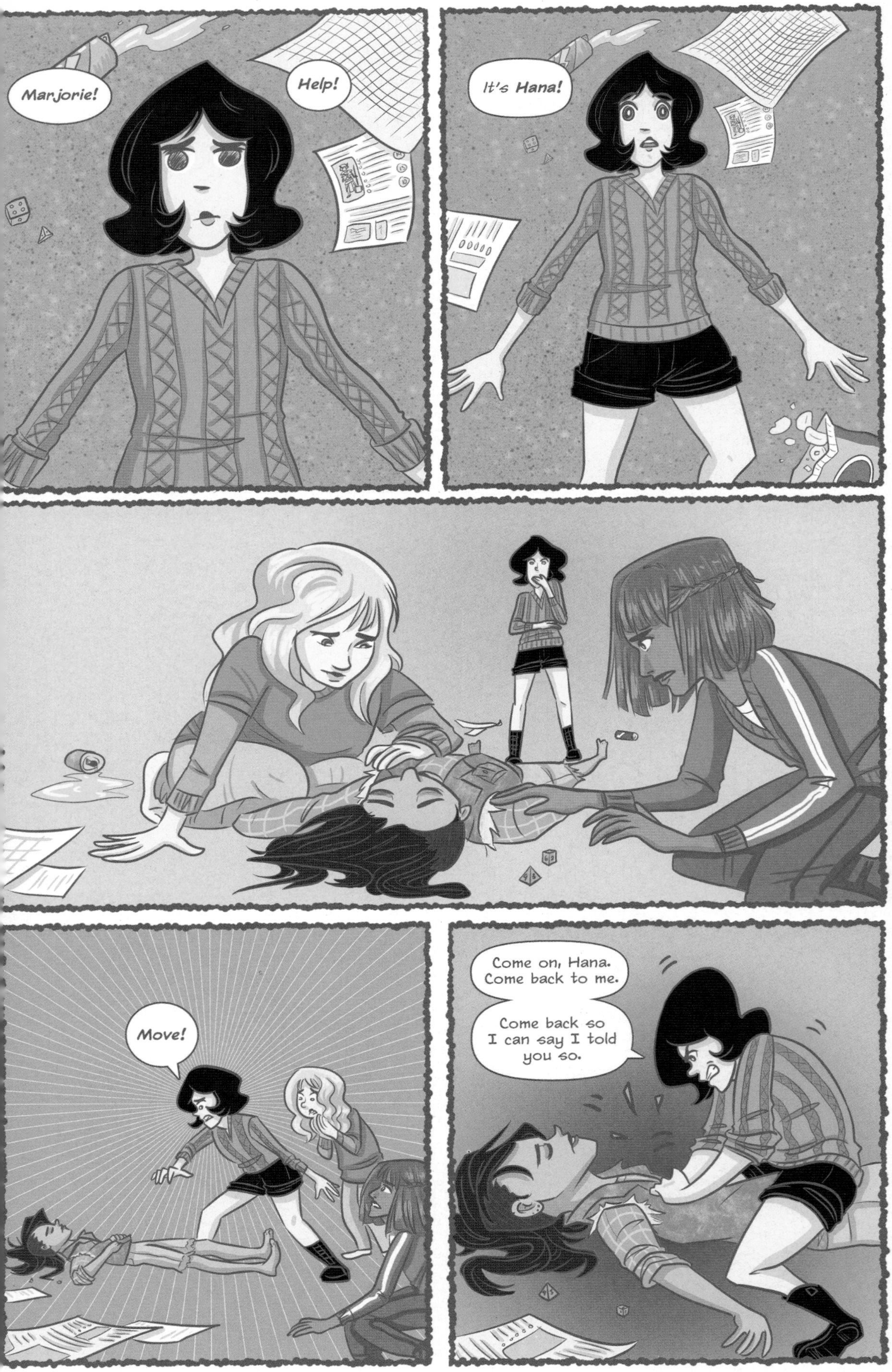
Marjorie!
Help!
It's Hana!
Move!
Come on, Hana. Come back to me.
Come back so I can say I told you so.

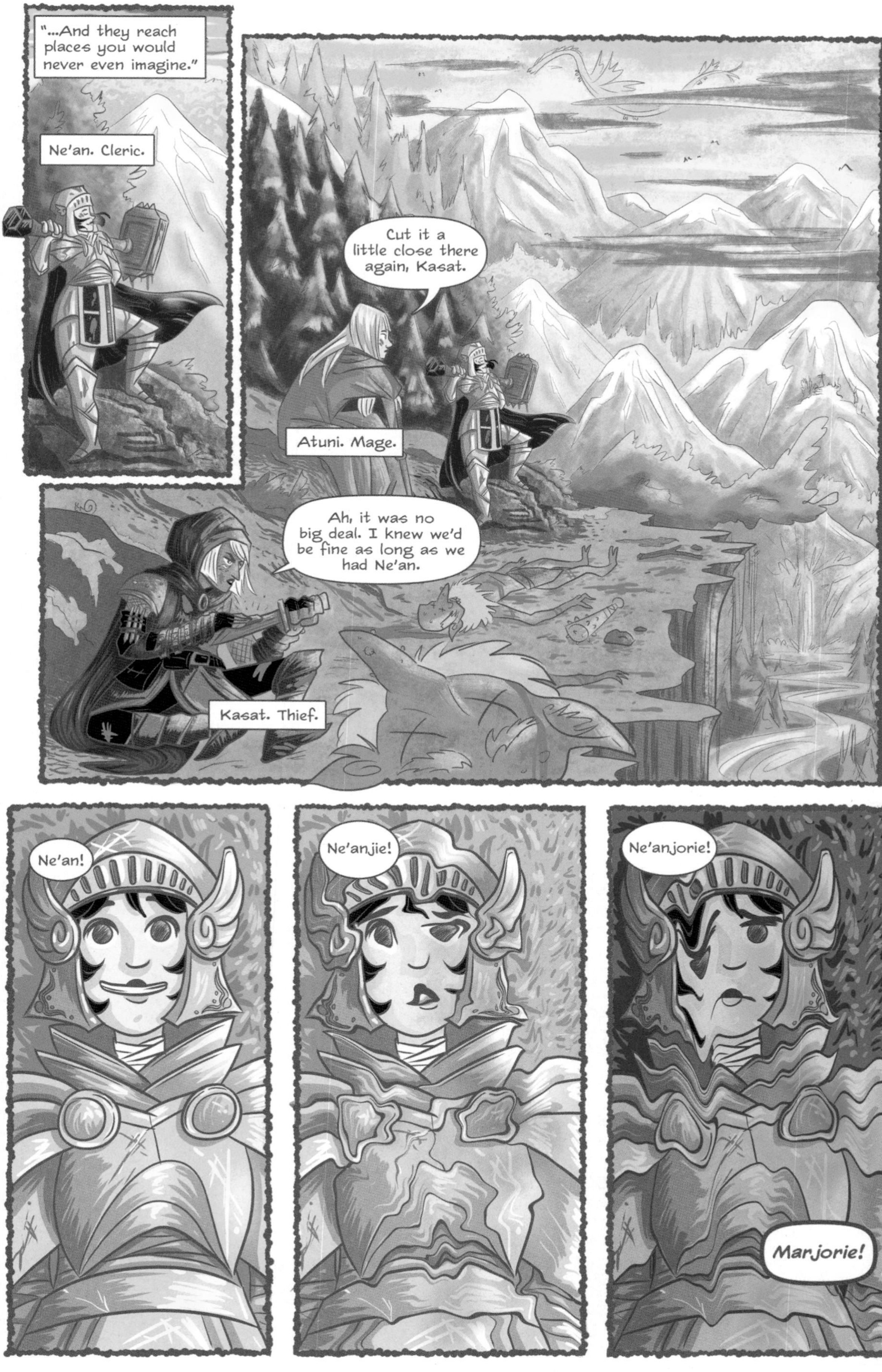
"...And they reach places you would never even imagine."
Ne'an. Cleric.
Cut it a little close there again, Kasat.
Atuni. Mage.
Ah, it was no big deal. I knew we'd be fine as long as we had Ne'an.
Kasat. Thief.
Ne'an!
Ne'anjie!
Ne'anjorie!
Marjorie!

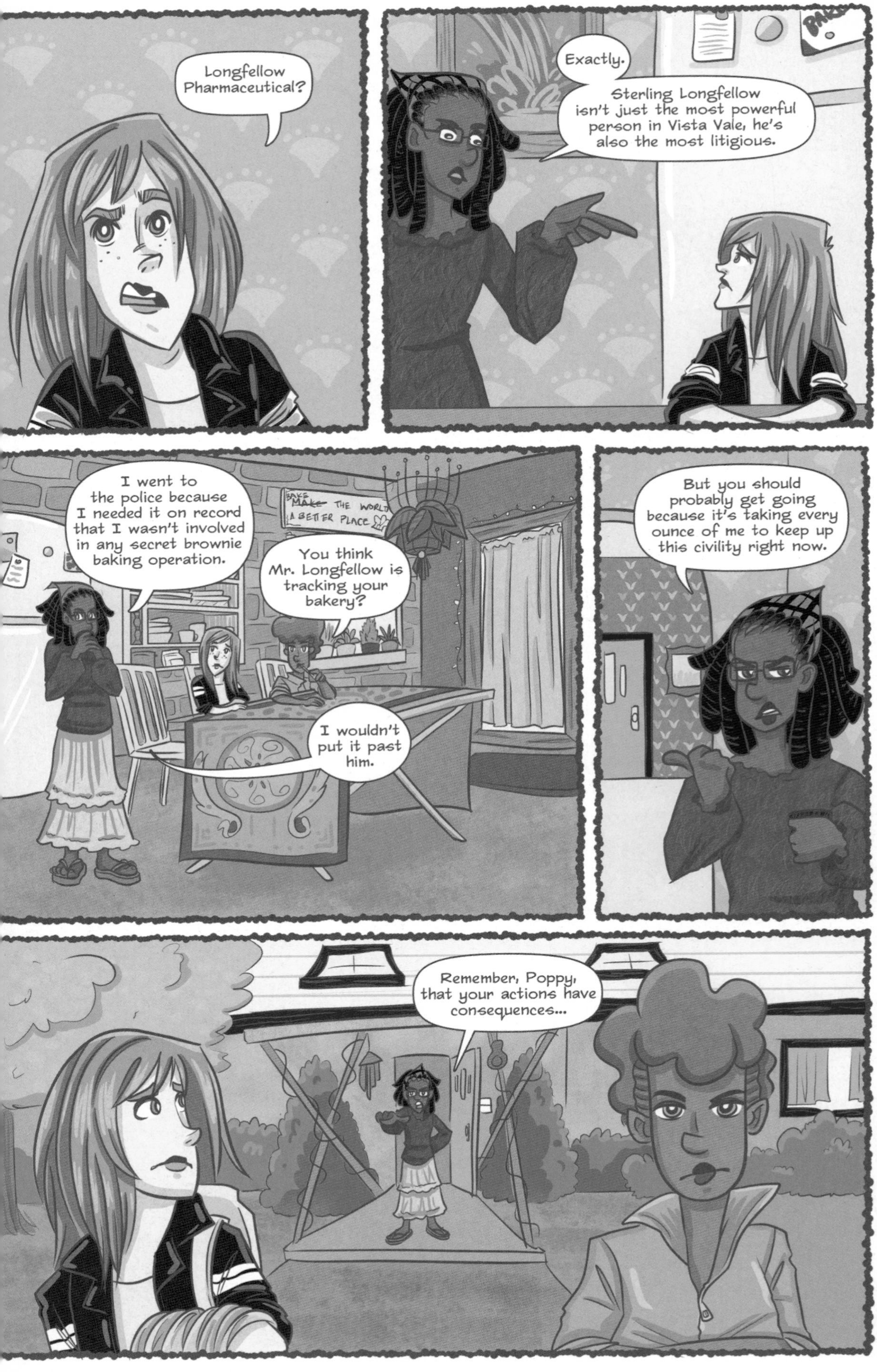

Longfellow Pharmaceutical?
Exactly.
Sterling Longfellow isn't just the most powerful person in Vista Vale, he's also the most litigious.
I went to the police because I needed it on record that I wasn't involved in any secret brownie baking operation.
BAKE MAKE THE WORLD A BETTER PLACE
You think Mr. Longfellow is tracking your bakery?
I wouldn't put it past him.
But you should probably get going because it's taking every ounce of me to keep up this civility right now.
Remember, Poppy, that your actions have consequences...

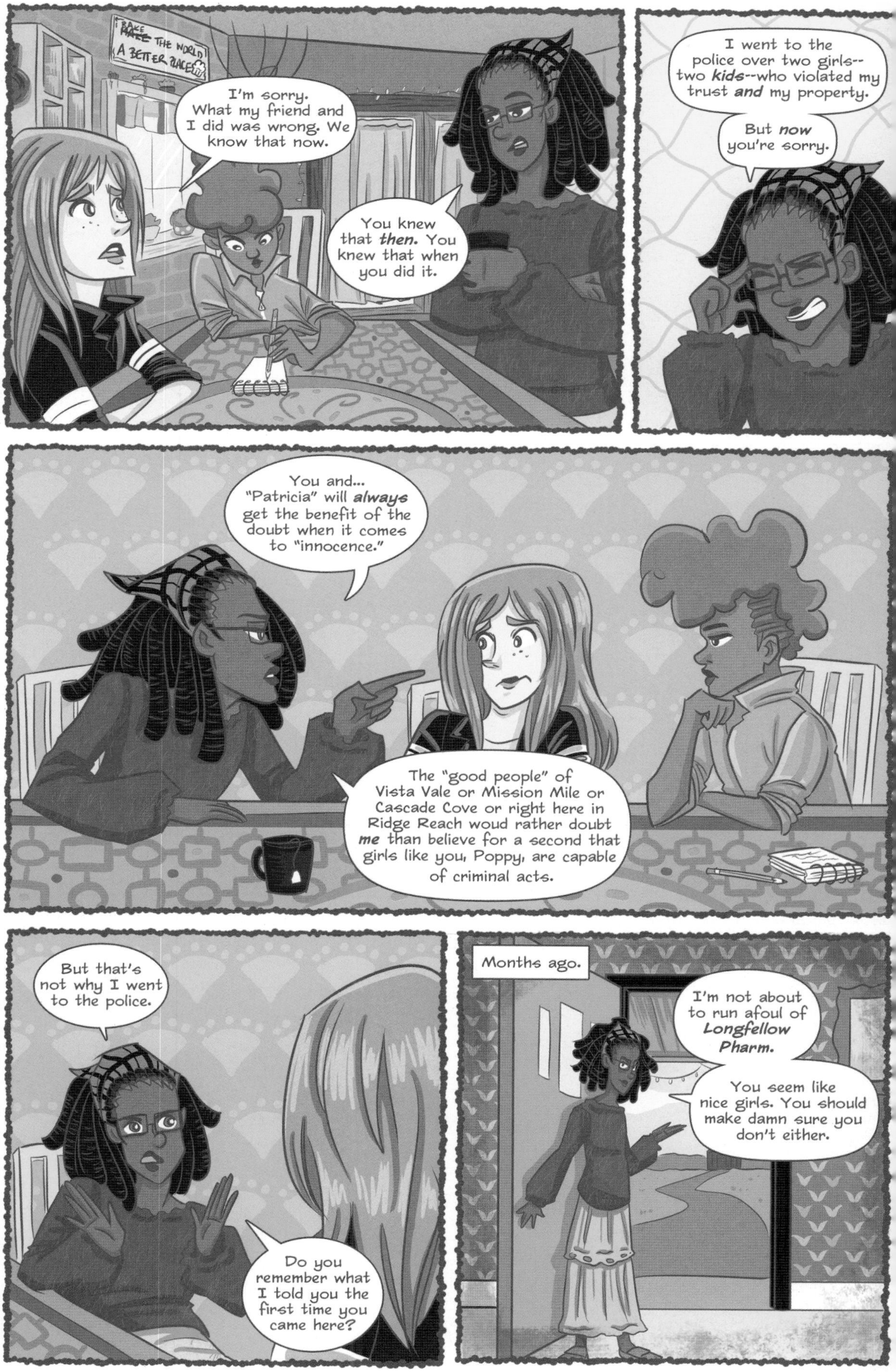

BAKE MAKE THE WORLD A BETTER PLACE
I'm sorry. What my friend and I did was wrong. We know that now.
You knew that *then.* You knew that when you did it.
I went to the police over two girls--two *kids*--who violated my trust *and* my property.
But *now* you're sorry.
You and... "Patricia" will *always* get the benefit of the doubt when it comes to "innocence."
The "good people" of Vista Vale or Mission Mile or Cascade Cove or right here in Ridge Reach woud rather doubt *me* than believe for a second that girls like you, Poppy, are capable of criminal acts.
But that's not why I went to the police.
Do you remember what I told you the first time you came here?
Months ago.
I'm not about to run afoul of *Longfellow Pharm.*
You seem like nice girls. You should make damn sure you don't either.

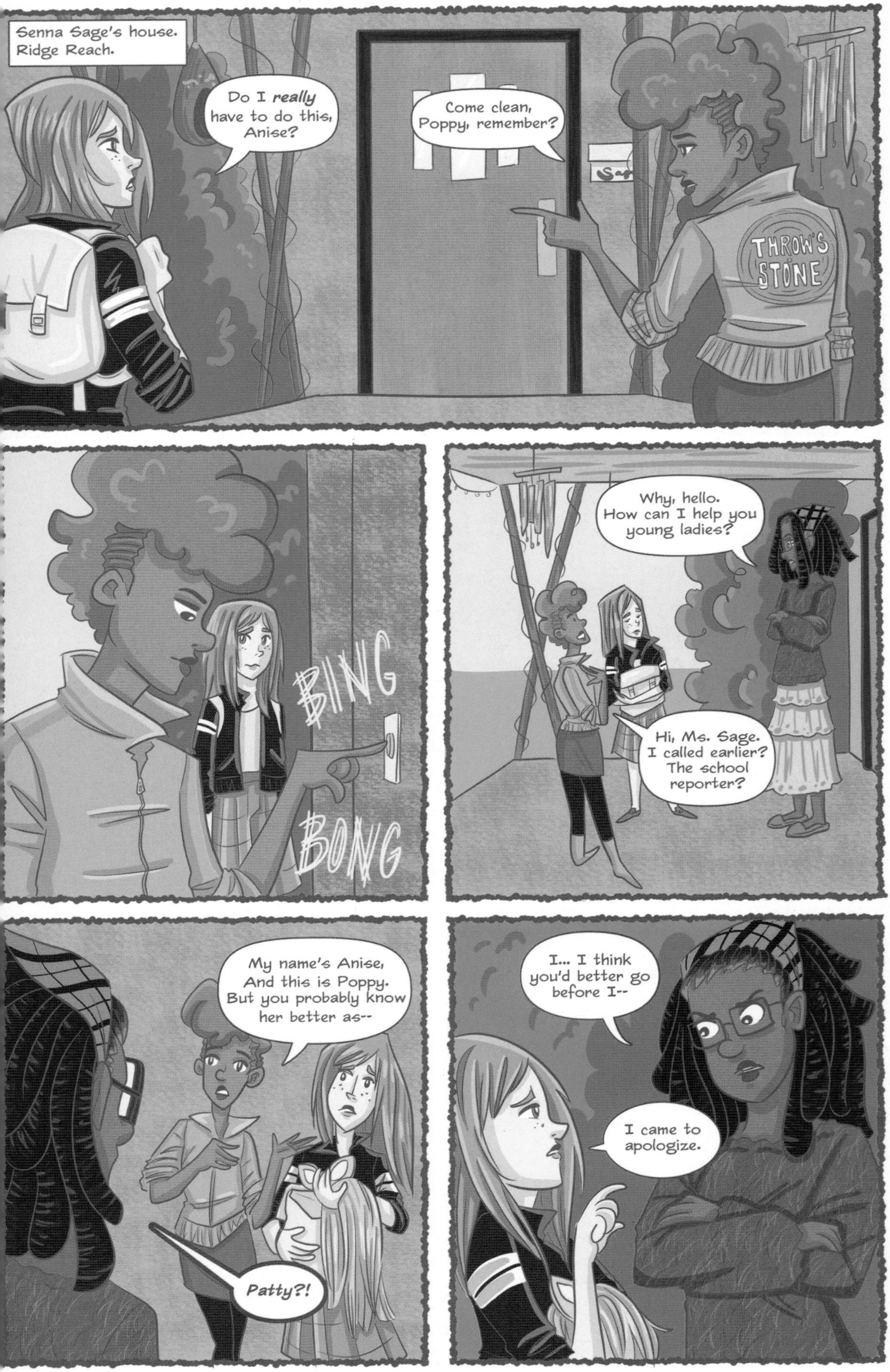

Senna Sage's house. Ridge Reach.
Do I *really* have to do this, Anise?
Come clean, Poppy, remember?
THROW'S STONE
BING
BONG
Why, hello. How can I help you young ladies?
Hi, Ms. Sage. I called earlier? The school reporter?
My name's Anise, And this is Poppy. But you probably know her better as--
Patty?!
I... I think you'd better go before I--
I came to apologize.

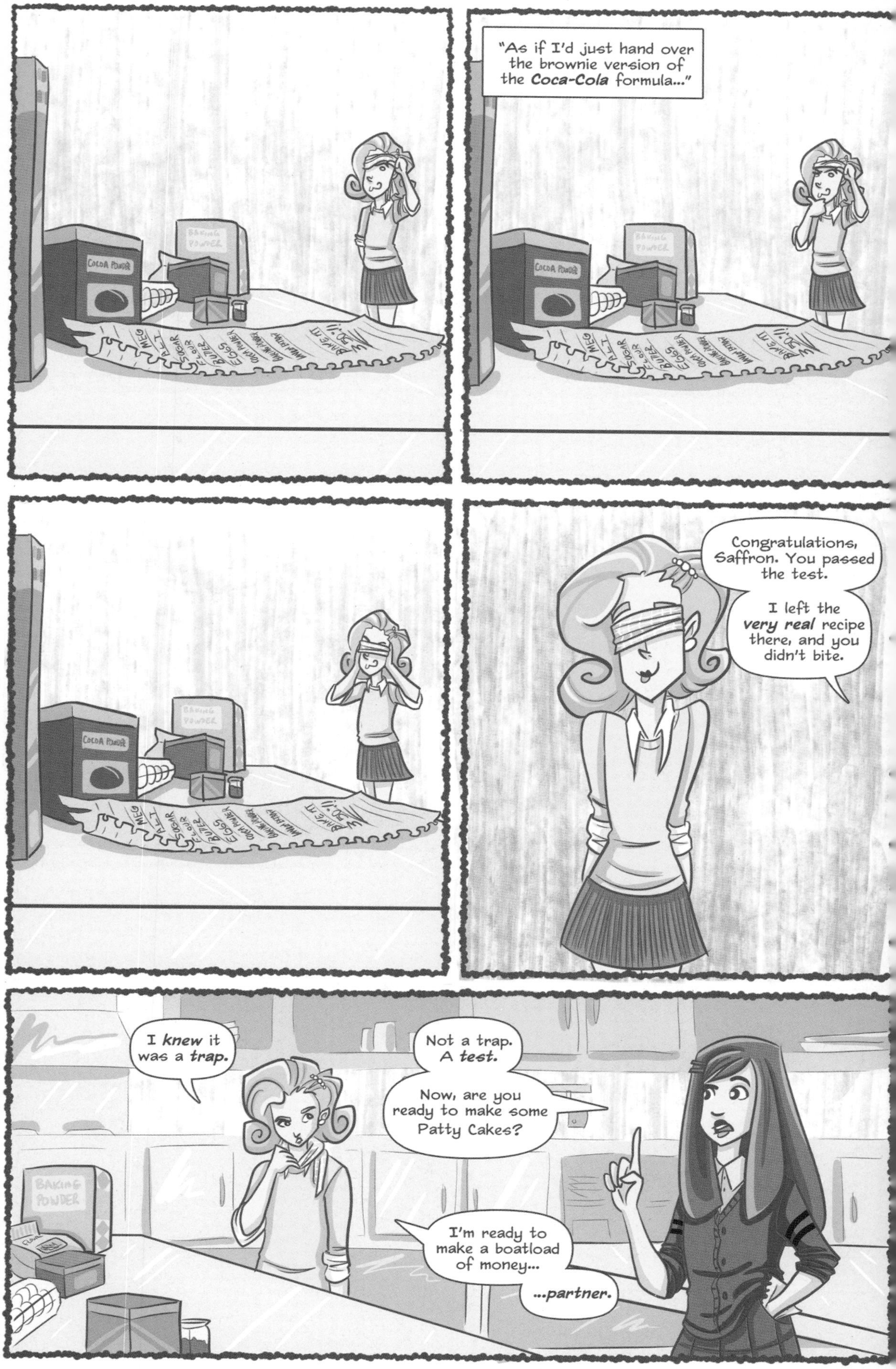

COCOA POWDER
BAKING POWDER
"As if I'd just hand over the brownie version of the *Coca-Cola* formula..."
Congratulations, Saffron. You passed the test.
I left the *very real* recipe there, and you didn't bite.
I *knew* it was a *trap*.
Not a trap. A *test*.
Now, are you ready to make some Patty Cakes?
I'm ready to make a boatload of money...
...*partner*.

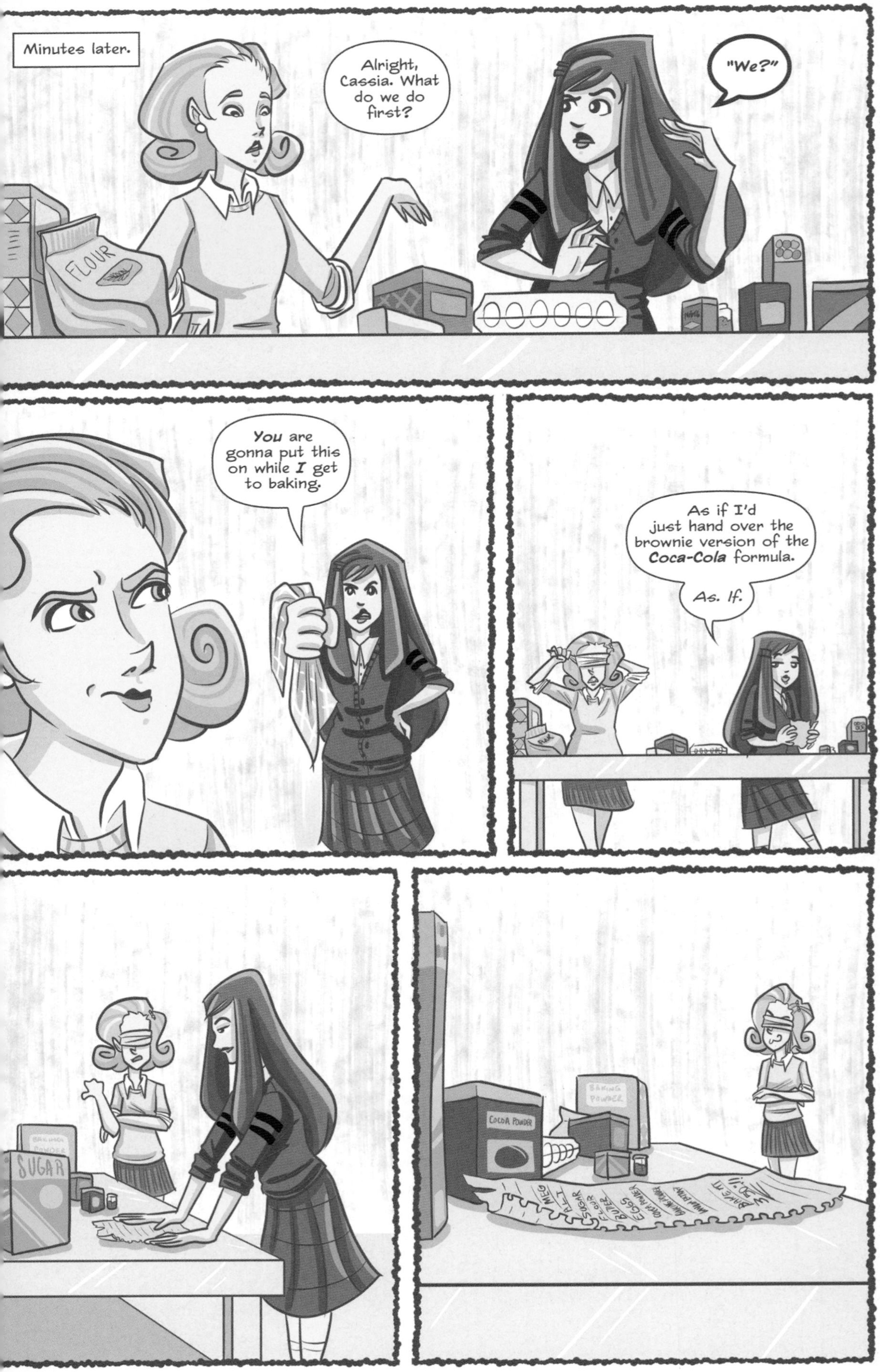

Minutes later.
Alright, Cassia. What do we do first?
"We?"
FLOUR
You are gonna put this on while *I* get to baking.
As if I'd just hand over the brownie version of the **Coca-Cola** formula.
As. If.
SUGAR
COCOA POWDER
BAKING POWDER

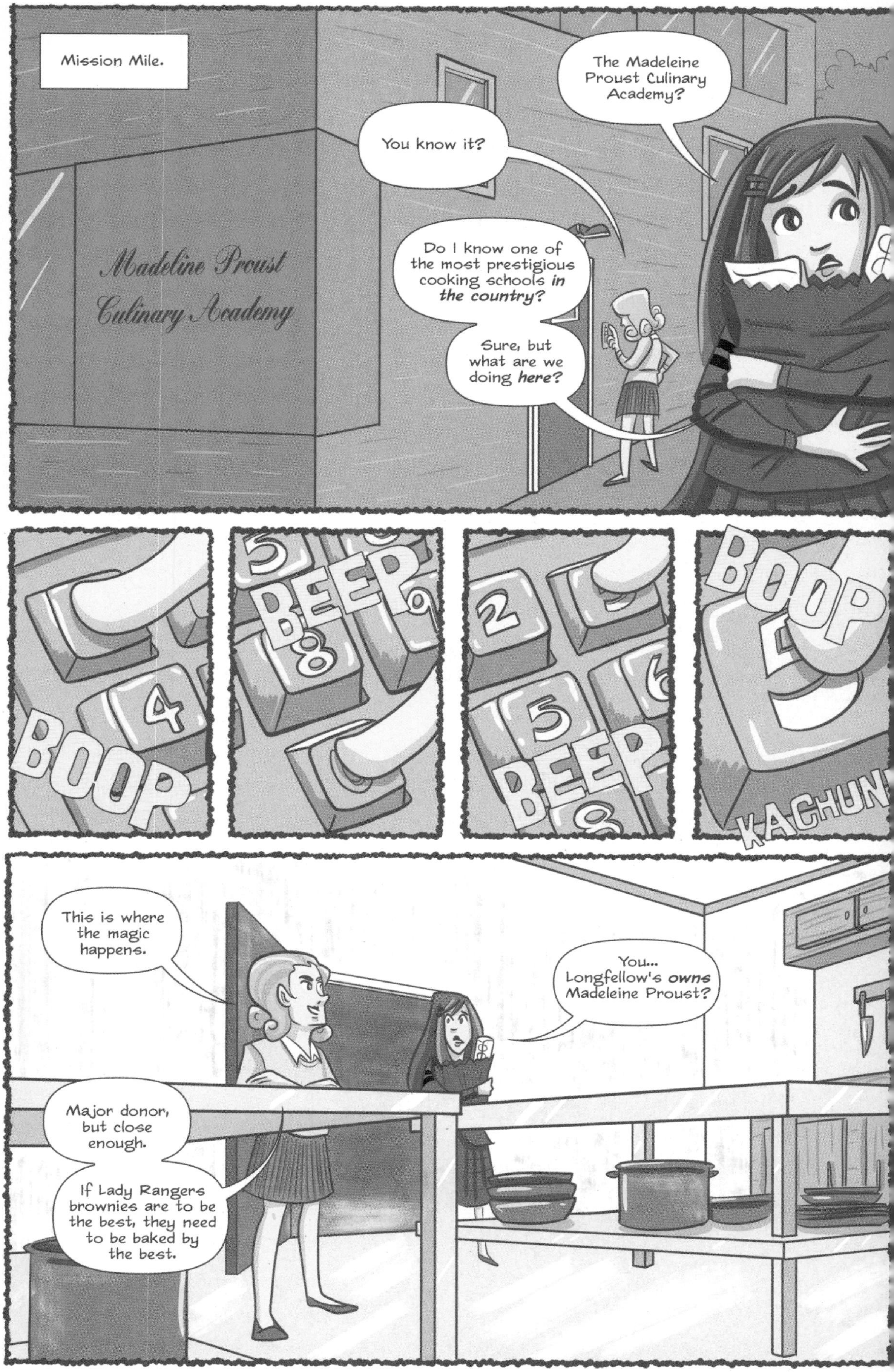
Mission Mile.
The Madeleine Proust Culinary Academy?
You know it?
Madeline Proust Culinary Academy
Do I know one of the most prestigious cooking schools *in the country*?
Sure, but what are we doing *here*?
BOOP
BEEP
BEEP
BOOP
KACHUN
This is where the magic happens.
You... Longfellow's *owns* Madeleine Proust?
Major donor, but close enough.
If Lady Rangers brownies are to be the best, they need to be baked by the best.

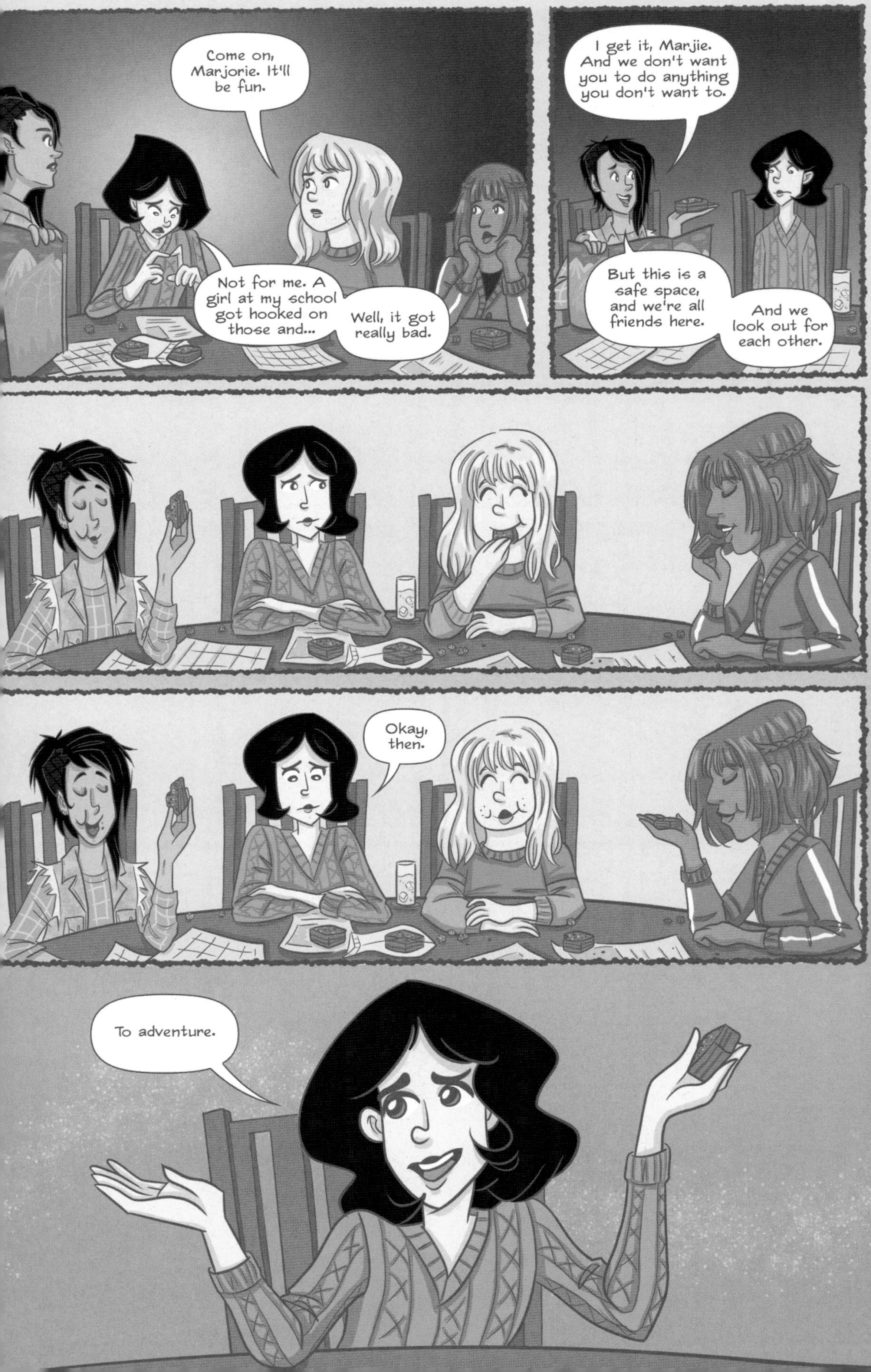
Come on, Marjorie. It'll be fun.
Not for me. A girl at my school got hooked on those and...
Well, it got really bad.
I get it, Marjie. And we don't want you to do anything you don't want to.
But this is a safe space, and we're all friends here.
And we look out for each other.
Okay, then.
To adventure.

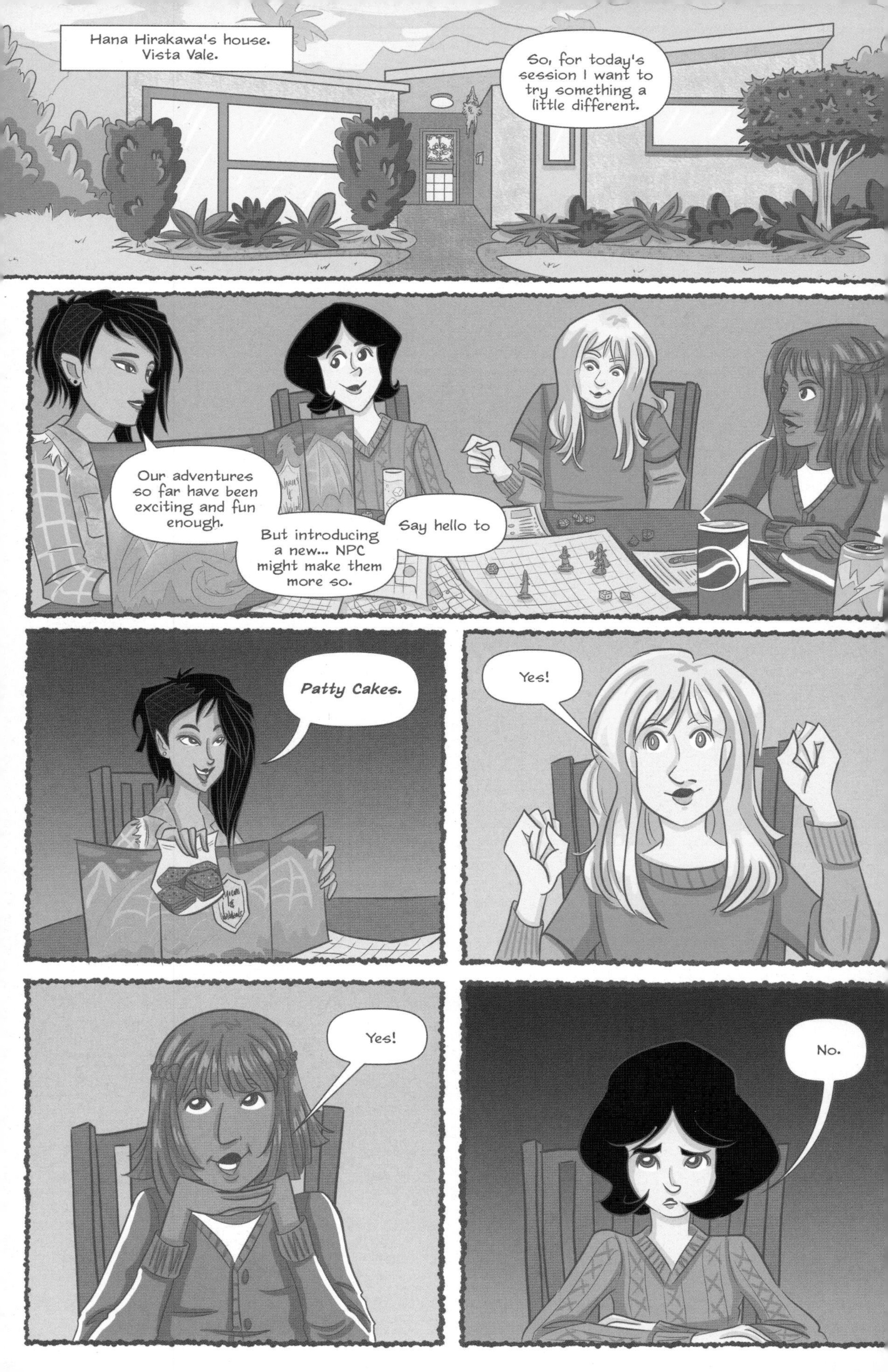
Hana Hirakawa's house.
Vista Vale.
So, for today's session I want to try something a little different.
Our adventures so far have been exciting and fun enough.
But introducing a new... NPC might make them more so.
Say hello to
Patty Cakes.
Yes!
Yes!
No.

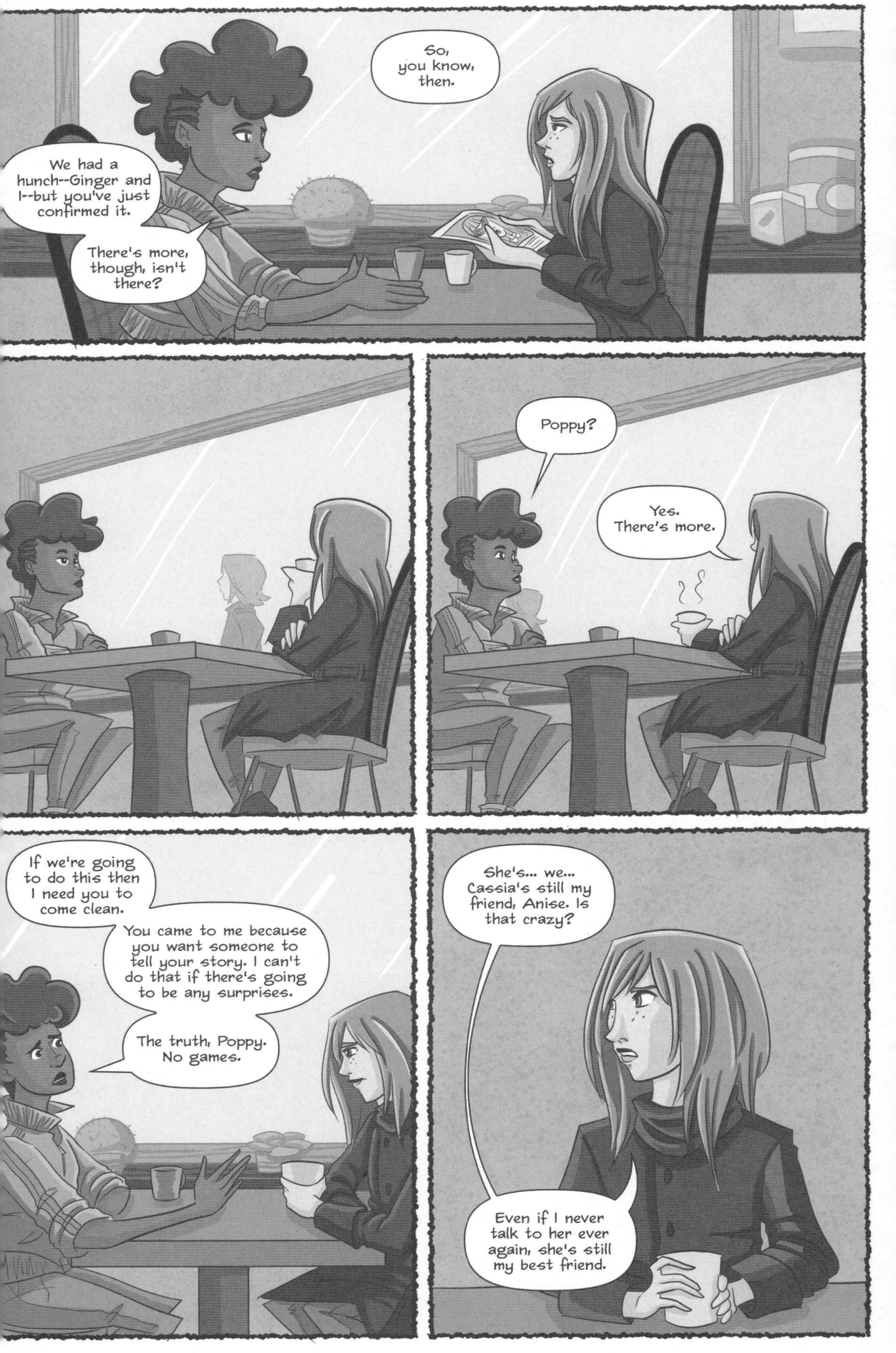
So, you know, then.
We had a hunch--Ginger and I--but you've just confirmed it.
There's more, though, isn't there?
Poppy?
Yes. There's more.
If we're going to do this then I need you to come clean.
You came to me because you want someone to tell your story. I can't do that if there's going to be any surprises.
The truth, Poppy. No games.
She's... we... Cassia's still my friend, Anise. Is that crazy?
Even if I never talk to her ever again, she's still my best friend.

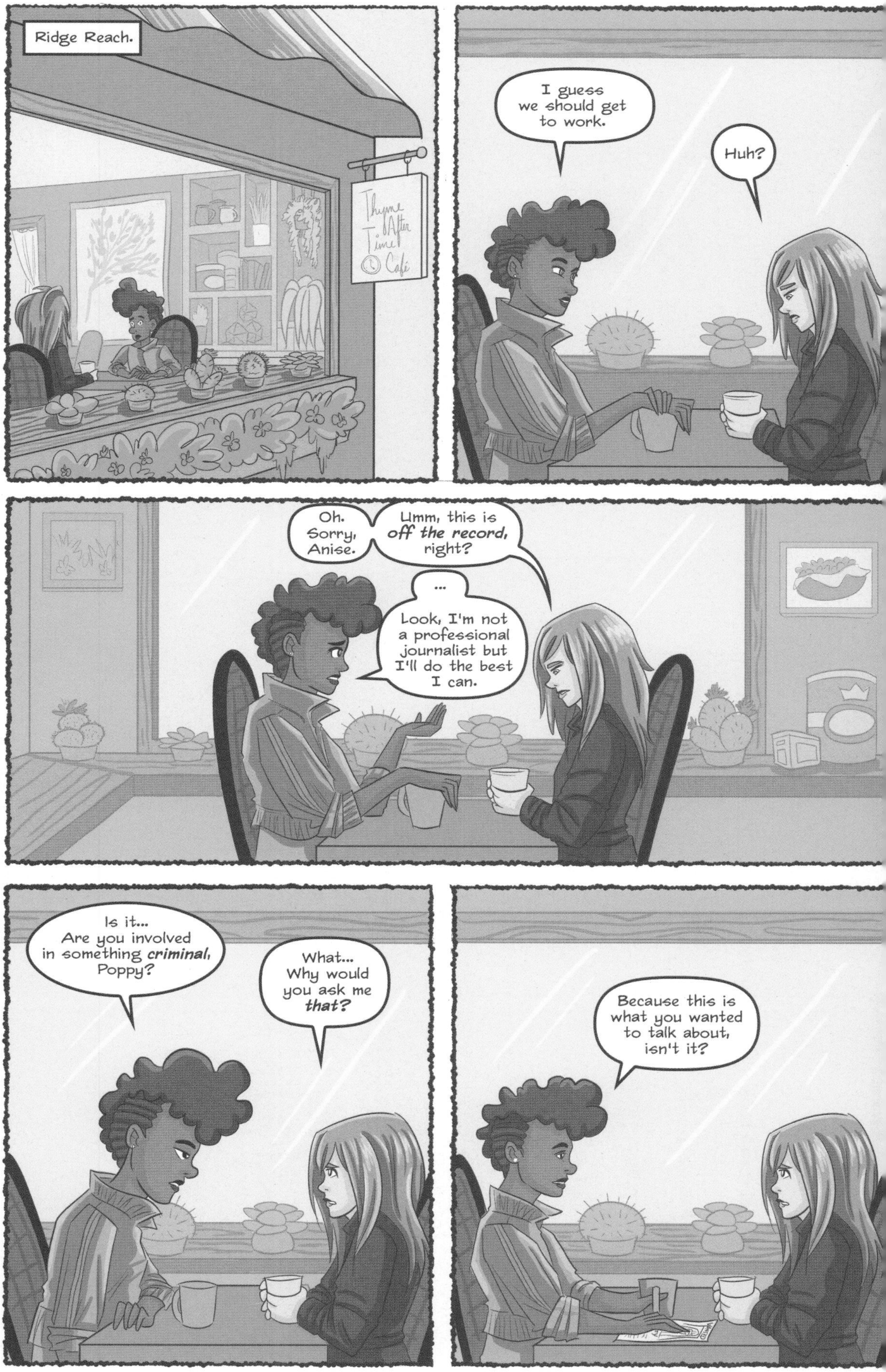
Ridge Reach.
Thyme After Time Café
I guess we should get to work.
Huh?
Oh. Sorry, Anise.
Umm, this is *off the record,* right?
...
Look, I'm not a professional journalist but I'll do the best I can.
Is it... Are you involved in something *criminal,* Poppy?
What... Why would you ask me *that?*
Because this is what you wanted to talk about, isn't it?

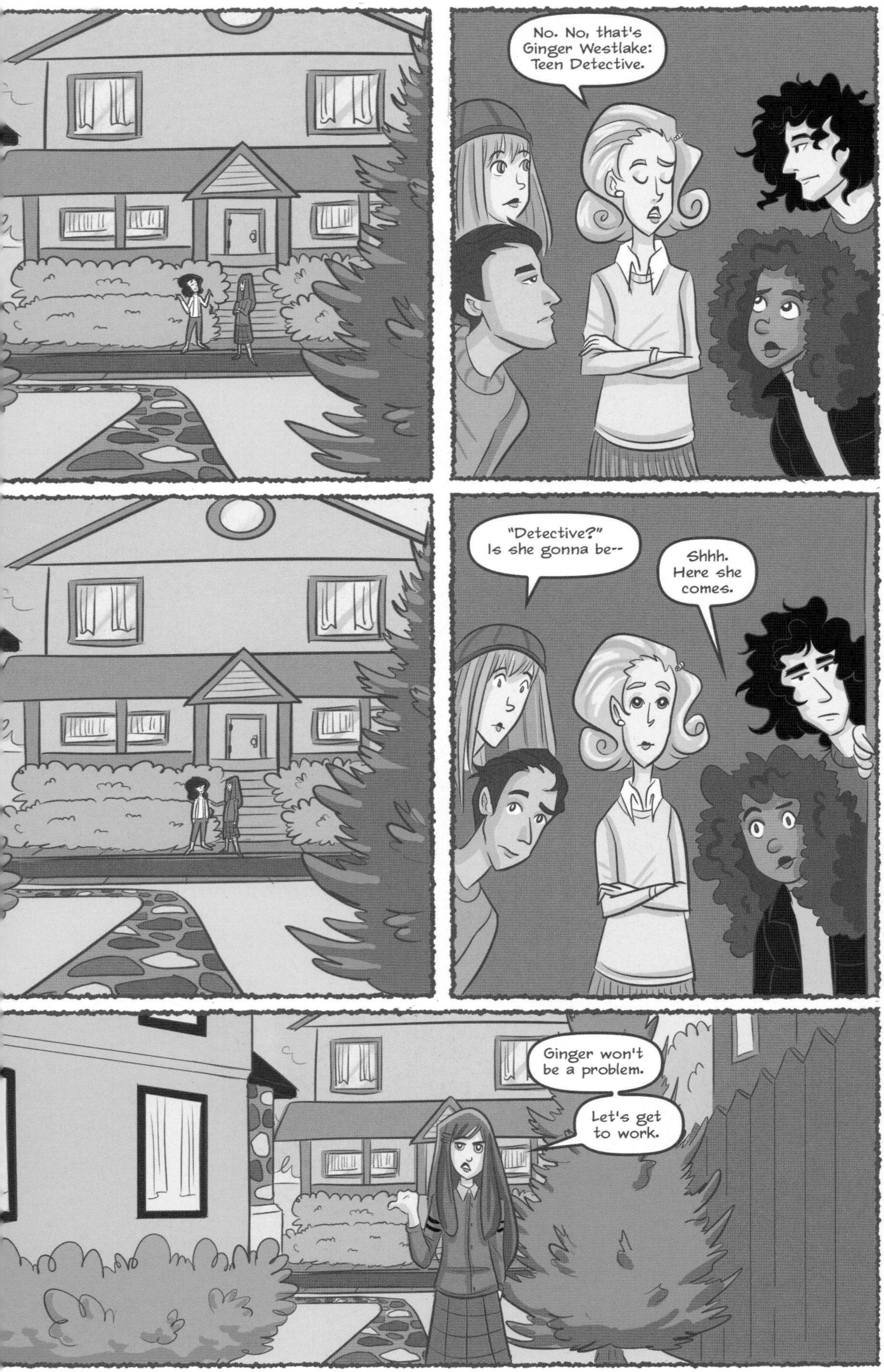
No. No, that's Ginger Westlake: Teen Detective.
"Detective?" Is she gonna be--
Shhh. Here she comes.
Ginger won't be a problem.
Let's get to work.

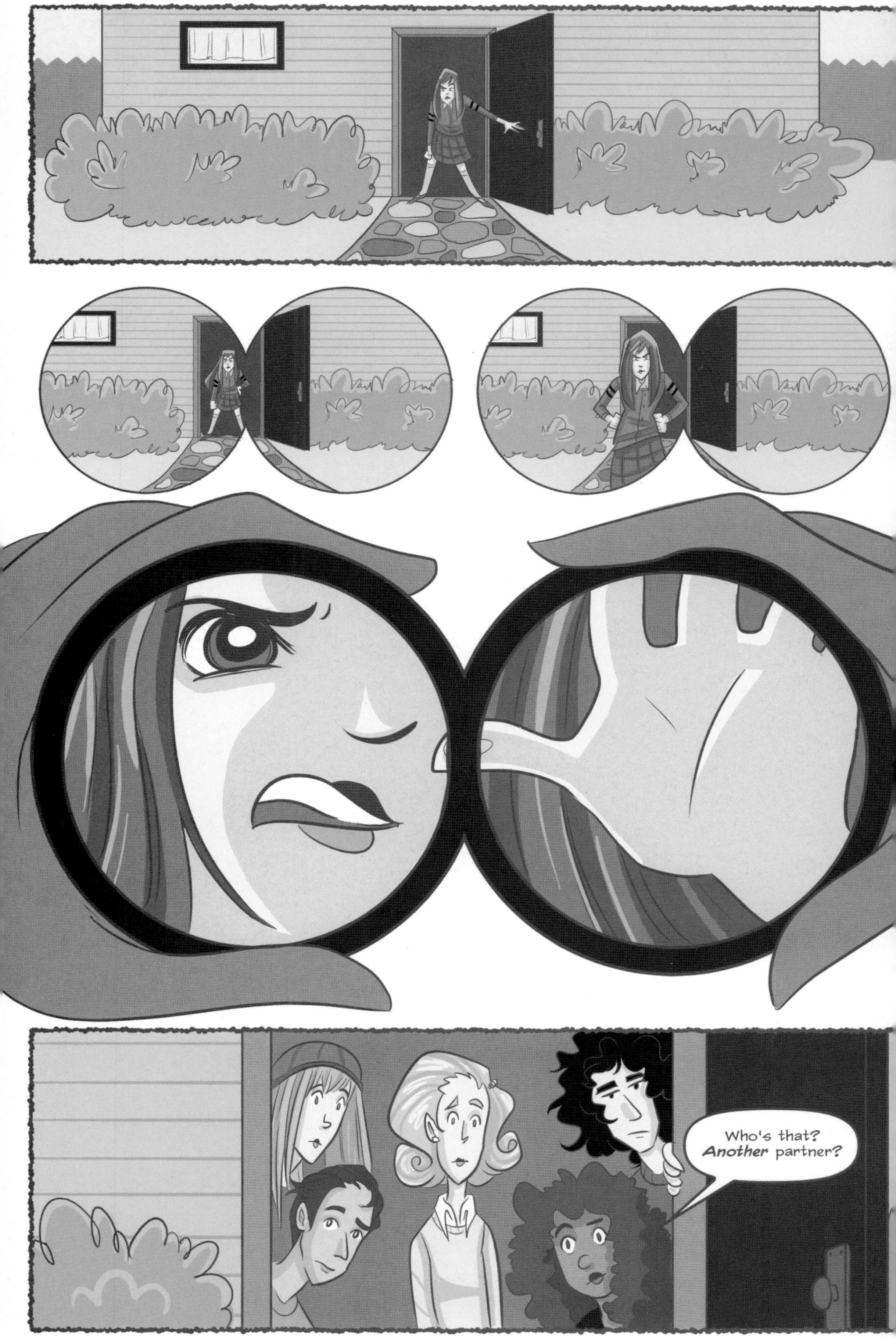
Who's that? *Another* partner?

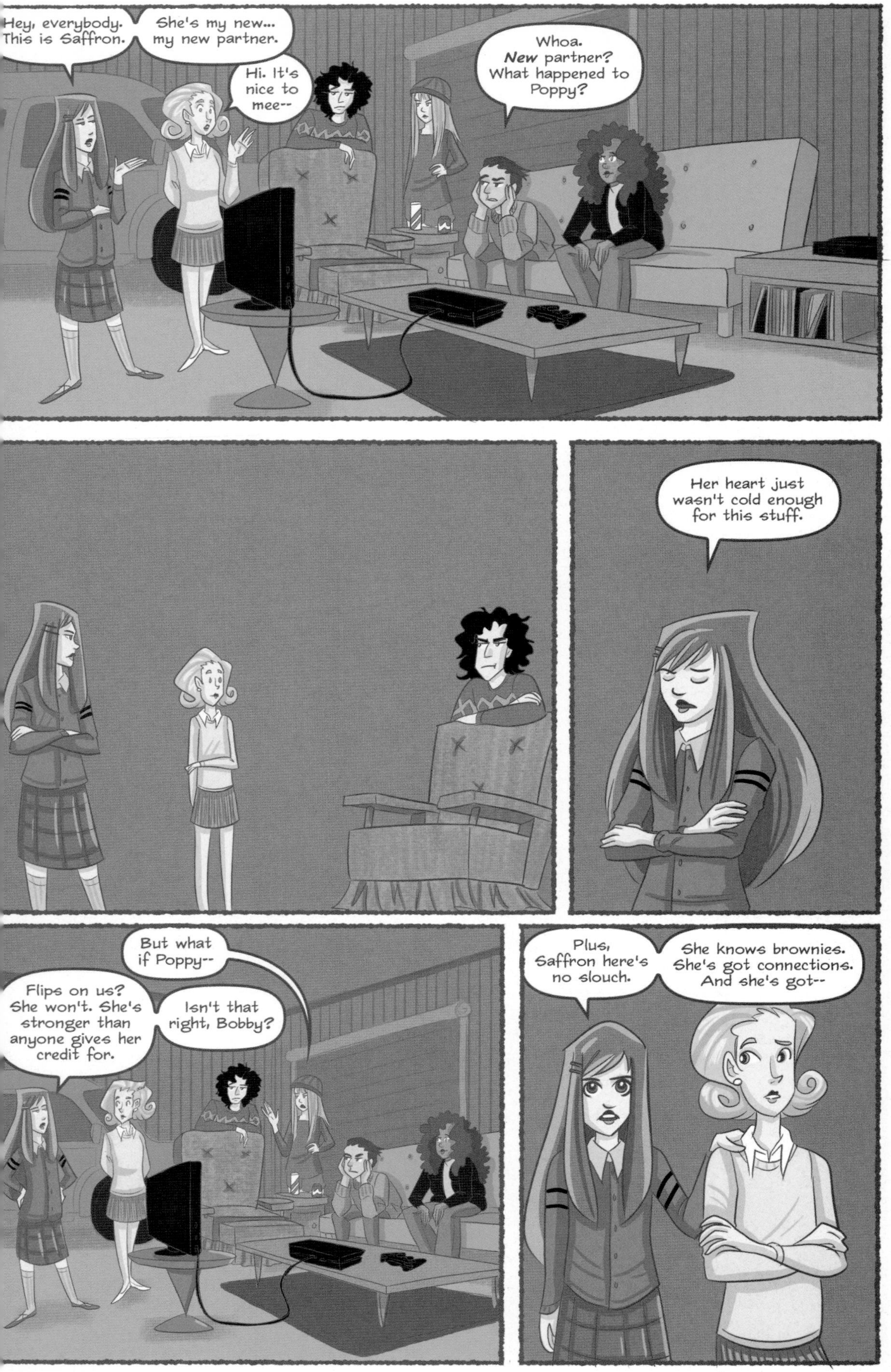
Hey, everybody. This is Saffron.
She's my new... my new partner.
Hi. It's nice to mee--
Whoa. *New* partner? What happened to Poppy?
Her heart just wasn't cold enough for this stuff.
But what if Poppy--
Flips on us? She won't. She's stronger than anyone gives her credit for.
Isn't that right, Bobby?
Plus, Saffron here's no slouch.
She knows brownies. She's got connections. And she's got--

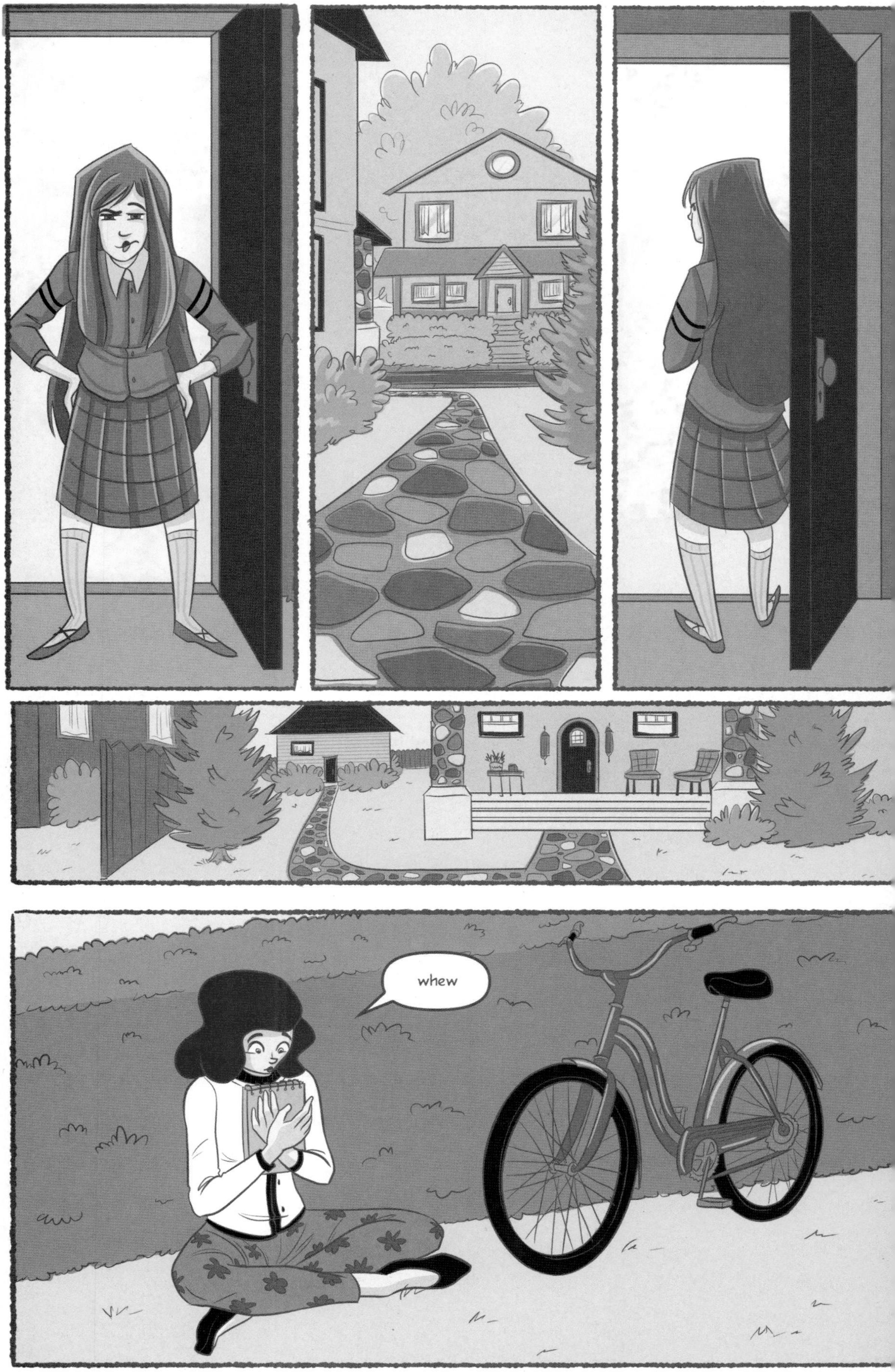
whew

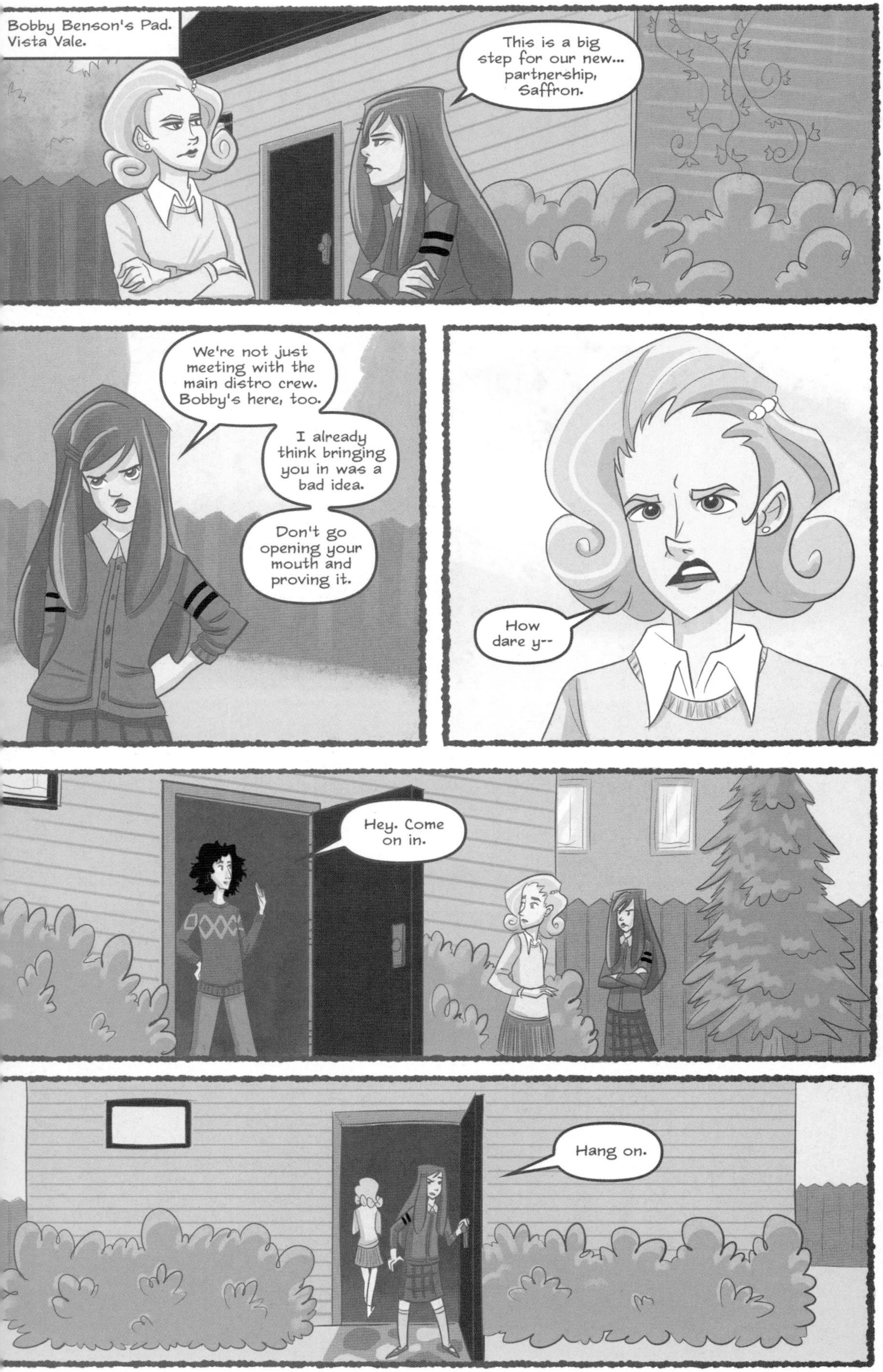
Bobby Benson's Pad. Vista Vale.
This is a big step for our new... partnership, Saffron.
We're not just meeting with the main distro crew. Bobby's here, too.
I already think bringing you in was a bad idea.
Don't go opening your mouth and proving it.
How dare y--
Hey. Come on in.
Hang on.

Bryan Seaton - Publisher • Kevin Freeman - President • Dave Dwonch - Creative Director • Shawn Gabborin - Editor In Chief
Jamal Igle - Co-Directors of Marketing • Chad Cicconi - ate all the brownies • Colleen Boyd - Associate Editor

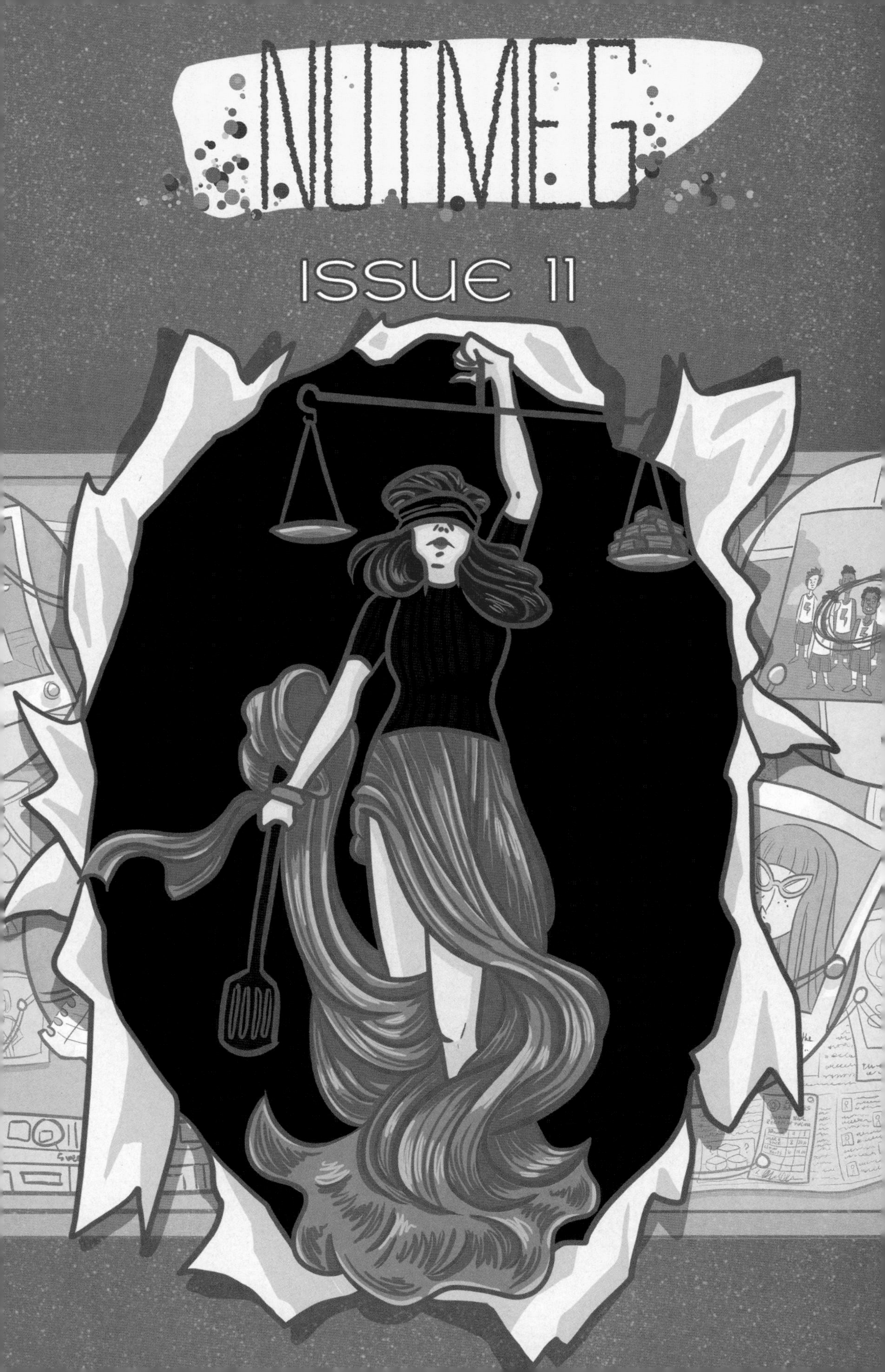
NUTMEG
ISSUE 11

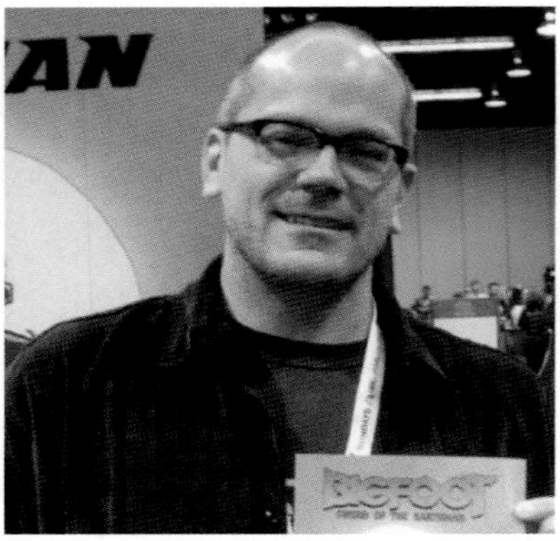
BIGFOOT

JOSH HENAMAN'S SAVORY TAVERN HAND PIES (FOR ADVENTURIN')

It's all in the crust! No joke. The joy of making hand pies (meat pie empanadas, etc.) is that you can fill them with pretty much anythin Sweet, savory, a combo of both, the world is yours. It really is the perfect food for when you need to get back to fightin' orcs!

INSTRUCTIONS

* Mix the flour, salt and fresh nutmeg together.
* Cut your sticks of butter into small pieces and then mix by hand with the flour (seriously, get your hands into the bowl and pinch with your fingers until the flour/butter mixture is all crumbled together. This move comes straight from Julia Child herself, so it's gotta be good! Just make sure your hands are clean.)
* Combine the vinegar and water together in a small bowl and drizzle a little of that mixture into the flour mix a tablespoon at a time.
* Using a fork, stir and mix the liquids and flour until the dough just comes together (don't worry, you'll have some of the water/vinegar left over. You don't want the dough too wet.)
* Divide the dough by half. At this stage, you can either make two whole 9 inch pies or continue on for hand pies!
* Preheat your oven to 400 degrees.
* Dust a workspace with flour so your crust won't stick.
* Roll out the crust until you get the rough shape of a 9 – 10 inch pie.
* Using a small cereal bowl (6-inch), cut out some circular pie shapes. After you roll out both crusts (and reshape the leftover scraps to roll out again,) you'll have about 11 circles.
* Add 1 – 2 Tbsp filling to the center of each 6-inch circle (see below for the filling I used). Combine the egg and 2 Tbsp of water in a small bowl (this is your egg wash/sealant for the crust.)
* Brush one half of the outer edge of each crust.
* Fold over the crust so that you make a nice little pocket.
* Using the tines of a fork, press along that outer edge so that you make a nice little seal. With the fork, poke a few holes in the top of that pocket so that any steam might escape (your hand pie might explode otherwise.)
* Cook the hand pies on a cookie sheet at 400 degrees for 35 - 40 minutes.
* Enjoy and get back to adventuring!

FOR THE DOUGH

2 ½ cups flour
1 tsp salt
½ tsp. freshly ground NUTMEG!!!
2 sticks butter (1 cup)
2 Tbsp. apple cider vinegar
½ cup cold water
1 egg (for the egg wash)
2 Tbsp water (for the egg wash)

SAVORY FILLING

1 lb. ground beef or spicy sausage

3 Tbsp. flour

1 ½ cups milk

Salt, pepper, seasoned salt

* The beauty of this filling is that you can use ground beef, sausage, ground turkey, bison, chorizo, etc. You can make it as spicy as you want. Nothing is written in stone.
* Brown your ground beef in a skillet.
* Once that's done, add your flour a table-spoon at a time and stir in the skillet until the meat is completely coated.
* With your skillet on medium, slowly add the milk and stir.
* Stir for 3 – 5 minutes until you have a thick gravy. The thicker the better, so don't be shy about letting it cook down (just keep stirring so as not to burn the milk.)
* Once you have a good, pudding-like thickness, remove from heat and stir in any combination of spices (I prefer salt, pepper and seasoned salt.)
* Set aside and make your crust. This is also how you make the military favorite S.O.S., so any leftover you can enjoy with toast!
* For an added little bit of cheesiness, add a cup of shredded cheese to the filling once it's cooled.

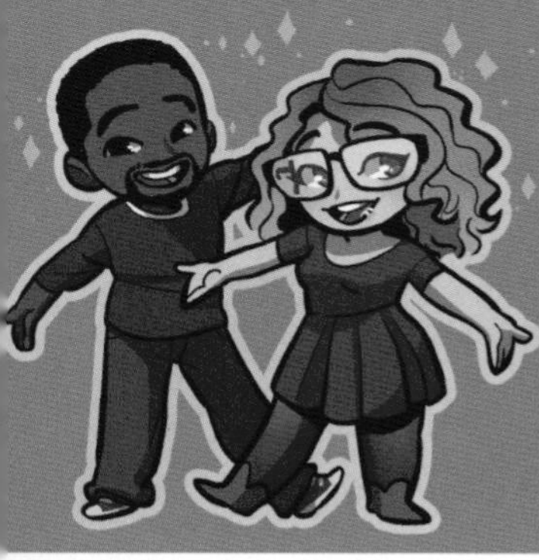

THE COOLING RACK

CONTACT: @NutmegComic NutmegComics@gmail.com

Avatars by Genue Revuelta

Did you miss us? We missed you! We're back with another edition of The Cooling Rack. And what better way to kick things off this go-round than with a wonderful piece of fan mail from series reader, Garry! Thank you so much for taking the time to write to us. (And if you'd like to write in, send us an email and mark it "okay to print!")

i there, creators of one of my favorite books!

originally purchased Nutmeg #1 thinking it might be something I could get my daughter to read, thus etting her hooked on my hobby, but I got completely sucked into it myself. I really enjoy the writing and haracterization, and also the parallels with Breaking Bad. (not that it's an exact copy, of course - it just eminds me of it a some). The art is definitely not the traditional comic book fare, and - probably for that eason - it's grown on me. If I'm not mistaken, I do believe I'm seeing Ms Crofts' work develop as the eries goes on, so that's an enjoyable thing to watch as well. Also, thanks for putting Josh Eckert's name n the cover - I like to see colorists and letterers getting more credit these days. Anyway, I never gave it to ny daughter - mostly because I didn't want to give her any bright ideas about starting her own middle chool criminal enterprise - but I've kept it on my pull list for the duration, and will continue to do so.

est wishes and may all your baked goodies be fresh!

Gary Gordon
Littleton, CO

And, as ever, we're always happy to get art from ans and friends. This month's pieces come via our pals Loki and Diana, whom we met at Emerald City Comicon in 2015 and have been close with ever since.

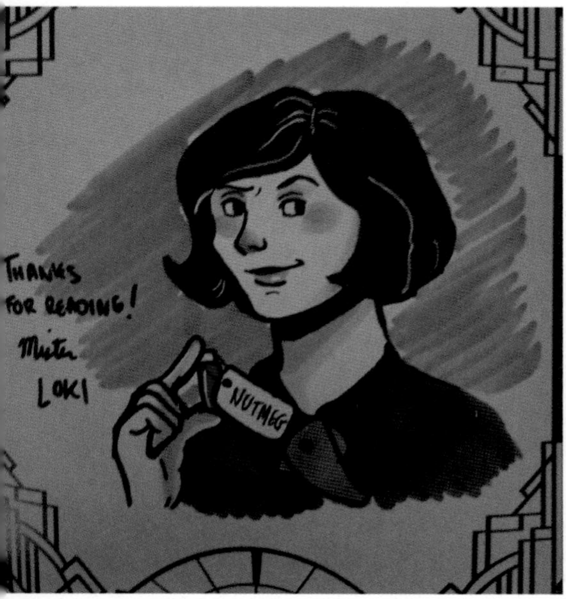
THANKS FOR READING! Mister LOKI
NUTMEG

arjorie" by Mister Loki, creator of *il the Last Dog Dies* **(lastdogdies.com)**

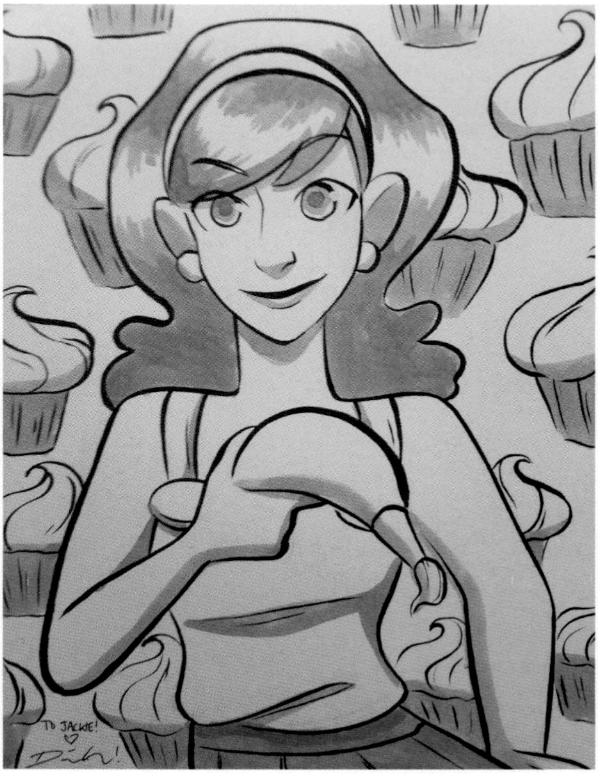
TO JACKIE!

"Poppy" by Diana Huh, creator of *The Lonely Vincent Bellingham"* **(lonelyvincent.com)**

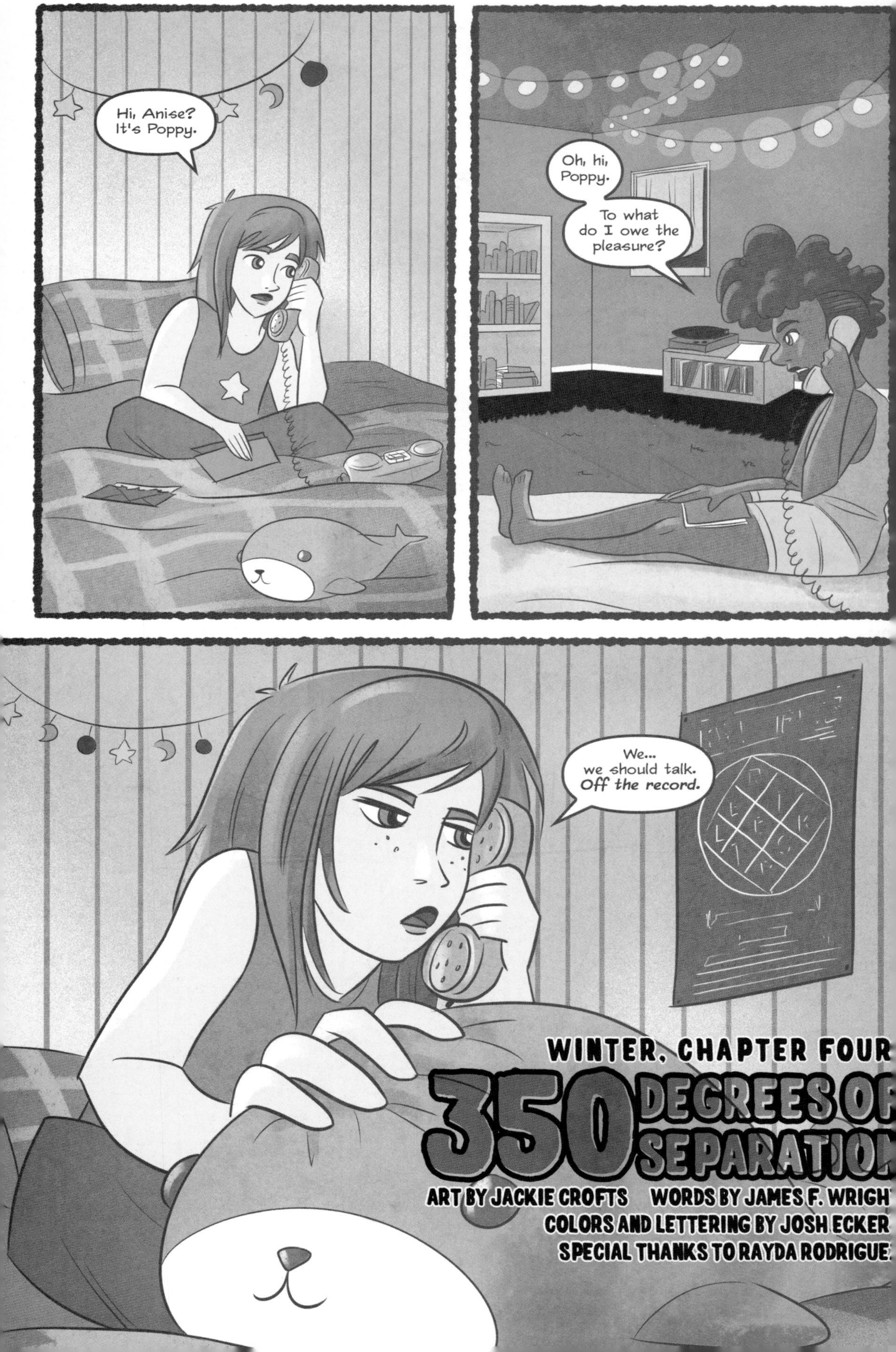

Hi, Anise? It's Poppy.
Oh, hi, Poppy.
To what do I owe the pleasure?
We... we should talk. *Off the record.*
WINTER, CHAPTER FOUR
350 DEGREES OF SEPARATION
ART BY JACKIE CROFTS WORDS BY JAMES F. WRIGHT
COLORS AND LETTERING BY JOSH ECKER
SPECIAL THANKS TO RAYDA RODRIGUES

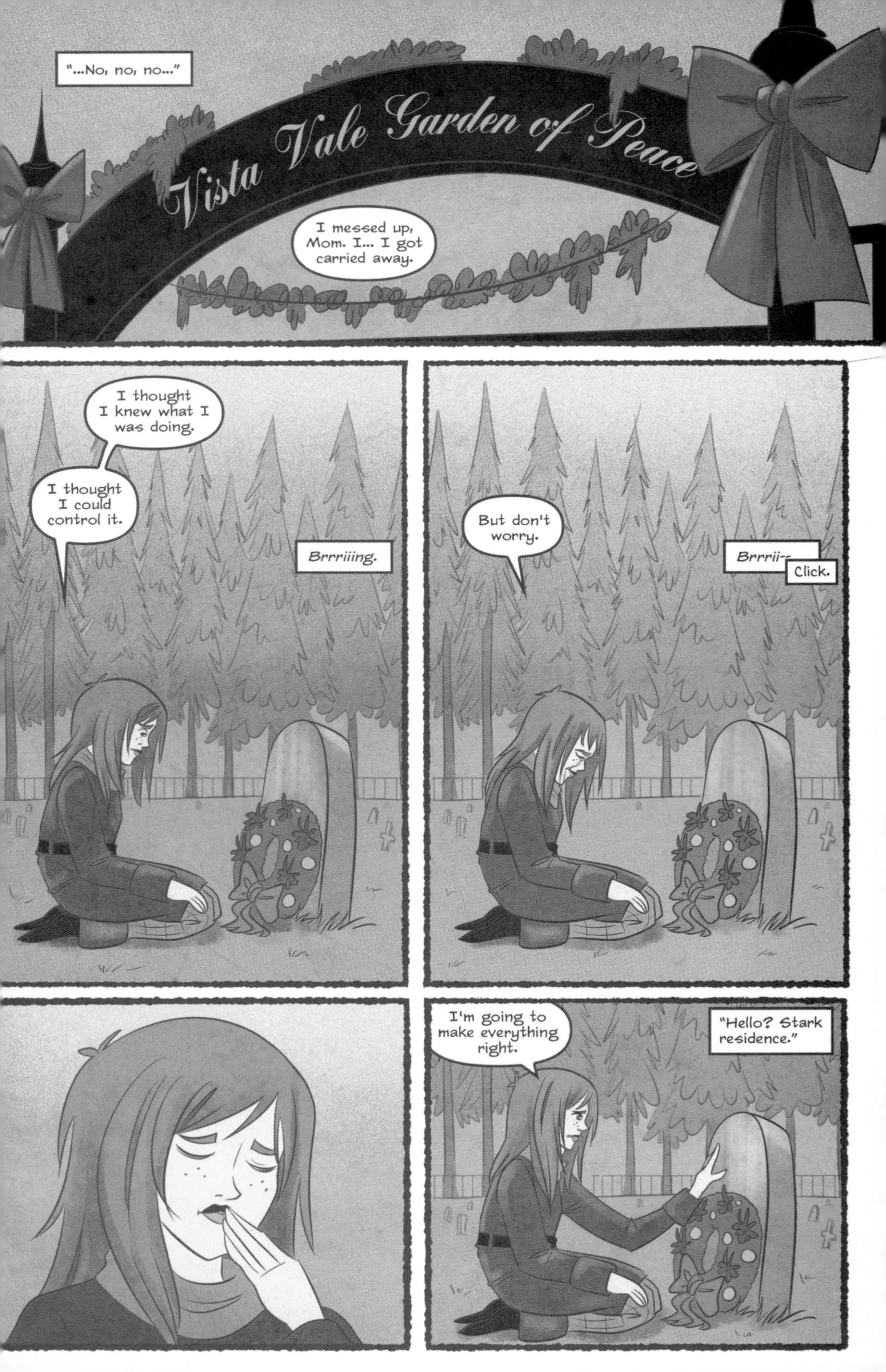
"...No, no, no..."
Vista Vale Garden of Peace
I messed up, Mom. I... I got carried away.
I thought I knew what I was doing.
I thought I could control it.
Brrriiing.
But don't worry.
Brrrii--
Click.
I'm going to make everything right.
"Hello? Stark residence."

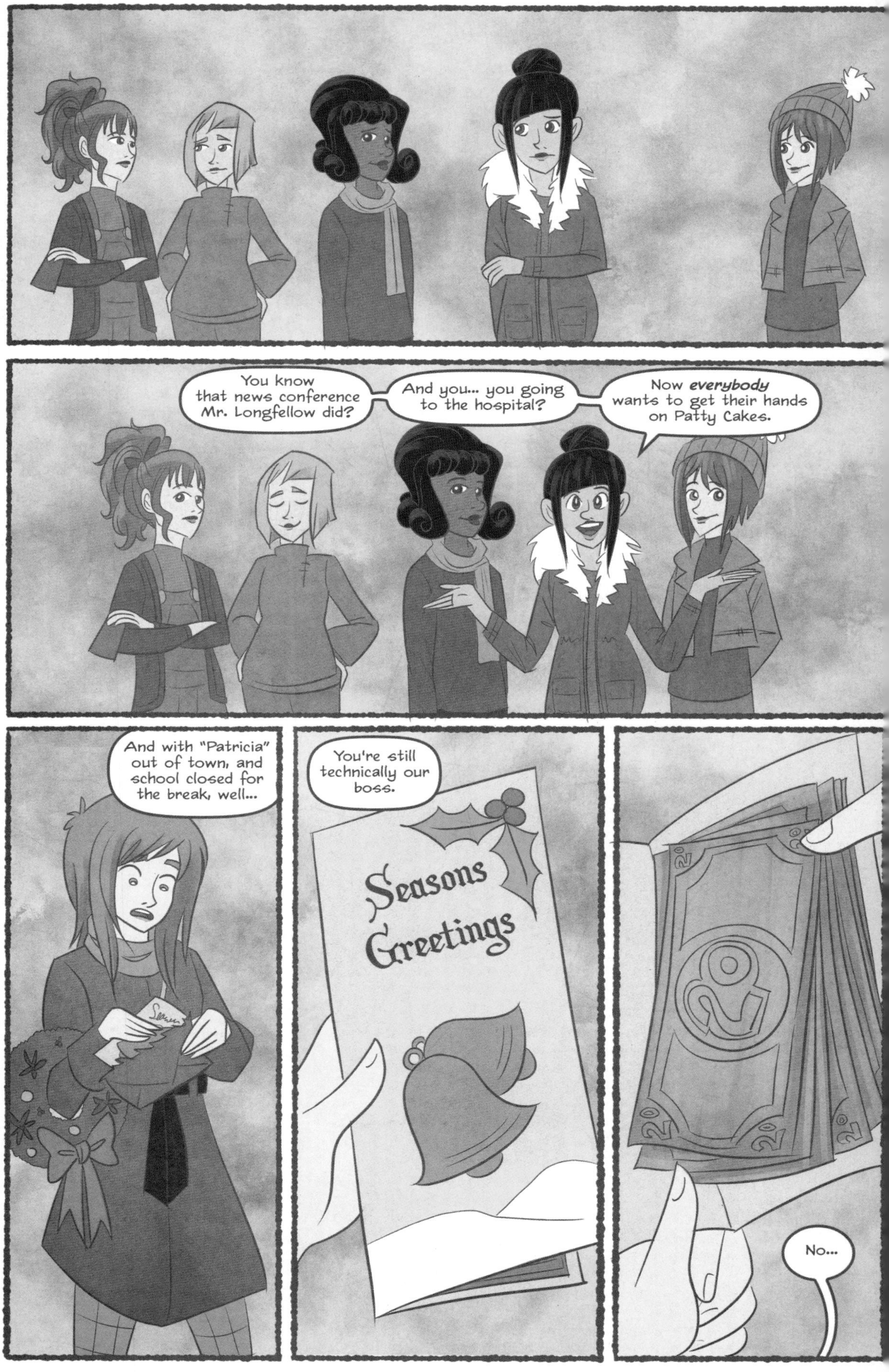
You know that news conference Mr. Longfellow did?
And you... you going to the hospital?
Now *everybody* wants to get their hands on Patty Cakes.
And with "Patricia" out of town, and school closed for the break, well...
You're still technically our boss.
Seasons Greetings
No...

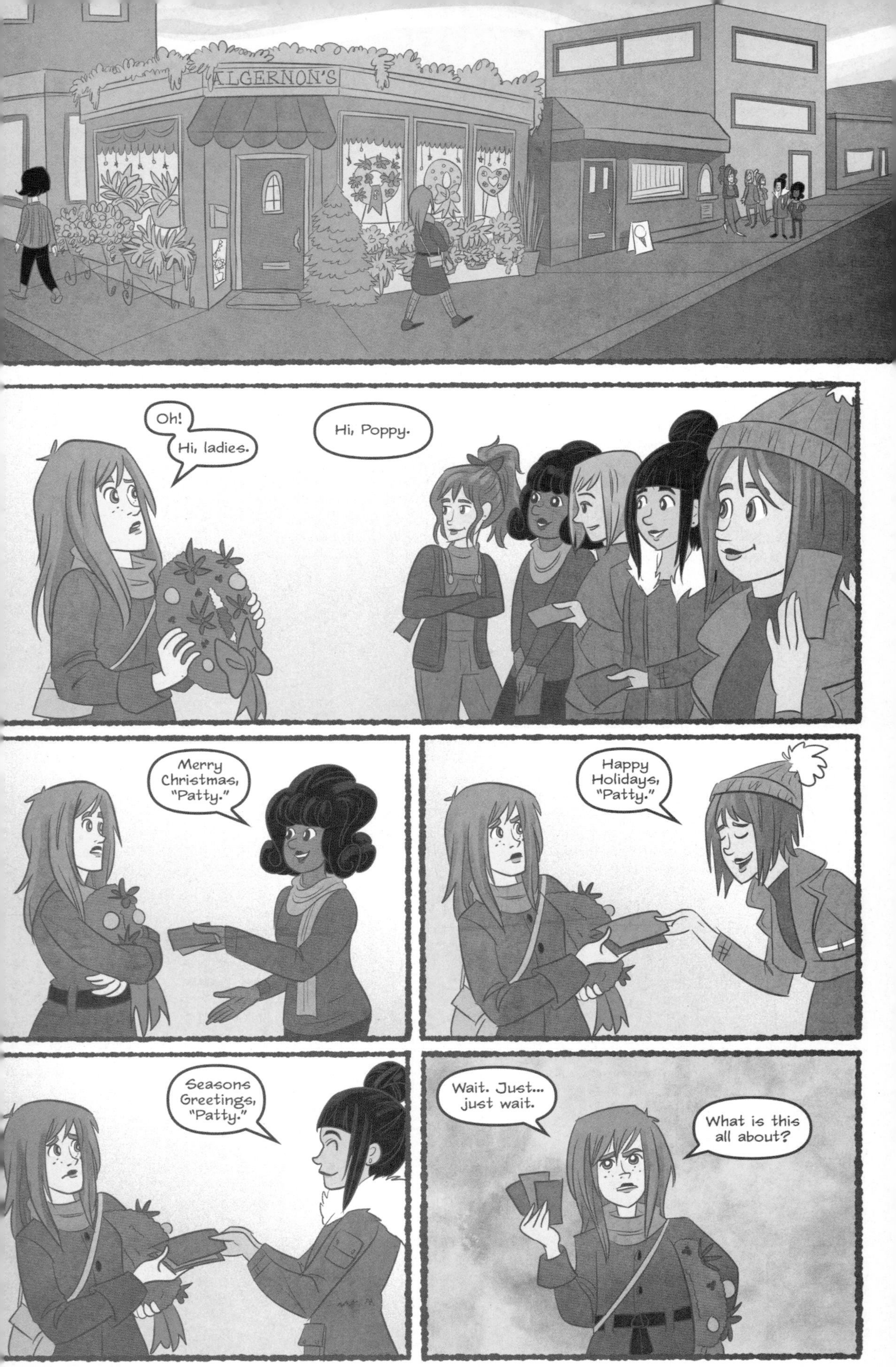
ALGERNON'S
Oh!
Hi, ladies.
Hi, Poppy.
Merry Christmas, "Patty."
Happy Holidays, "Patty."
Seasons Greetings, "Patty."
Wait. Just... just wait.
What is this all about?

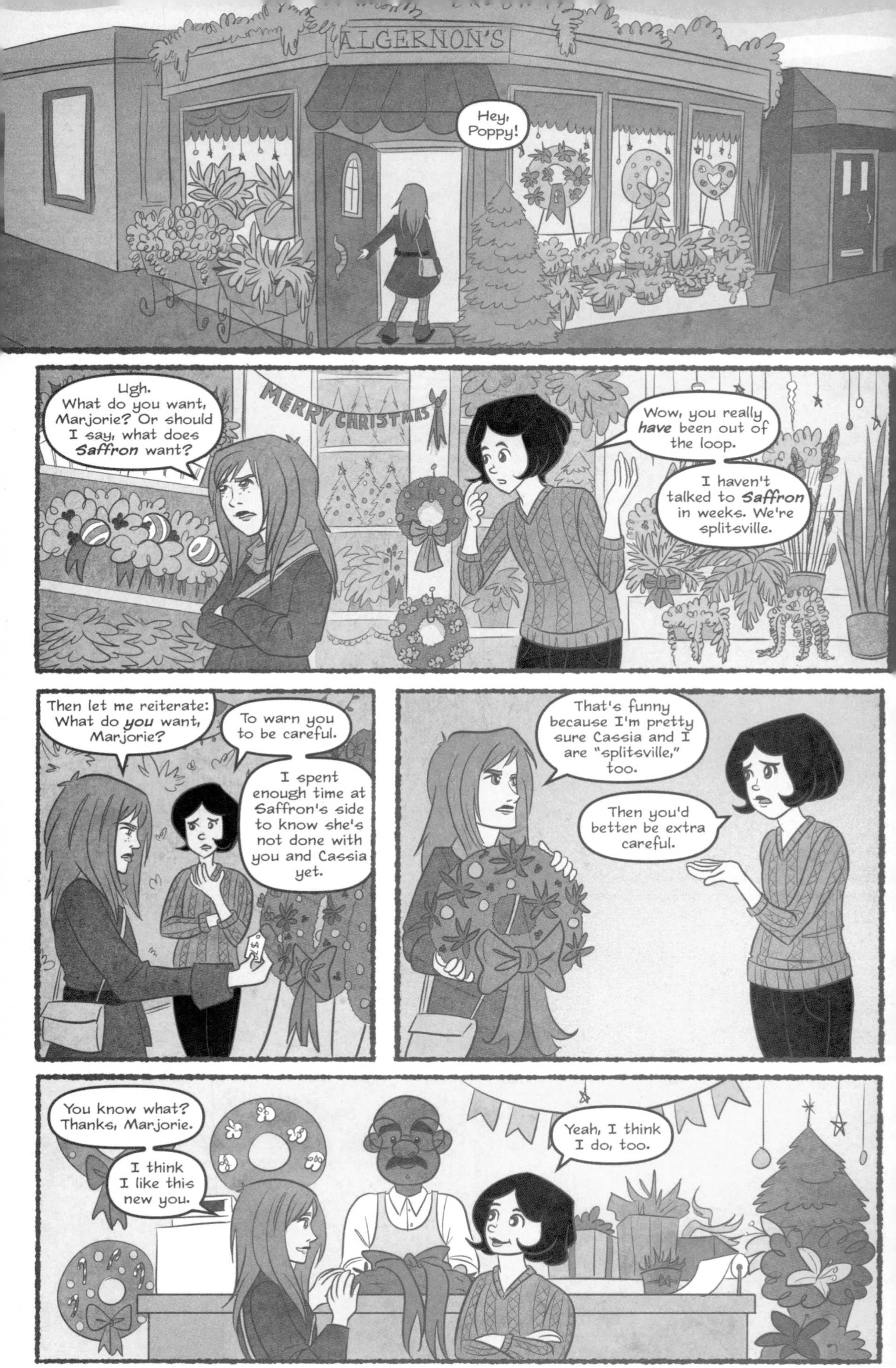
ALGERNON'S
Hey, Poppy!
Ugh. What do you want, Marjorie? Or should I say, what does *Saffron* want?
MERRY CHRISTMAS
Wow, you really *have* been out of the loop.
I haven't talked to *Saffron* in weeks. We're splitsville.
Then let me reiterate: What do *you* want, Marjorie?
To warn you to be careful.
I spent enough time at Saffron's side to know she's not done with you and Cassia yet.
That's funny because I'm pretty sure Cassia and I are "splitsville," too.
Then you'd better be extra careful.
You know what? Thanks, Marjorie.
I think I like this new you.
Yeah, I think I do, too.

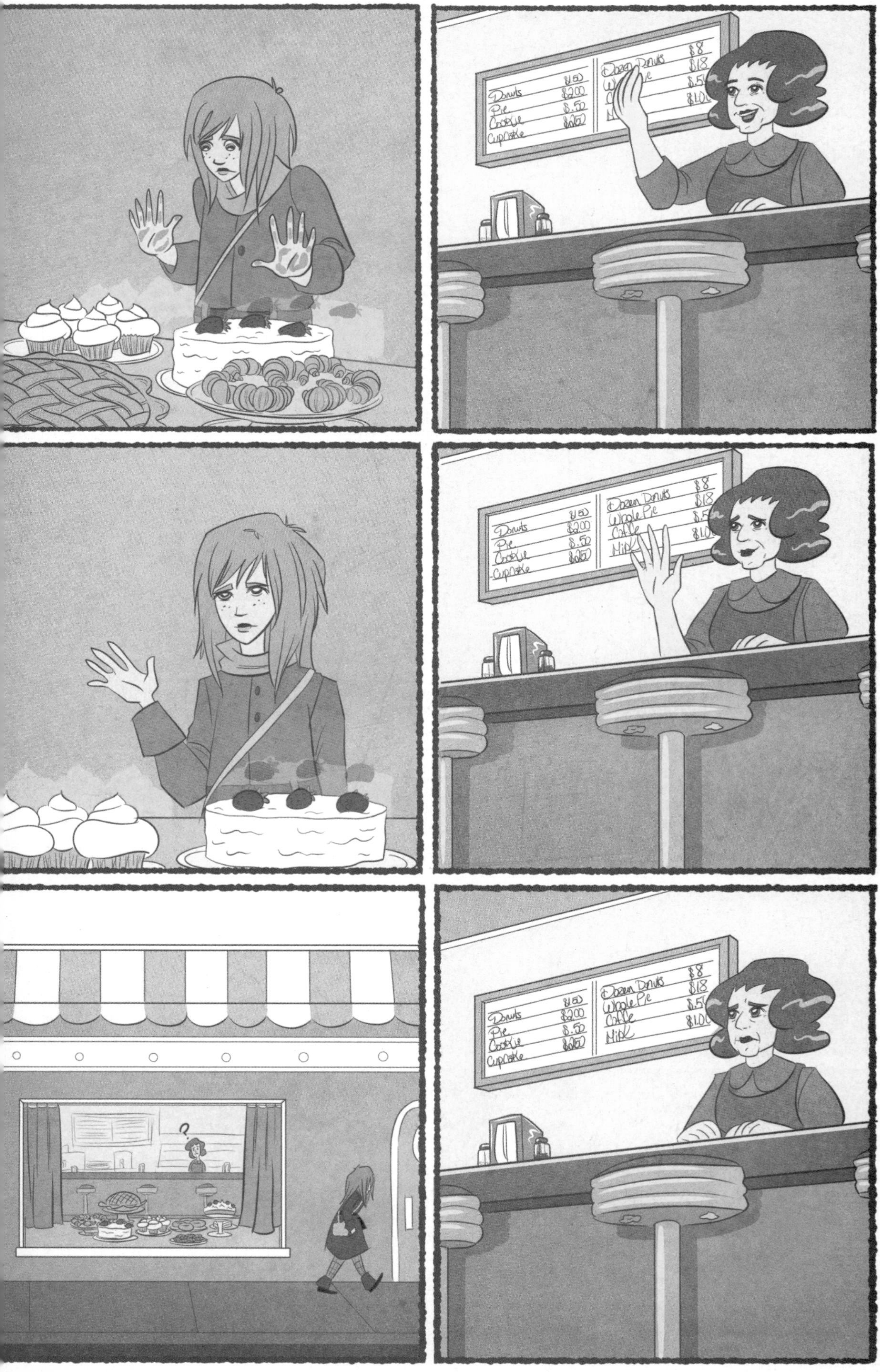
Donuts
Pie
Cookie
Cupcake
$2.00
$.50
Dozen Donuts
Whole Pie
Milk
$8
$18

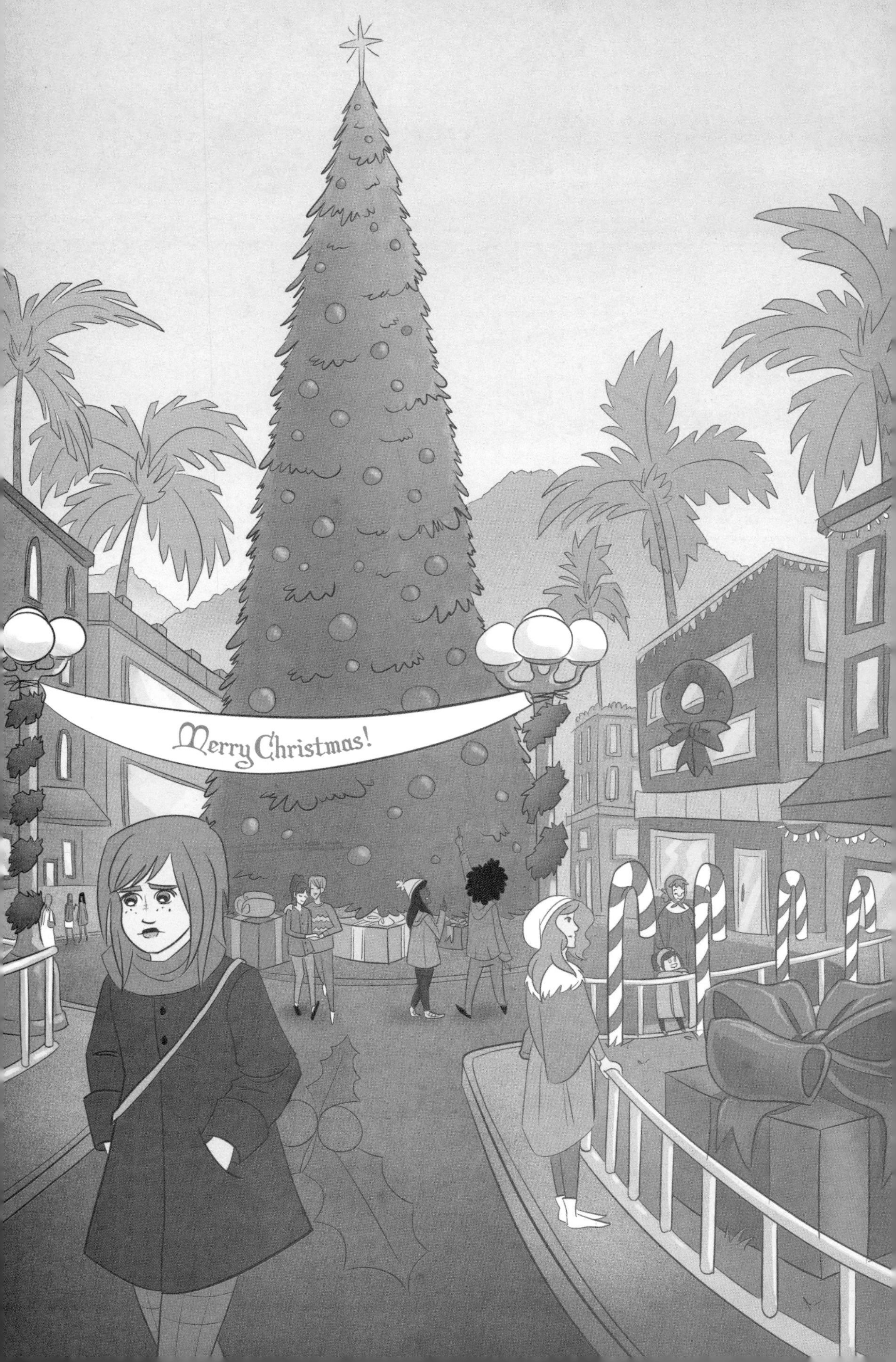
Merry Christmas!

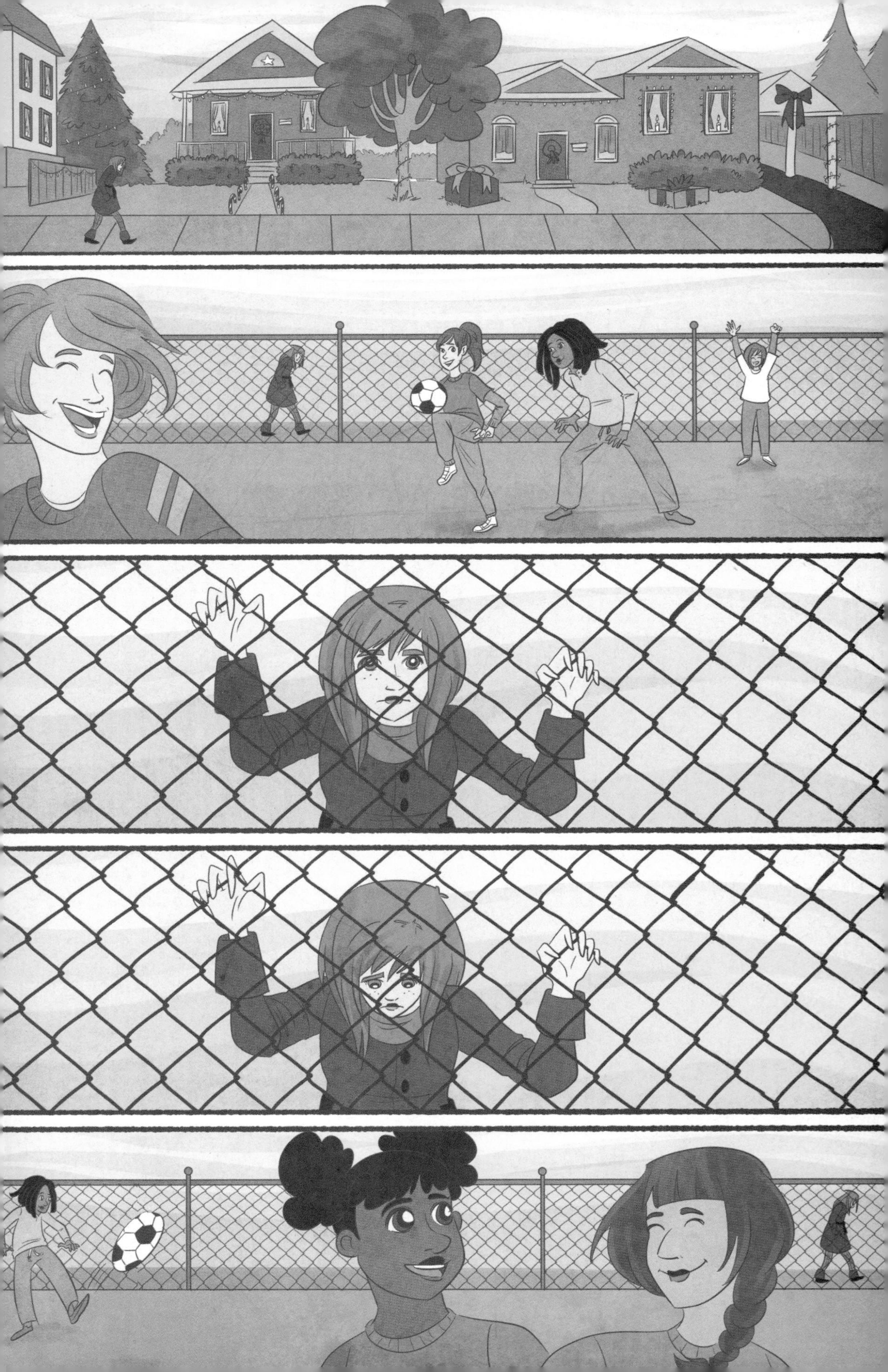

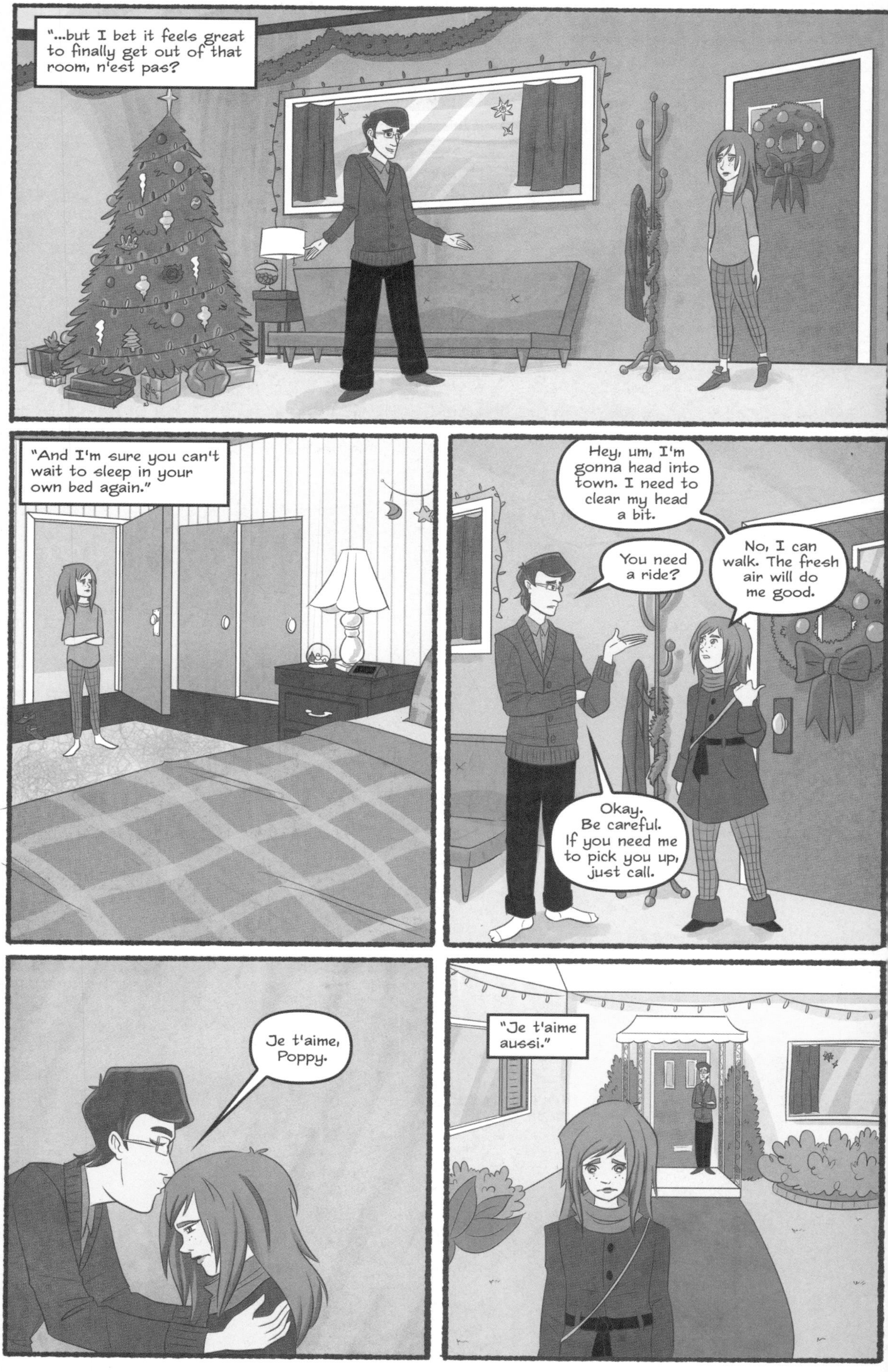
"...but I bet it feels great to finally get out of that room, n'est pas?
"And I'm sure you can't wait to sleep in your own bed again."
Hey, um, I'm gonna head into town. I need to clear my head a bit.
You need a ride?
No, I can walk. The fresh air will do me good.
Okay. Be careful. If you need me to pick you up, just call.
Je t'aime, Poppy.
"Je t'aime aussi."

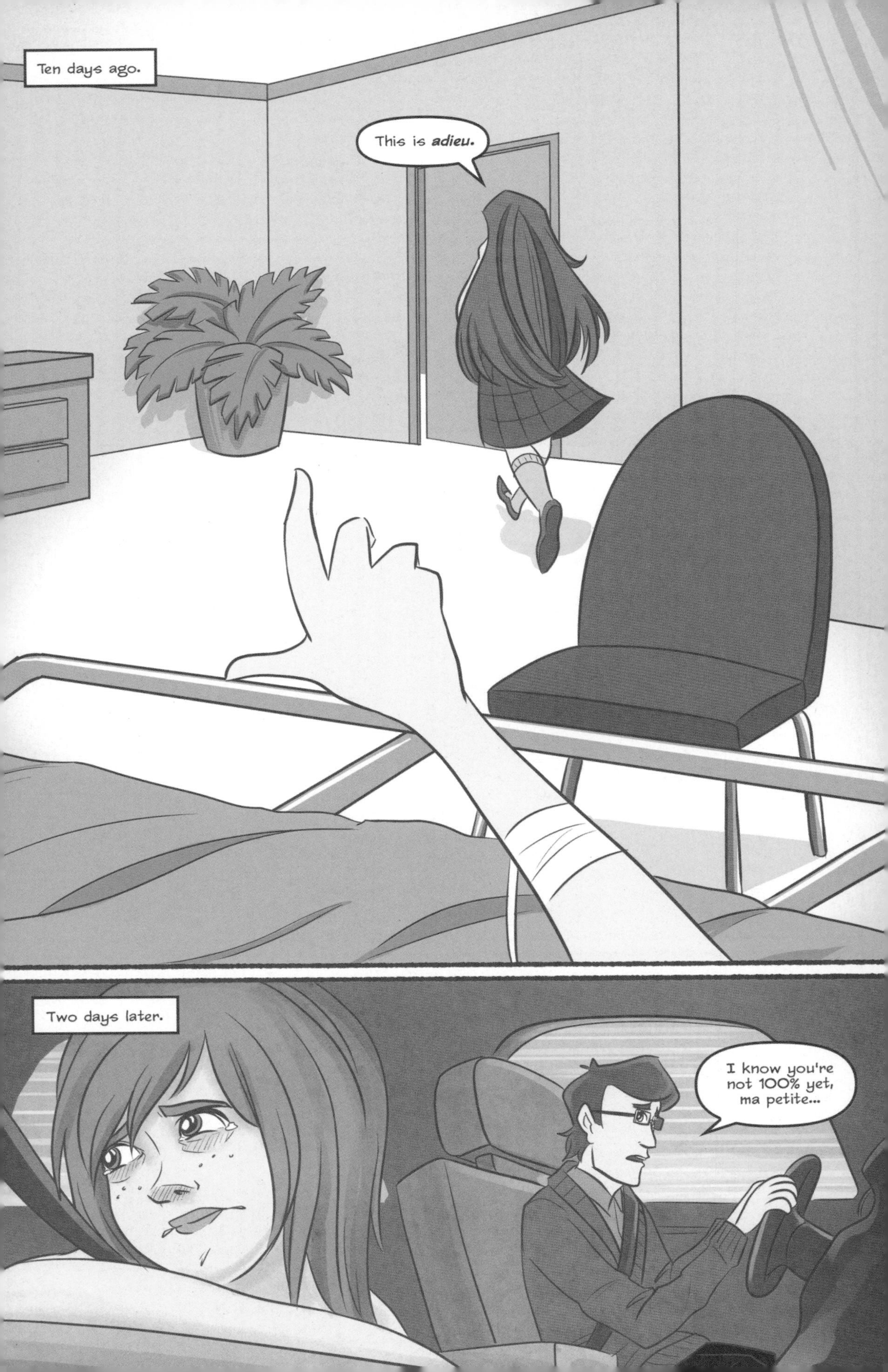
Ten days ago.
This is *adieu.*
Two days later.
I know you're not 100% yet, ma petite...

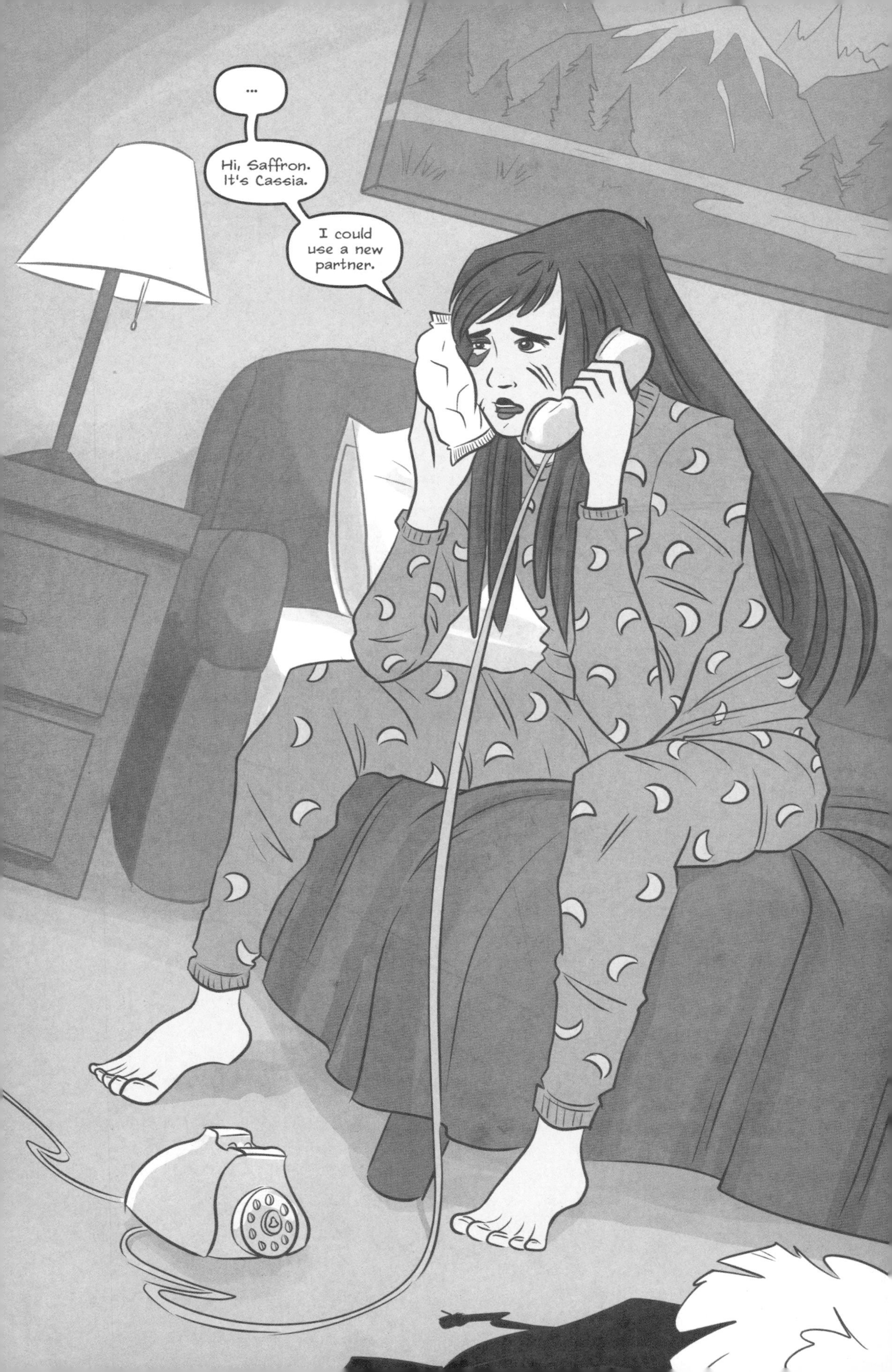
...
Hi, Saffron. It's Cassia.
I could use a new partner.

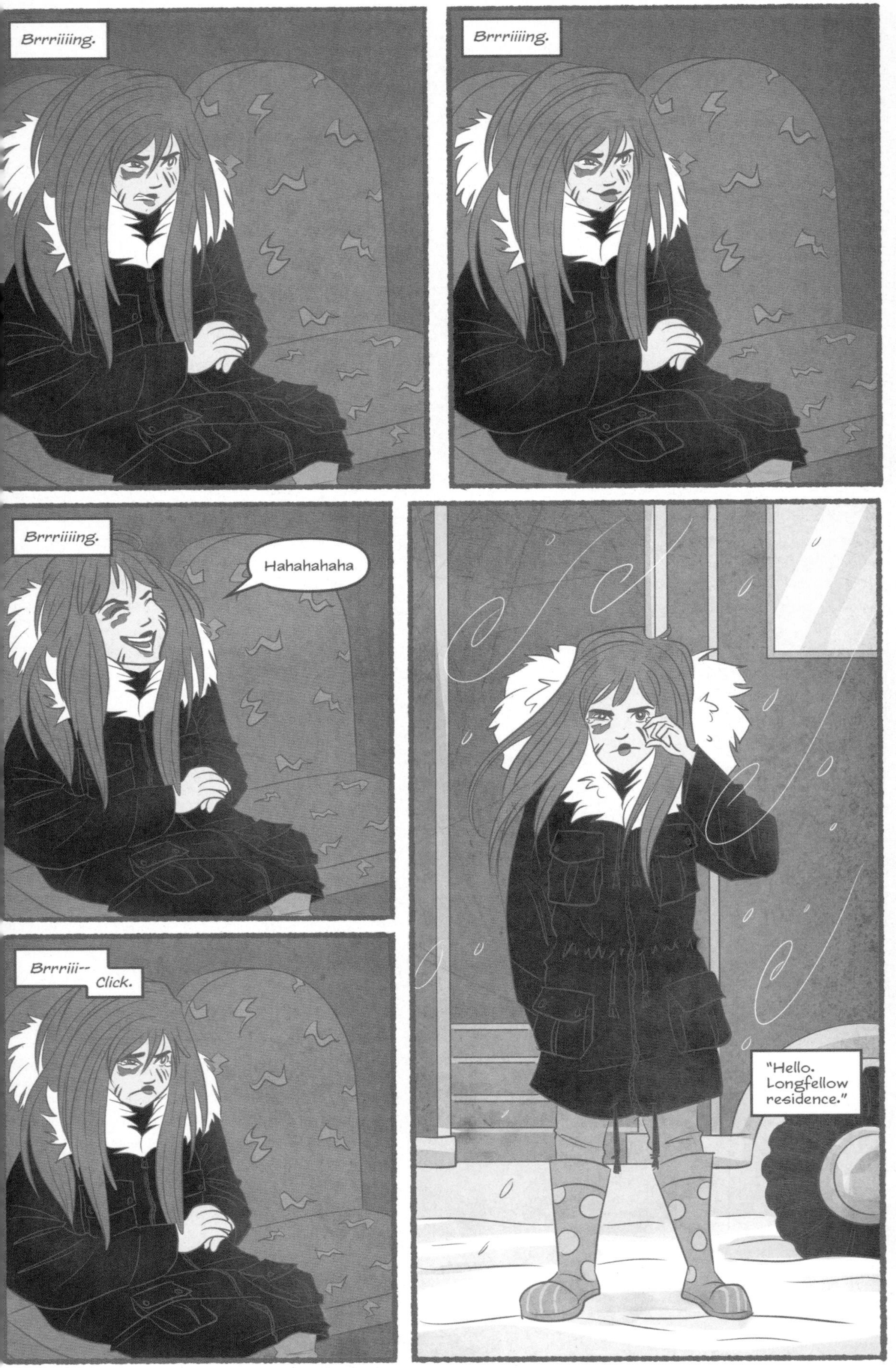
Brrriiiing.
Brrriiiing.
Brrriiiing.
Hahahahaha
Brrriii--
Click.
"Hello.
Longfellow
residence."

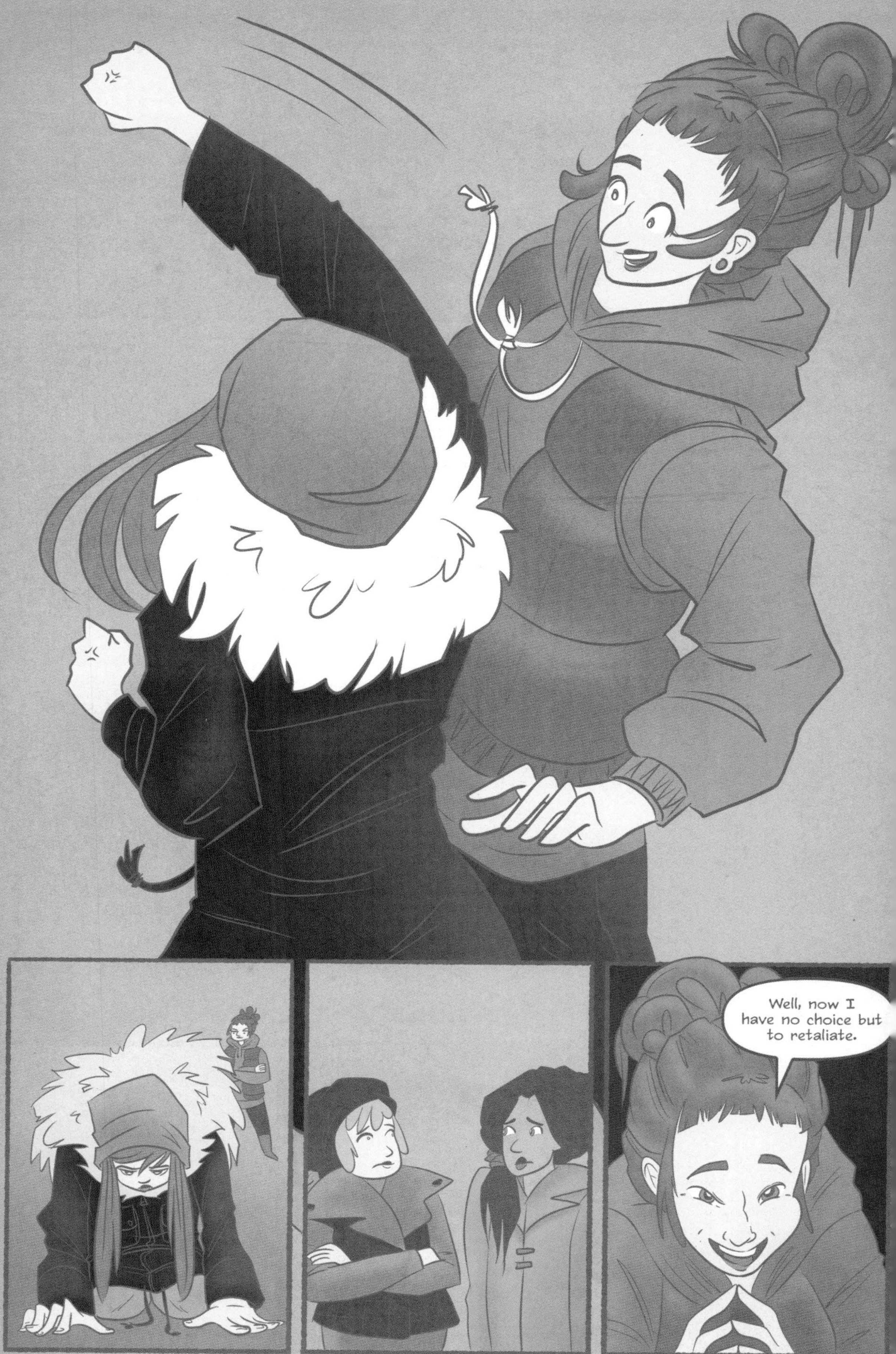
Well, now I have no choice but to retaliate.

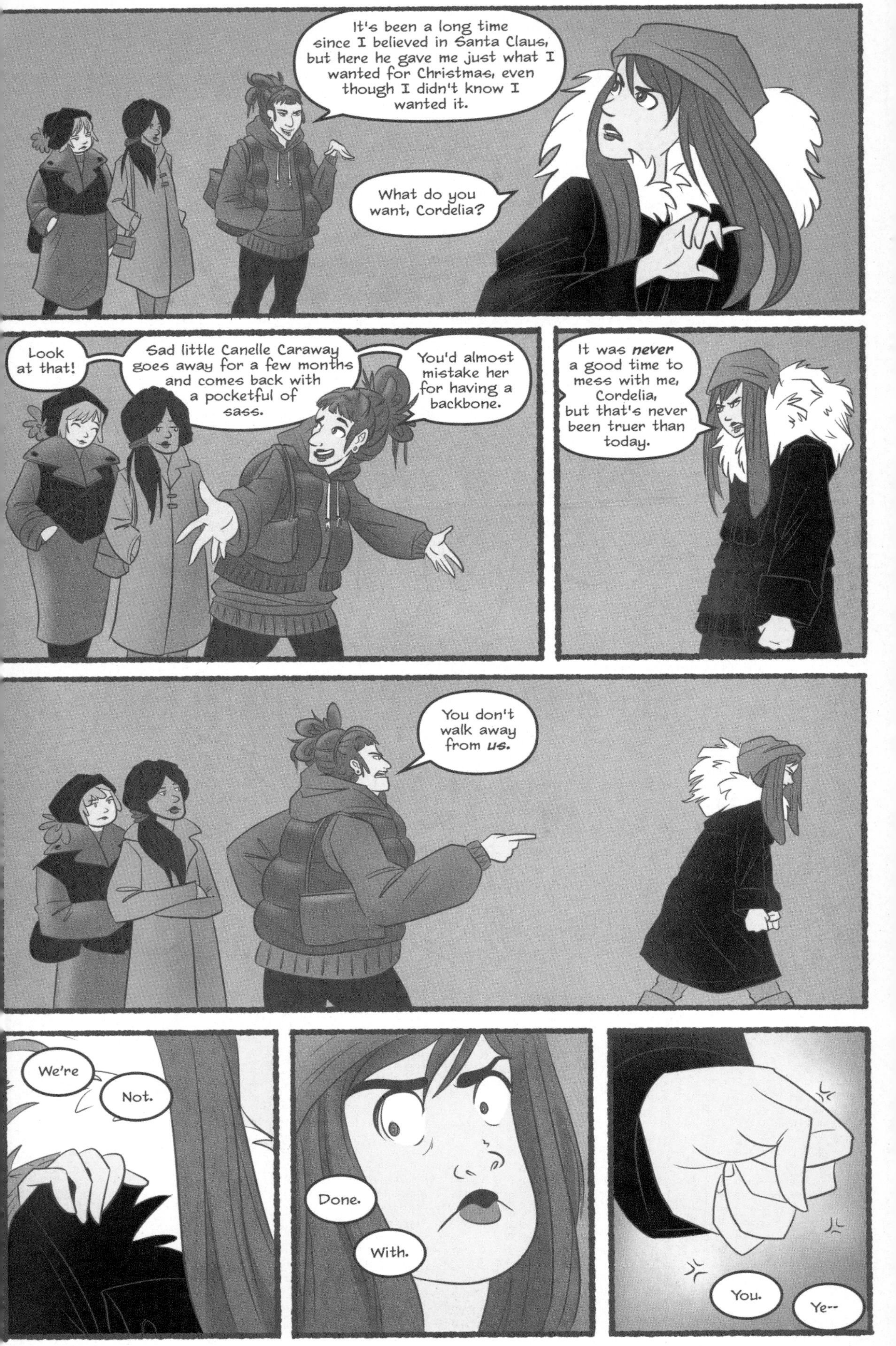
It's been a long time since I believed in Santa Claus, but here he gave me just what I wanted for Christmas, even though I didn't know I wanted it.
What do you want, Cordelia?
Look at that!
Sad little Canelle Caraway goes away for a few months and comes back with a pocketful of sass.
You'd almost mistake her for having a backbone.
It was *never* a good time to mess with me, Cordelia, but that's never been truer than today.
You don't walk away from *us.*
We're
Not.
Done.
With.
You.
Ye--

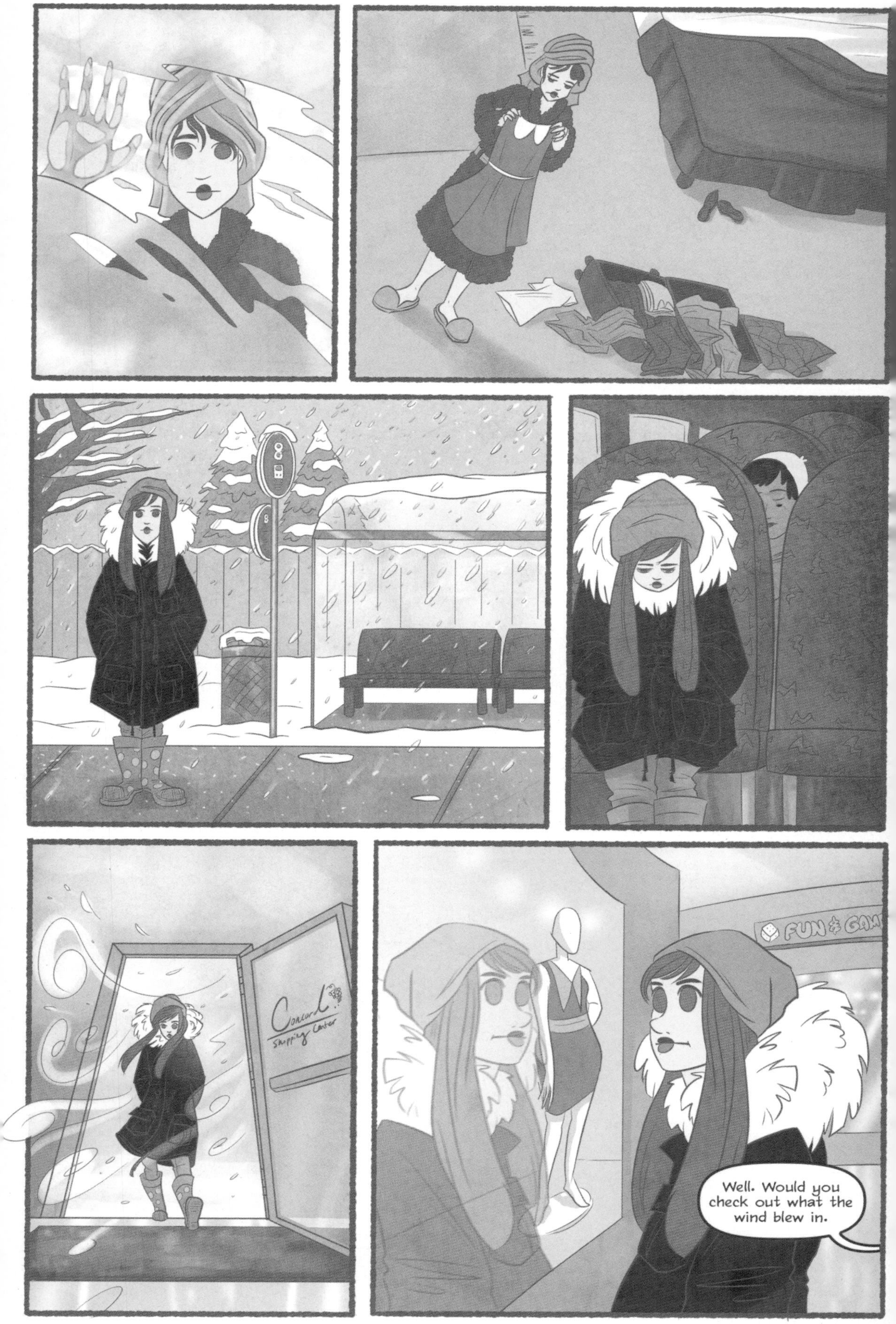
Concord Shopping Center
FUN & GAM
Well. Would you check out what the wind blew in.

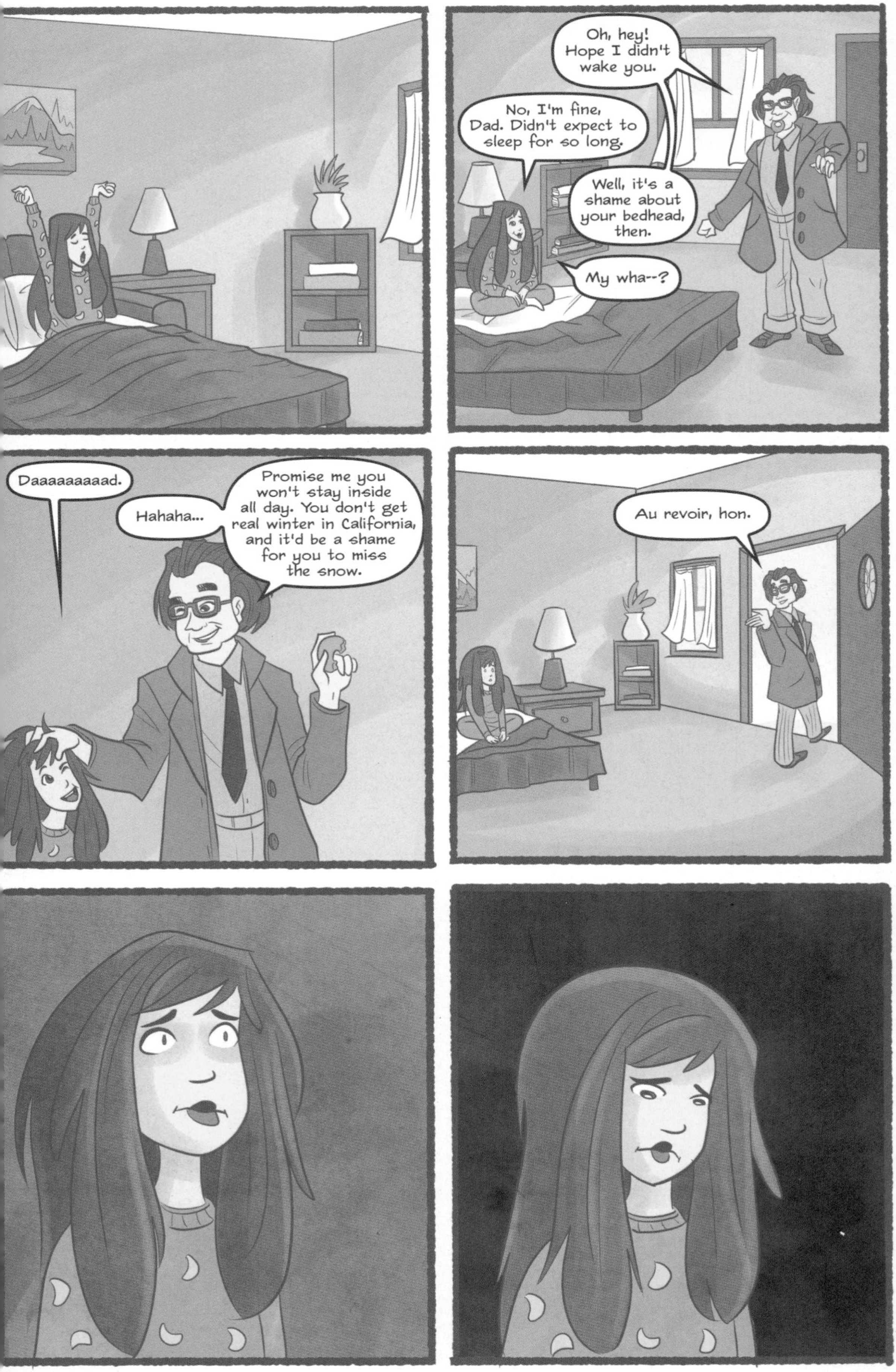
Oh, hey! Hope I didn't wake you.
No, I'm fine, Dad. Didn't expect to sleep for so long.
Well, it's a shame about your bedhead, then.
My wha--?
Daaaaaaaaad.
Hahaha...
Promise me you won't stay inside all day. You don't get real winter in California, and it'd be a shame for you to miss the snow.
Au revoir, hon.

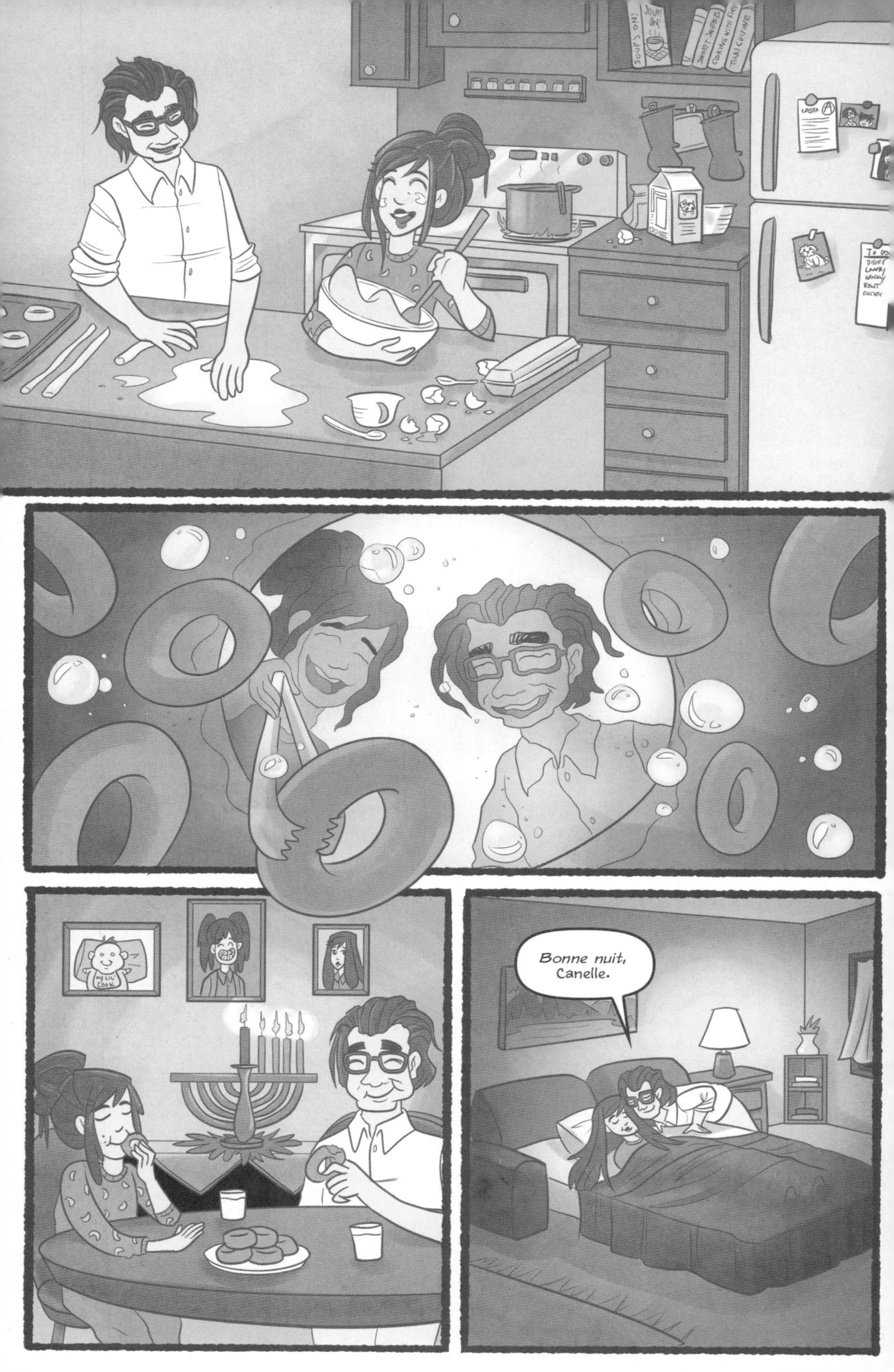
SOUP'S ON!
THAI CUISINE
Bonne nuit, Canelle.

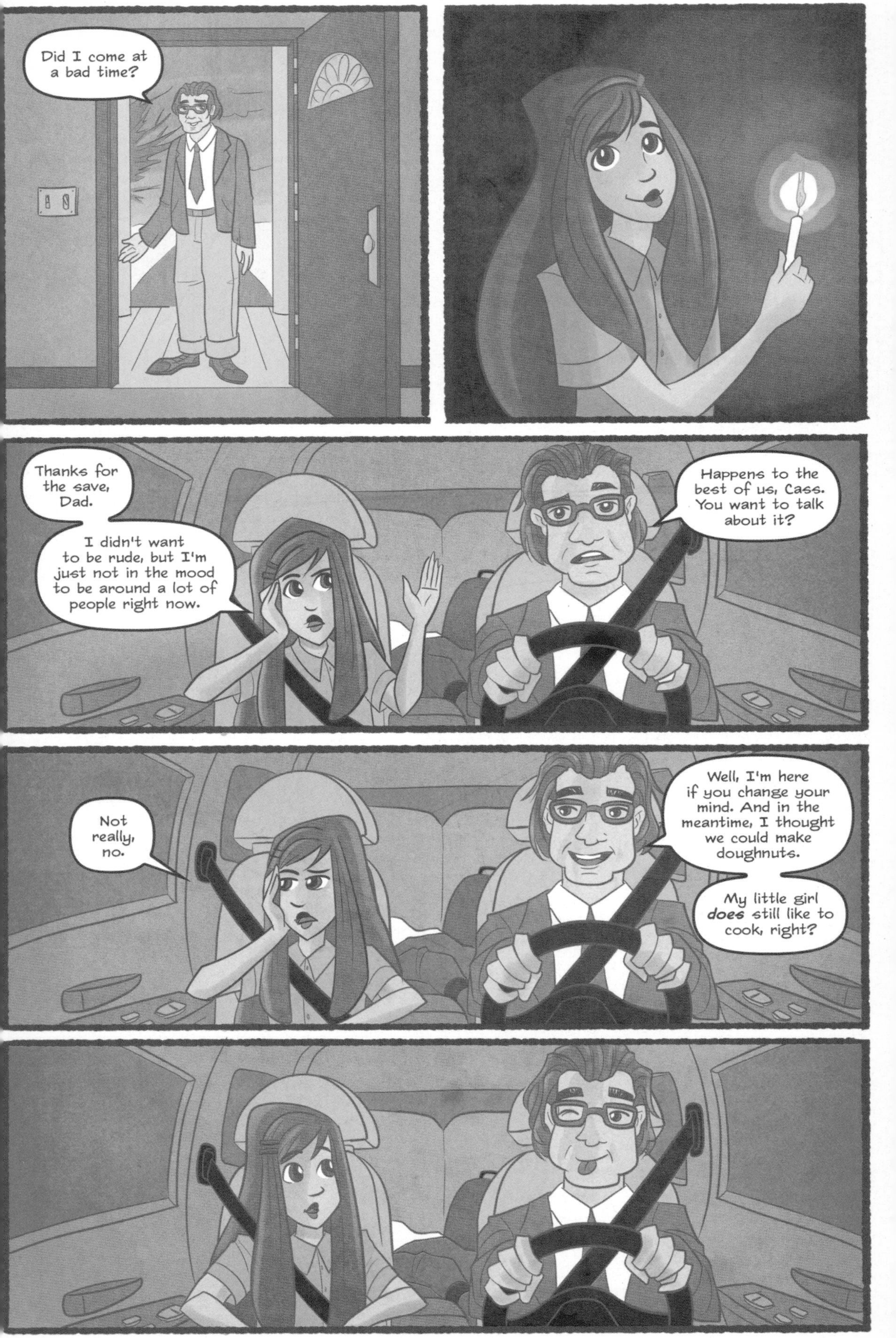
Did I come at a bad time?
Thanks for the save, Dad.
I didn't want to be rude, but I'm just not in the mood to be around a lot of people right now.
Happens to the best of us, Cass. You want to talk about it?
Not really, no.
Well, I'm here if you change your mind. And in the meantime, I thought we could make doughnuts.
My little girl *does* still like to cook, right?

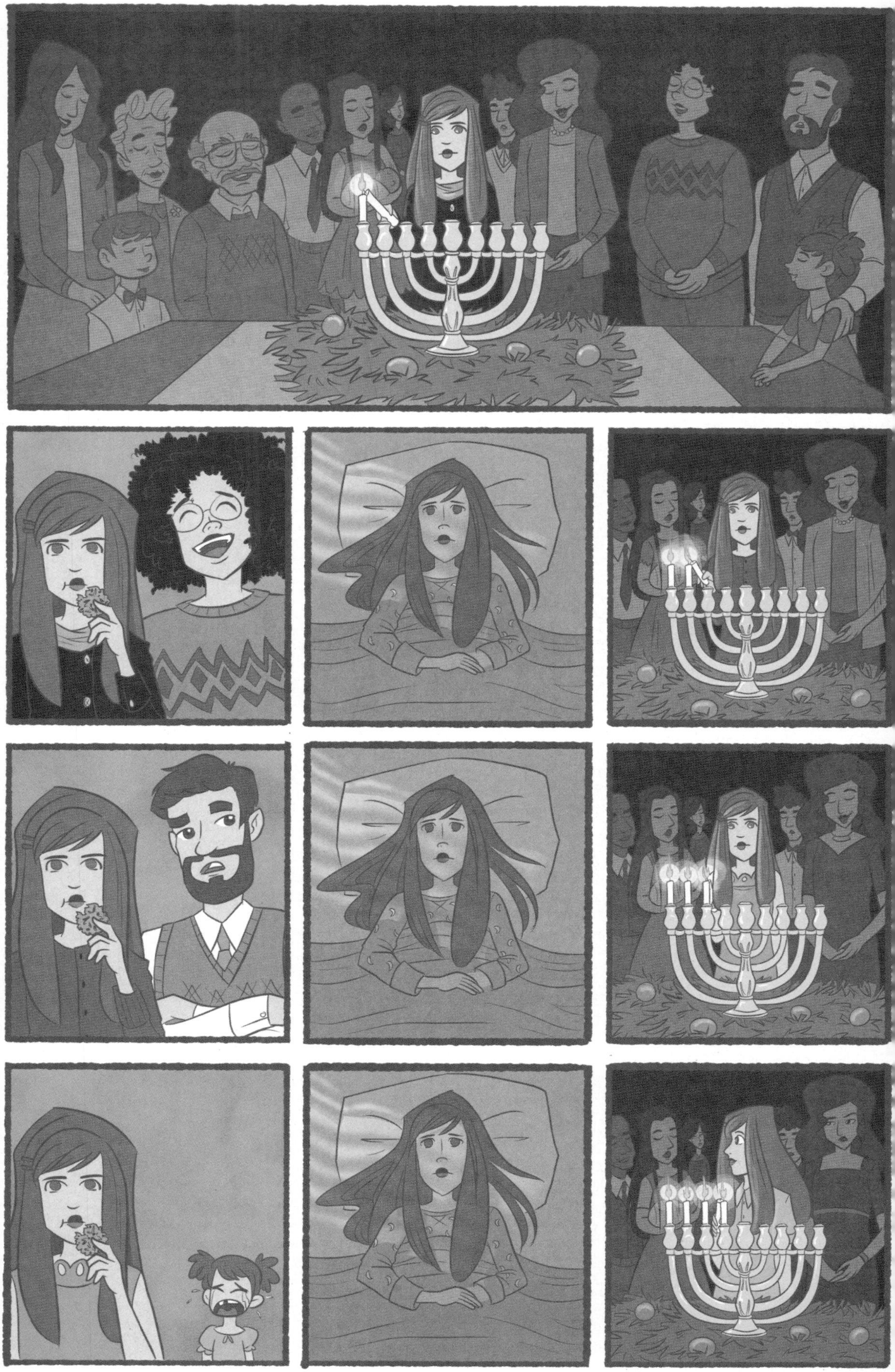

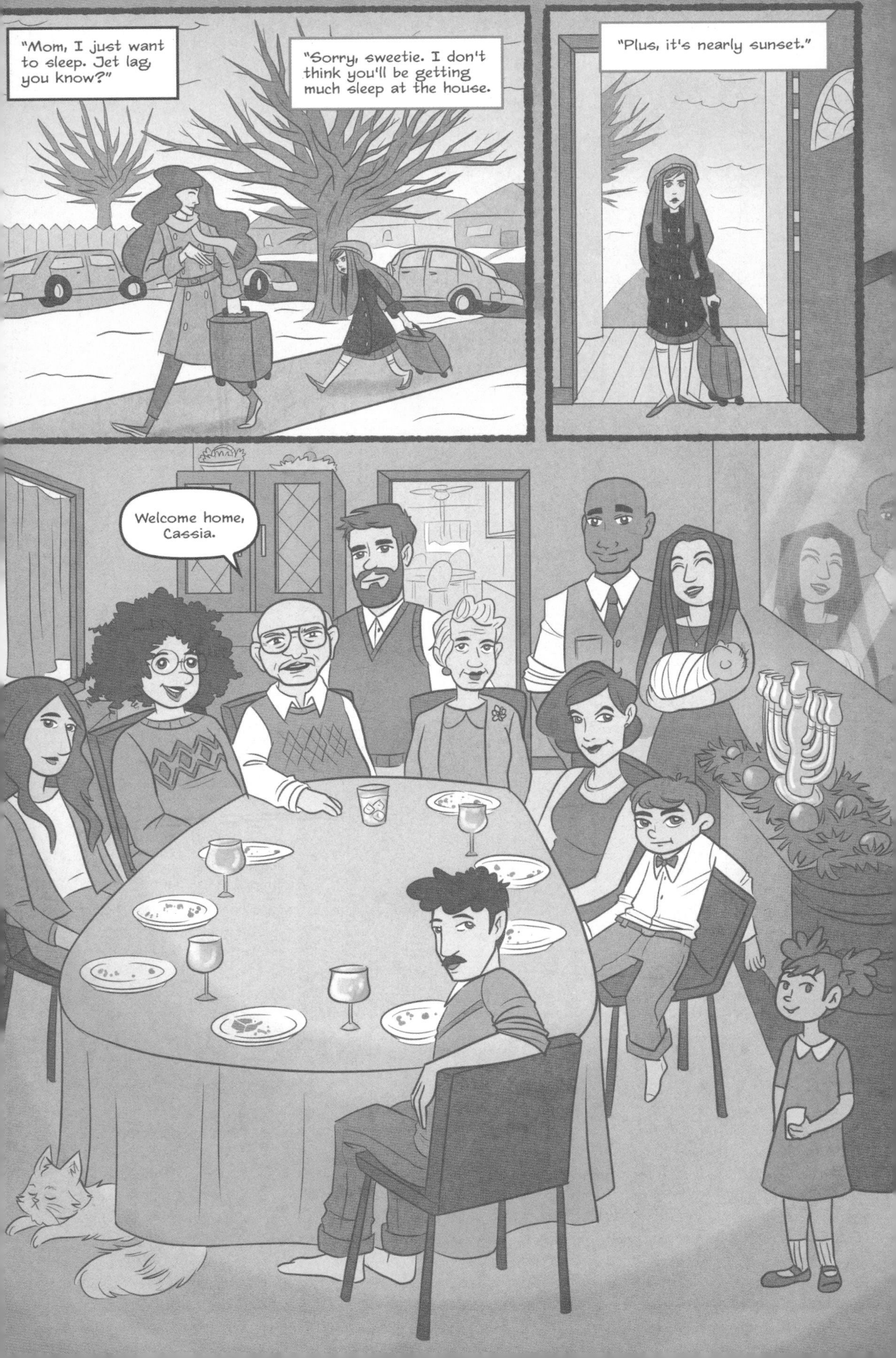
"Mom, I just want to sleep. Jet lag, you know?"
"Sorry, sweetie. I don't think you'll be getting much sleep at the house.
"Plus, it's nearly sunset."
Welcome home, Cassia.

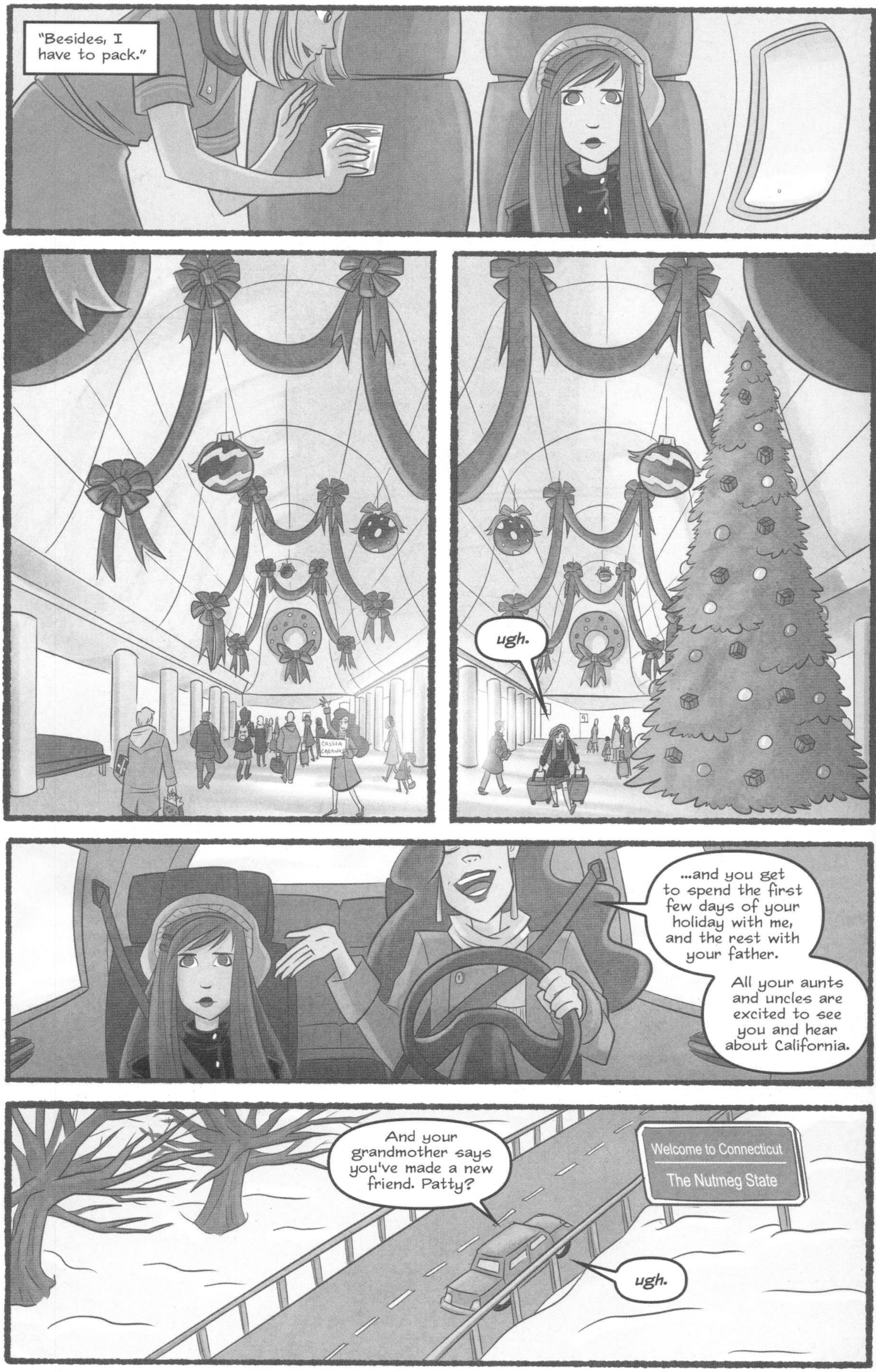
"Besides, I have to pack."
ugh.
...and you get to spend the first few days of your holiday with me, and the rest with your father.
All your aunts and uncles are excited to see you and hear about California.
And your grandmother says you've made a new friend. Patty?
Welcome to Connecticut
The Nutmeg State
ugh.

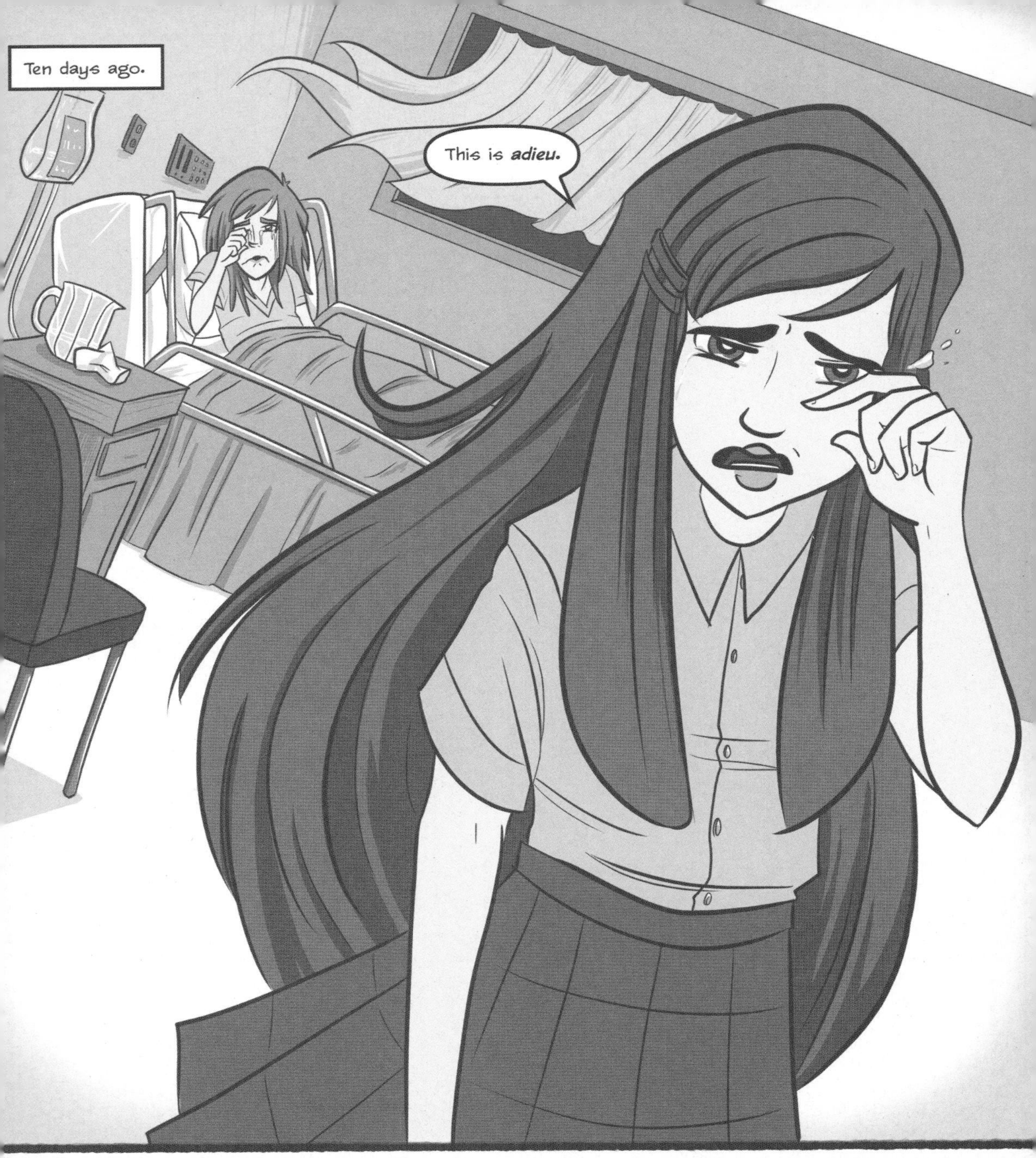
Ten days ago.
This is *adieu.*

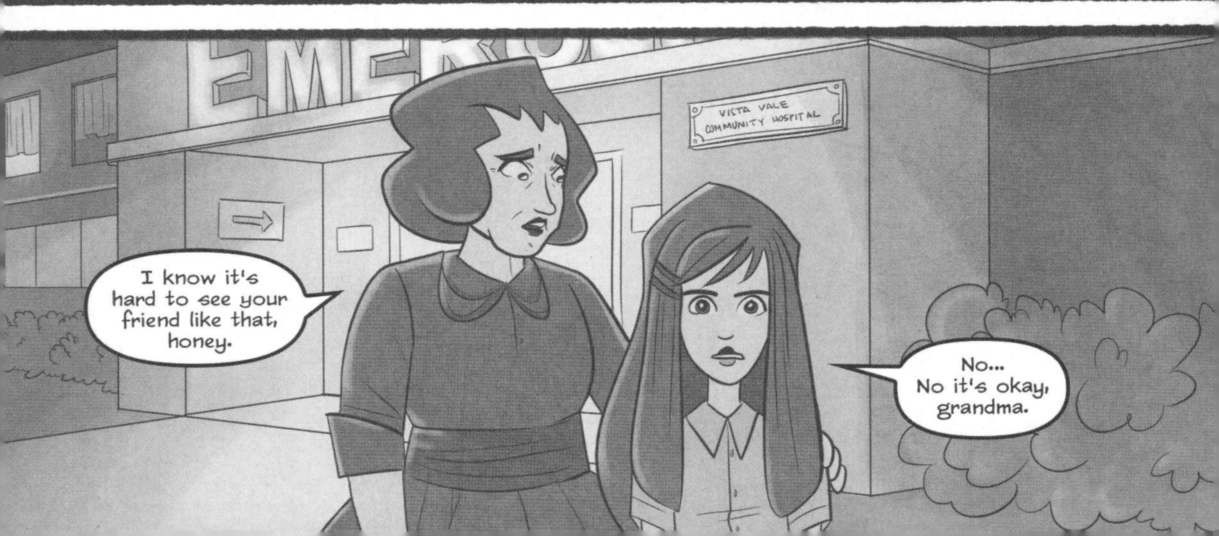
VISTA VALE COMMUNITY HOSPITAL
I know it's hard to see your friend like that, honey.
No... No it's okay, grandma.